DEATH
IN THE
OZARKS

DEATH
IN THE
OZARKS

A SALLY WITHERSPOON MYSTERY

ERIK S. MEYERS

LEVEL
BEST BOOKS

Author Photo Credit: Walter Fogel (https://www.walterfogel.com/)

First edition

ISBN: 978-1-68512-520-2

Cover art by Level Best Designs

This book was professionally typeset on Reedsy.
Find out more at reedsy.com

To my mother, my stepfather and my sister for their love and support.

Chapter One

Sally Witherspoon dropped onto the sofa in her office with a sigh, the cracked brown leather groaning as she settled herself, and ran her hand through her graying chestnut ponytail. What a night. The fights in the bar on Saturday nights were getting worse. Sally loved her bar, Sally's Smasher, and her adopted town of Berry Springs, but the violence was getting to her. She had come to live in the small town fifteen years ago. An old college friend, Bill Arnold, was from there, and he had always urged her to come for a visit. With a population of two thousand, one hotel, two bars, two diners, and a few arts-and-crafts shops, it was very different from her high-powered life in finance in Atlanta, but now it was definitely home.

A home that didn't include her husband, mind you. They had divorced soon after the trip to Berry Springs. Putting her life's savings into buying an old run-down bakery—with a lot of financial help from Bill—and turning it into Sally's Smasher had been quite a gamble, but life here was different. The thought of living in the beautiful Ozark mountains in Arkansas and still sitting in an office like back in Georgia hadn't been an option for her, and the bar seemed like the perfect alternative. Running it meant she had more time to explore and hike the local area. Yes, the nights were long, but the town had come to love Sally and her biker bar, and she'd made many friends.

With only two bartenders, Jay and Magda, to help, it took a lot to run the place. Most Saturday shifts were hard slogs, but that night had been an especially long evening, as she had to deal with three bar fights, each uglier than the last. First, her business partner, Bill Arnold, had gotten into a heated argument with his biker club, The Mountaineers, over who would get to ride Bill's vintage Vincent Rapide next. As it was on display at the bar in a large metal cage, it was often a topic of contention. Bill was always worried it would be stolen, it was worth a lot, or worse, one of his buddies would ruin the perfectly restored and polished leather seat and shining metal. Then Bethany Wells, the school assistant, had accidentally stumbled into Mayor Jennifer Milkowski on her way to the bathroom. Bethany did love her wine, and there had been a bit of a misunderstanding. Bethany got easily annoyed when she had had too much to drink. Jennifer was not the easiest to get along with, for sure, but she was always watching her image, and being involved in a bar fight would certainly not fit her mayoral brand, and she quickly defused the situation. The third fight almost resulted in Sally calling the police. Her friend Jeff Bartholomew, a teacher at Clinton High School, was sitting with their local Catholic priest, Father O'Malley, and had become pissed off by the bikers yelling at each other next to their table. Jeff stood up, his fists at the ready. One of The Mountaineers lobbed him in the jaw, and Jeff swung in return. Jeff had had too many beers to be in top form, and his swing missed. As he swiveled around, he fell hard, knocking over a table full of glasses and falling on a metal chair in the process, which his broad six-foot-two frame bent out of shape. If it weren't for Bill stepping in and throwing Jeff out of the bar at that moment, Sally's Smasher would have been truly and royally, well, smashed up.

Unfortunately, this was not something completely unusual; the rough-and-ready people living in the remote town rising to conflict more than she'd seen in the city, but the fights that night had been more violent than normal. They'd completely torn up one corner of the place. Her insurance would pay for now, she hoped. She didn't really have the funds to fix it up herself.

But reviewing the events of the evening wasn't going to change matters, nor was it helping Sally relax. She pushed herself up from the couch to finish cleaning up and readying the place for the next night. She'd sent Jay and Magda home at half past twelve, not needing their help in finishing off the last of the jobs. Plus, she didn't want to overwork them. If they quit, she would be up the proverbial creek without a paddle.

Sally went over to her desk to tally up the night's receipts, making a note of the amount of cash in the drawer and putting all of it in the safe. While the overall accounting at the bar wasn't as perfect as she wanted it to be—far too much red ink for her finance background's liking—she always made sure the cash drawer was perfect.

She then headed back out into the bar to put the glasses away she had washed before closing for the night. Pushing all the tables and chairs back in their proper places, Sally made one final sweep of the bar before checking all the windows and doors. Casting her eyes over the decorations around the bar always made her smile. The deer antlers above the door came from one of her hunting trips. Bill's vintage bike was a real pull. And the red wooden paneling had been specially made by the local lumberyard. She was so proud of what she had accomplished, though it wouldn't have happened without Bill's help, and his money.

As she did every night, she went to each window from left to right, making sure the catches were secure. Then she locked the front door. Back in her office, she grabbed her backpack and shut off the lights. Just before leaving through the back door, she set the alarm. The reassuring red light always calmed her nerves. After four break-ins in one month the previous year, she finally broke down and bought an alarm, a huge expense, but so far, worth it.

In the parking lot, she headed to her car, looking forward to falling into bed. She threw her red backpack in the back of her old blue Datsun and started the engine.

Damn, I forgot to put out the trash. She turned off the car and reluctantly headed back across the parking lot. Looking up, she frowned. Bill's fiery-red Harley-Davidson motorcycle was still parked in the back of the building near the trash bins. Bill didn't have a car, so he couldn't have taken that. And she had definitely checked everywhere inside to make sure no one was passed out in one of the bathroom stalls. Maybe someone had given him a lift home. Bill was her business partner, but he acted like a very loyal customer most nights, drinking up the Murphy's stout imported from Ireland for him.

She walked over to the motorcycle and was surprised to find the engine warm to the touch. *That's strange*, she thought. She glanced around the parking lot and the woods behind for Bill. Though, why would he be waiting outside?

At that point, she was too tired to think about the motorcycle any further. Bill was a big boy, and he'd make his own way home, and she went to get the trash bags.

She stomped back inside. Annoyed with herself, she had to switch the alarm off. She'd left the damn things by the door but must have walked straight by them. There were three huge bags, so she would have to make two trips. To make it easier for herself, she moved the bags outside before locking up and turning on the alarm again.

She then grabbed two of the bags and lugged them across the lot.

Why hadn't she put the trash bins closer to the door? This was one of her many to-dos that never reached the top of the priority list. She should get Jay to do it for her next week.

At the dumpster, she opened the lid and threw the bags in without looking, brushing her jeans against some grease on the side. Jeans were pretty much her go-to outfits, or sweatpants at home. Everything else was a waste of money, as it got dirty so easily at the bar. And she didn't do much beyond hiking, working, sleeping, and eating.

She went back and grabbed the third bag from the door, and returned to the dumpster. Her long night would finally be over.

As she opened the lid again, she realized the bags she had just thrown in were too close to the top. The dumpster had been emptied the day before, so what was under the bags? If someone else was dumping their rubbish in her bin, she'd be having words.

Sally fumbled in her pocket for her cell, switched on the flashlight, and peered inside. Waving the flashlight, the light landed on something that was definitely not trash.

She brought her hands to her mouth, dropping the trash bag, and screamed.

Staring back at her were the gray, unseeing eyes of Bill Arnold.

4

Chapter Two

Bill's body was lying motionless inside the dumpster. Sally still had her hand over her mouth in shock. Bill had been so full of life such a short time ago. And he had been one of her oldest friends besides being her business partner. She retched, her stomach tied in knots.

Tentatively, Sally leaned into the trash bin to feel for a pulse. Her mother had been a nurse, so her medical side always activated in situations like this, adrenaline coursing through her body, but she was still unnerved by the look in Bill's eyes. The floodlights behind the building didn't reach that far, so it was only her flashlight that was available to see anything.

No pulse. He was definitely dead. But his body wasn't cold, so he couldn't have been dead long. As Sally withdrew her fingers, she saw blood on the side of Bill's head.

She shuddered. Spinning around to go back inside to call the police, she tripped on the trash bag that she had dropped when she found Bill's body. She fell, banging her knee on his motorcycle, sending it crashing to the ground. She rubbed her knee for a few seconds through the tear in the jeans. A sickening realization came over her. Whoever killed Bill—because Bill hadn't ended up in the dumpster by accident—might still be there. And knocking over the bike, she'd alerted them to her being there too. Adrenaline took over, and she jumped up. She glanced around her to make sure she was alone.

She hobbled back inside as quickly as she could, locking the doors, and called the police. She grabbed some ice from the freezer out front, moving with difficulty, wrapped it in a blue towel, and held it on her throbbing knee.

Then she collapsed on her office sofa sobbing.

She lay there for a while, the pain in her knee was still too intense to move. She was also in shock. Every great memory of Bill from college, or from the life in Berry Springs, came rushing back to her. He had been a huge bear of a man with a heart just as big.

Why would anyone want to kill Bill? she thought. Wiping her eyes with a tissue, she waited for the police to get there.

In spite of the small town, the cops still took twenty minutes to arrive at the bar. Sally's Smasher, housed in the old bakery, was outside town on Route 10, heading south, but it was still only five miles from the town center.

When the two cop cars finally arrived at around 2:30 a.m., Sally managed to limp out front to meet them at the entrance of the bar. She raised her eyebrows when she saw Detective John Finnegan, accompanied by Sergeant Mark Soder, get out of one of them. The other held two officers who stood at the front door looking menacing. Finnegan barely left his desk most days—or he was in the coffee shop "working on a case." It was a miracle any crimes got solved in the town. But then again, a murder case was pretty high profile. And it was well known he'd been trying to get promoted to chief for years.

Finnegan was a hulk of a man, weighing at least two hundred and fifty pounds, the buttons on his shirt straining to stay closed. His brown hair was thinning to the point of nothingness, though he tried to hide it with a poor attempt at a comb-over. He wasn't married, except to his job.

Soder, on the other hand, had been a wrestler in college twenty years before, and he was still full of muscles covering his six-foot frame. Soder's wife, Candy, was a teacher at the elementary school in town. While Finnegan was in his standard detective's outfit of ill-fitting gray suit and mismatched tie, Soder was wearing the standard county police uniform, his belt full of cuffs, revolver, and pepper spray. There wasn't a lot of violent crime in Berry Springs, but the cops liked to show off their power. Soder removed his hat as he stepped inside the bar, revealing his thick blond hair.

"Thank you for getting here so quickly," Sally said, a crack in her voice.

"Just show us the body," Finnegan replied, pushing Soder aside, showing who was boss.

Sally led them through the bar and out to the back parking lot and then over to the dumpster.

Finnegan surveyed the scene, his eyes glancing over the crashed motorcycle and the bag of trash that had fallen open.

"Was the bike like this when you found him?" Detective Finnegan asked.

"Um, um, no, I knocked it over with my knee when I jumped back from the dumpster," Sally replied.

"Okay, we'll need to get your full statement. First, we have to wait for Forensics. Soder will take you inside. I'll be in soon," Finnegan growled. *Always a pleasant guy.*

Sally and Soder waited in her office while Finnegan remained outside, reviewing the scene.

"Do you want a coffee?" she asked.

Soder nodded, and she went out to the front to make a pot. She was glad to have something to do to keep her mind off what she had found in the dumpster.

Back in the office, she handed Soder a mug and sat down across from him on the couch, sipping her own steaming cup.

"Sally, I'm so sorry about Bill. I know you were close," Soder offered.

Sally smiled. "Thanks, Mark. It still seems like a nightmare that, in a few minutes, I'll wake up from. Bill was so full of life tonight. And now he's gone."

Sally stared down at her cup, and Soder didn't interrupt her thoughts further.

How did she always manage to get into these situations? Wherever she was, whether at work, at home, on vacation, visiting her aging parents in Oklahoma, or just getting her groceries at the local food mart, trouble followed her there. Her analytical mind was always looking for a solution, and somehow, this had resulted in her trying her luck as an amateur detective on previous occasions. She didn't want to be the person solving crimes, but people came to her with their troubles, like a modern-day Sherlock Holmes. This was the first time she'd been faced with a murder, though. And worse, the murder of one of her closest friends.

Admittedly, the last incident she had solved was the poisoning of her neighbor's dog, but this was in a whole other league. Bill was one of her best friends, her colleague, and the person who had helped her build Sally's Smasher from the ground up.

Detective Finnegan finally appeared, carrying a small bag, and sat down on the one chair left in the office, which barely bore his weight. Sally was worried the creaky wooden chair would collapse under him. He looked through the back window for a few seconds before turning his attention to Sally. He pursed his lips and pulled out his notebook with a heavy sigh. The walk from the dumpster had clearly been more steps than he had taken in a while. He had a nervous twitch in his left hand. Every time the hand jumped, Sally tried to look away. He was nervous, but Sally couldn't understand why. Soder seemed oblivious to it.

"So, tell us how you found the body," Finnegan prompted.

Sally took a deep breath and began to tell the officers what had happened.

Finnegan nodded his head toward the coffee cups. "Can I get a coffee, too?" he asked, raising his voice.

Sally sighed and got him a cup from the bar. She handed him the coffee, and he took it without thanking her. She felt the detective was somehow annoyed she had found the body, like he was putting her out. Maybe he was worried she would try to solve the crime. Sally knew the police didn't like amateurs getting involved.

"Carry on, Ms. Witherspoon."

Sally began her story again, relating the events leading up to finding Bill's body. He took a couple of notes while Soder scribbled furiously.

"Your window here looks onto the back lot. You didn't hear anything while you were working back here?" Finnegan asked.

Sally felt like he wanted her to give him all the answers and solve the murder for him.

"No, I was concentrating on the accounts," she replied.

"What time was that?"

"Must have been about one a.m."

"And when was the last time you saw Bill?" Finnegan asked again. He hadn't let Soder get a word in the entire time and seemingly wasn't about to start.

Maybe that was why Soder was keeping his head down and noting every word, Sally thought. He knew better than to step on Finnegan's toes.

"Hmm, good question," she answered. "I think it must have been about ten thirty. We had a brief chat after we broke up a bar fight and kicked a customer out. Jeff Bartholomew, actually."

Finnegan seemed surprised when Sally mentioned Jeff, everyone's favorite teacher. "What did Jeff do?" he asked.

She told him about the fight. "But most nights, Bill usually leaves earlier than me. There were quite a few people until about eleven, so I guess he must have left before then. Or not, as it turns out."

"So why did you think Bill had left?" he continued.

It had only been a few questions, but Sally was ready to leave. She sighed. "Well, after eleven, the place cleared out, and there were only a few customers left. I would have seen him in the bar."

"So who was left after eleven?"

Sally knew Finnegan would expect her to name everyone left. She had many regulars, and she knew most of the people in town. She put down her coffee cup that she had been clutching the whole time.

"Well, let's see," she began. "Father O'Malley was still here. He had been sitting with Jeff when Jeff was thrown out, but stayed until closing."

Everyone knew the Catholic priest liked to imbibe every Saturday night. But no one knew how he managed to be up bright and early the next day for the seven a.m. service. The hand of God perhaps, Sally mused. Jeff led the youth group at St. Elspeth's, so he was well acquainted with the priest, and he would often drink with him.

"Go on," Finnegan prodded.

Sally thought for a second.

"Sitting next to them were Mayor Milkowski and Margaret Jackson."

Margaret Jackson was head of the town's sanitation department, so this also made sense.

9

"That's it?" Finnegan scribbled in his small brown notepad. Every time he raised his pencil, he panted. *He really needs to lose weight*, Sally thought.

"Yup. Oh wait, one of Bill's Mountaineers was still there," Sally replied. She wouldn't need to explain the biker gang to the officer; they were well-known in the community.

"Who was it?" Soder asked, getting a frown from Finnegan.

"Zeke Parker. He was the one Jeff tried to punch. I would have thrown him out earlier when Bill chucked Jeff out, but Bill wouldn't hear of it."

Although they didn't always see eye to eye, Sally always did what Bill said. He had helped keep her afloat the first few years, knew the town and its people well, and still was her official business partner, owning forty percent of the bar. It had served her well so far. But now, who was she going to turn to for advice? Sally had to stop her lip from wobbling.

Finnegan was scribbling in what seemed like shorthand while Soder took down every word.

Sally was hoping the questioning would be over soon. She needed to be by herself.

Finnegan flipped back through his notes as if he were looking for something.

It made Sally nervous.

After a couple of minutes, he reached down to the small bag he had placed on the floor next to the chair. He lifted it up and placed it on the table. Inside was a syringe.

"I found this under the dumpster. Do you know where it came from?" the detective asked.

Sally continued to stare at it. "I have no idea."

"Any junkies come to your bar?"

Sally turned red. The man could be so rude.

"It's a biker bar, not a druggie hangout." Her voice had been louder than she had wanted it to be, but she hated the undertone in Finnegan's voice.

"Take it easy. It's just a routine question."

"Sorry." Sally took a few deep breaths. She knew she needed to stay on the detective's good side. Particularly if she really wanted to try and solve

10

Bill's murder. "Do you think it's related to how Bill...." She couldn't finish the sentence.

"Could be unrelated, but we'll have Forensics check the syringe. Bill was definitely hit on the head, as you no doubt noticed, but we'll see what this clue has to tell us." He tapped the plastic bag.

Sally noticed that he seemed somehow gleeful as if he could already see himself sitting in the chief's chair after having solved this case so quickly.

She yawned, hoping this would be a signal. It worked.

Finnegan stood up. "Okay, that's enough for now. We'll be in touch once we have the forensic analysis. We can send a counselor over to talk to you, if you need it."

"Thanks, Detective, but I just want to get home and go to bed."

Finnegan shrugged and motioned for Soder to follow him out but turned back for a second.

"Oh, Sally. Would you hold off speaking with anyone? We'll be heading to the Arnold place to inform the family, and we wouldn't want it all over town before they've been notified."

"Um, I'm not a gossip, Detective," Sally replied a bit too loudly.

Finnegan stared at her as if he didn't believe her. She definitely heard a lot working at a bar, but she tried to be discreet. Though she was one of the few people in town who didn't gossip about everything. Small towns tended to be like that.

But then it hit her where they were going, and her hand went to her mouth.

"Oh God, Bill's family. They won't know. Poor Gillian," Sally cried.

Gillian was Bill's only sister, and the two of them were close. His two brothers, Steve and Jack, were much older and almost out of the house when Bill and Gillian had been born. Gillian, being the last child, was still the baby in the family. Her heart also went out to Momma Arnold, the family matriarch. Her husband had died years ago, and she had been left to raise the four children by herself.

Sally was exhausted, but she couldn't even begin to imagine the pain they would all feel when they heard the news. She had to do something.

"Could I come with you?" she asked.

Finnegan hesitated while staring down Soder, who looked like he was about to say something.

"I've known Bill and his family since college. I know they would want me to be there when they are told."

"Well, it's not strictly procedure—"

"Please, Detective. It would mean a lot to me."

Finnegan stared at his shoes for a few seconds.

"All right. We could do with help with the family, I guess," Finnegan offered.

"Thank you," Sally replied.

As they walked out of the bar, Detective Finnegan stopped to talk to the officer that had arrived with them and had him stay with the body until the coroner arrived.

Then he led Sergeant Soder and Sally out to his police car to drive to the Arnold place just outside of town.

Chapter Three

It was still what could be described as the early hours of Sunday morning when the police officers and Sally pulled up in front of the Arnold home. They would all still be at home at this time, which was some comfort, but Sally didn't know how much. All the children still lived with Momma Arnold in the big old log cabin. Well, everyone called it a log cabin, but actually only part of the original 1860 log cabin remained. Instead, what was left was dwarfed by a gaudy Victorian compound built between 1880-1900 with wings and windows jutting from everywhere. This told the observer all they needed to know of the family's long-held wealth and standing in the community. From a modest beginning, Great-Grandpa Jesse Arnold had built a logging empire in this corner of northwest Arkansas. And when it was time to expand the house, he had let his wife and mother have free rein. Unfortunately, they couldn't agree on styles, so besides the Victorian, there were also two sides that resembled a medieval castle. Luckily, Jesse's wife was able to convince her mother to place these at the back of the house, which couldn't be seen from the driveway. Although everyone knew the Arnolds were loaded, their sense of modesty meant that the entrance to the driveway and the driveway itself were kept as original as possible. No lions standing at the gate or anything of the sort. You only got to know the real Arnolds once you were invited in.

Finnegan let Sally lead the way to the door once the three of them had climbed out of the car. The sound of the gravel under their feet might as well have been cymbals crashing in the still early-morning air.

Sally knocked, but there was no answer. It was four in the morning, so this wasn't surprising. Sally knocked again, this time a lot harder.

A few seconds later, Momma Arnold opened the door. She was small but rotund, with heaps of gray hair that stuck up all over the place. She had obviously just thrown on an old bathrobe, which was only partially closed, and she wasn't wearing slippers. She didn't look pleased to be woken so early.

"What is going on? Why are you all here at this hour?" she asked while peering behind Sally to see the police car and the officers.

"Sally, what are you doing here? What has Bill done now?" his mother asked.

Sally teared up, but Finnegan moved in front of her, and she let him speak.

"Ma'am, could we come in?"

Momma Arnold looked like she was going to protest. She didn't take orders from anyone, and her red face told them exactly how she was feeling about this early-morning intrusion.

"Well...."

"It's important, Momma Arnold," Sally added.

After a slight pause to consider, Momma Arnold stood aside and ushered them into the living room at the front of the house. Well, it was more like a great room, with high walls covered in antlers. The family hunted as often as possible. On the wall across from the doorway was a large leather sectional with a carved wooden table in front of it. Momma Arnold indicated the three should sit down there, but it was hard to find space among all the throws and pillows and blankets that covered it.

She didn't wait to see if they got comfortable and turned to go upstairs to get the rest of the family down.

Momma Arnold returned with Bill's younger sister, Gillian, and his two older brothers, Steve and Jack. They all looked pretty angry at being woken at that hour. Due to the family's influence in the town, the Arnold family was used to getting their own way—and not being disturbed if they hadn't invited the people.

Steve, fifty-five, was the biggest, always angry and like Bill, was balding. He had the worst temper and had been known to pull a shotgun on trespassers.

14

Jack, fifty, was just as tall as Steve, but rather than fat, he was solid muscle. Gillian, thirty-five, was the opposite, almost too thin. They all had the blackest hair Sally had ever seen. Steve's just a few tufts left, Gillian's in a perm. All three were wearing their bathrobes and slippers. Well, except for Steve, who was wearing a bathrobe, but for some reason had on his cowboy boots.

Momma Arnold took a seat on a lounge chair—more like a throne—across from the couch. The three siblings stood around her and waited.

Sally looked back at them. She felt like the Spanish Inquisition was sitting across from her. She loved Momma Arnold, and Momma Arnold had a soft spot for her, but the siblings had always been wary of her presence. Probably because they thought Sally was trying to marry Bill, which would not do. Arnolds always married within Berry Springs.

"Okay, Detective. What's going on?" Momma Arnold began.

Finnegan looked across at her with a grim look on his face.

"I'm sorry to have to tell you, ma'am, Bill was found dead this morning." He was never one to mince words.

There was the briefest moment of silence, as if Momma Arnold was still registering what had been said before she brought her hands to her face and shrieked, "My baby!"

Gillian leaned down, and they grabbed each other in a bear hug while sobbing. Steve and Jack just stared straight ahead.

"Who found him? What happened?" Steve asked.

Finnegan looked over at Sally.

"It was me, Steve, in the back parking lot at the bar," she said, tears beginning to well in her eyes. "The police think he was murdered."

"How did he die?" Steve asked.

Sally and Soder looked at Finnegan for a cue.

"Well, ma'am. It looks like he was hit over the head. And we found a syringe under the dumpster...," Finnegan said.

Sally felt he had just dumped this on the family, implying a possible overdose without any real evidence to support it.

Steve swore.

15

Sally was surprised Finnegan had given so much detail, even if nothing was confirmed yet. Then again, this was the Arnold family, and Finnegan would definitely not want to be accused of holding information from them. Particularly if he wanted their help to get elected chief.

"We thought it was weird he wasn't home by the time we all went to bed last night, though sometimes he would go with his biker buddies to their clubhouse after the bar closed. We just thought it was one of those nights," Jack said.

"Oh, who would want to kill my baby, my Bill?" Momma Arnold cried, still in tears.

Sally was wringing her hands, wondering whether she should get up and hug Momma Arnold. She decided against it and to just let the family grieve.

Soder stood up, surprising everyone, "Um, how about I go and make us all some coffee?" he offered.

Momma Arnold tried a smile, and this seemed to lessen the tension in the room a bit.

"Oh, thank you for offering, Mark, but Gillian will do that for us," she answered.

She looked up at Gillian, who reacted quickly to that silent order and left the room.

The rest turned back to the detectives, who had now gotten out their notepads.

Finnegan began chewing on his pencil.

"Did Bill seem all right last night, before he went to the bar?" Finnegan continued.

"What does that mean?" Momma Arnold asked.

"Well, just wondering whether he seemed his usual self," Soder added, looking over at Finnegan for approval.

"Of course, why wouldn't he be?" Momma Arnold replied.

"What was he doing yesterday before he went to the bar?" Finnegan asked.

Each family member looked at the other. No one seemed to want to speak for some reason.

"No idea, Detective," Steve finally offered after what seemed like hours, voice raised. "We all do whatever we want and don't need to check in with one another every five seconds. And there's plenty of space in our compound, so we might not see each other for a while."

Finnegan ignored the antagonistic comment.

A few questions later, Gillian returned with a pot of coffee and several mugs on a tray, along with a pot of sugar and some milk.

The pouring and serving took a couple of minutes, and it let everyone gather their thoughts.

"When was the last time you saw Bill?" the detective asked.

Gillian spoke up.

"It must have been at breakfast yesterday. We often eat together and then head out. Bill was going on a long motorcycle ride, and then he said he would head straight to the bar to get ready for the evening," she explained.

"Did he say the same to all of you?" Finnegan asked.

The family members looked up at him, and all nodded.

"Okay. And where were you all last night and the early hours of this morning?" Finnegan asked.

Sally felt the tension in the room at this question. She thought Finnegan could have been a bit more tactful with his choice of words and his tone. They were only just told that their son and brother had died, but it came out like an accusation.

Momma Arnold glared at the detective while her children remained silent, waiting to see whether she was going to answer the question, and how.

The older one took a deep breath. "We were here all last night having dinner, and then we watched an old Cary Grant movie on TV. What was it, Gillian?"

"Oh, *Arsenic and Old Lace*," Gillian explained. Sally saw in her face she realized the irony of the choice of movie. A movie about two old biddies who poison their guests.

Detective Finnegan seemed to notice this as well. "Interesting. When was the movie over?"

"Around eleven, I think," Gillian answered.

"So, none of you left the house last night after that?" Finnegan asked.

17

Everyone shook their heads.

"Can you think of anyone who would want to hurt Bill?" Soder interjected, which got him a look from Finnegan.

"No way, everyone loved Bill," Gillian replied.

Finnegan looked at the rest of the family. All he got was headshakes.

"I understand that Bill worked for the family business. Were there any disgruntled employees that you know of, Mrs. Arnold?" Finnegan asked.

Momma Arnold furrowed her brow. "Detective, my son worked in accounting at the family business. I have made all the important decisions since my husband passed. God rest his soul. If anyone was 'disgruntled,' as you say, and wanted to kill someone at the company, it would be me," she declared, crossing her arms.

"Well, if you think of anyone, let me know. Someone killed Bill. Whether it was someone from town or a stranger passing through, that's what we need to find out."

That is the small-town mentality. That everyone in the town is perfect, and if anything bad happens, it must have been a stranger, even if only from the town five miles away. These were the moments that Sally was glad she had lived in Atlanta. It had given her a much broader outlook on life.

"But who?" Gillian said sobbing, "Everyone loved him."

Well, obviously not, thought Sally.

"That's what we are going to work out, miss," Finnegan said.

Sally could almost see the ambition dripping from him. It disgusted her.

They all sat in silence for a few minutes. Steve and Jack looked like they might cry too, but Sally knew that wasn't going to happen with the police there.

"I want to bury my boy as soon as possible."

Sally's heart was in her throat when she heard Momma Arnold's cracking voice.

"Well, we need to finish the investigation, which I'm sure will be fast. Then you can bury your son."

Sally's stomach lurched. Finnegan was really laying on the emotion and the ego.

"If it's not fast enough, I will be calling the mayor, Detective." Everyone knew that Momma Arnold had been Mayor Milkowski's fifth-grade teacher, and for some reason, she still had quite a sway over her, even if the Arnold name wasn't enough.

This was the first time during the meeting that Finnegan scowled, but he kept his mouth shut. Momma Arnold's threat registered.

Steve now turned to Sally. "What the hell happened, Sally?"

Sally had tried to make herself as small as possible on the edge of the couch, hoping she wouldn't be dragged into the conversation. She was tired. She was in shock. And she wanted to collect her thoughts before she said too much.

"Um, well, Steve, I have no idea. He was in such a great mood last night, as he always is. There were a few bar fights, but that didn't bring him down," Sally answered as she began to sob.

Momma Arnold finally got up and gave her a big hug and then turned to the officers.

"You better find who did this to my son," she almost growled, crossing her arms.

This seemed to indicate the end of the interview. The officers got the message. Finnegan closed his notepad and stood up. Soder did the same. Sally remained seated.

"Thank you for your time, ma'am," Detective Finnegan said. "I'm sorry for what has happened, and I want to let you know I will do all in my power to solve Bill's murder as quickly as possible. You have my word."

Sally looked at the Arnolds as Finnegan said this. She didn't think they thought he was up to the task.

"Thank you, Detective, for coming here. And Sally, it was nice of you to be here too. I know how close you and Bill were." Momma Arnold, the business woman had taken over.

Sally was glad she had come with the police to inform the family. She stood up finally and joined the officers in the hallway. Gillian led them out.

Chapter Four

S oder drove Sally home from the Arnolds', which was fortunate as she was exhausted and probably wouldn't be safe to drive herself back. It was only a fifteen-minute drive, and returning to the bar first would have taken longer. They made the journey in silence, Soder leaving her with her thoughts, and she waved him off as he backed off her driveway and headed back to the station.

Sally lived on Maple Street on the east side of town in a rambling old Victorian set back from the road. It was one of the last homes of this type built in the town, in around 1900, and she had gotten it for a steal, meaning she needed to spend a lot of time and money restoring it.

Fifteen years later, and still not all the rooms were done. At the back of the first floor, she had a large kitchen full of every kitchen appliance one could want. The room was even big enough for a large wooden table in the center with six chairs. She often ate her meals there and even entertained friends in the warm kitchen. And in the summer months, she'd invite her guests through to the stone patio with a large open grill. Well-seasoned grilled meat was her specialty, washed down with plenty of wine, or beer, as one preferred.

In the front of the house was a vast living room with an adjoining office. A large squishy sofa was set against the front window with two equally comfy easy chairs across from it. She had a TV mounted on the wall to the left, but she rarely watched it. The rest of the room was covered in wooden shelving, mainly books but also souvenirs of her many trips abroad. She loved Europe most of all, having spent a lot of time exploring Ireland. She had even tried to learn Gaelic, but hadn't gotten very far with that. It was hard to learn a language when you had no one to practice with.

Across from her living room, she had turned the original salon into an ornate dining room, replete with crystal chandelier. She loved to entertain, but didn't have much of a chance these days. The long mahogany table with ten chairs had belonged to her New York grandmother, who had bought it in Savannah when she got married in 1924. The sideboard along the far wall, covered in candlesticks and old family photos, was bought at the same time. Sally loved the atmosphere and history of this room.

On the second floor, only her bedroom and a small guest room were finished. Every room was decorated in different light pastels, the colors she loved.

Once inside, she threw her keys on the ornate wooden table in the hall and padded straight into the kitchen. It was six in the morning, and it was definitely too early for a glass of red wine, but seeing as she'd never actually gone to bed, it totally counted as late rather than early, and darn it, her friend had died. She sank into the couch, sitting with her head in one hand and a glass of wine in the other.

Bill was dead.

Bill Arnold, her friend and business partner for over fifteen years. Dead.

But why?

She always told herself she was a strong person, and a lot had happened in her life to make her that way, but finding your best friend dead in the dumpster behind the bar you owned with him was just too much.

She dropped her head and wept, spilling red wine on the carpet.

After a few minutes, she raised her head, took a deep breath, and put the wine glass on the coffee table in front of her.

Okay, *Sally*, she thought. *Pull yourself together.*

It was time to end the very long day and for her to get the rest she desperately needed. Sleeping wouldn't bring Bill back, but it would help her relax and focus.

The focus she would need to figure out what happened and catch her friend's killer.

Chapter Five

Sally woke early as usual. It was already ten, but the bar was closed on Sundays, so she could sleep all day if needed. She had only gone to bed three hours earlier, so a little lie-in wouldn't be scandalous. For a moment, she relaxed in the warmth of the covers.

Until reality hit her like a punch in the face.

Bill. Oh, Bill.

She was determined not to cry again, her eyes and face already sore and puffy from last night's sobbing, and took a deep breath and jumped out of bed. Opening the windows, she let the still-warm September air hit her face. Her bedroom faced east, and she loved to feel the bright sun. Her legs were still shaking from the night before, but the sadness and anger would give her the strength she needed to go on.

Down in the kitchen, she made a pot of coffee, poured herself a cup into her favorite green ceramic mug—black, no sugar. She buttered a couple pieces of toast and took everything on a wooden tray out to the back patio, on the same side of the house as her bedroom. The sun shone there in the morning, and she enjoyed the peace and quiet. Every year, as the summer faded, she tried to eat breakfast outside for as long as possible, even if that meant a blanket and a heavy sweater. The fresh air always did her good.

Chewing her somewhat burnt toast, she considered the events of last night. She still couldn't accept the fact that her friend, her best friend, was dead. And yet he was. Her eyes pricked with emotion, but she stopped herself. She couldn't give in to her grief yet, not until she'd discovered who'd killed Bill. She knew the police wouldn't do it; she didn't have too much trust in the local police after they were discovered taking bribes from the local wealthy so their kids would be safe from arrest, no matter what they did. Maybe Finnegan and Soder weren't as bad as the gossip tended to imply—Detective Finnegan (to Sally's surprise) and Sergeant Soder weren't included in newspaper reports when the scandal hit, but in Sally's opinion, the apple may not fall far from the tree. That was small-town life, she told herself. So she'd have to do it herself.

Nursing her slowly cooling coffee, she ran through the events of the evening in her head to figure out if there was something she had missed. Bill had seemed his usual gruff but funny self at the bar the night before. Though he seemed more annoyed than usual when he had to break up the bar fight. She couldn't figure out if he had been more irritated at Jeff Bartholomew for taking a swing at one of his Mountaineers or for his biker-club buddy having swung at Jeff. But maybe she was reading too much into this.

But then again, maybe he had had something on his mind, though she would never find out now. Her eyes watered again, but she brought herself up with a strong sniff and continued to stare off into the small woods behind her property as her mind wandered.

Jay and Magda, her young bartenders, had worked as hard as they usually did, and she didn't notice anything strange with them. Jay was his usual overly friendly self. She felt kind of flattered, and he was very good-looking, with the dark wavy hair and big brown eyes of a 1940s movie star, but his interest bordered on sexual harassment at times.

She thought back to the question Finnegan had focused on. Who was still in the bar at closing? There had only been four customers remaining after Bill left, though she wasn't sure exactly when that was.

Let's see, she thought. There was Father O'Malley. He had sat Zeke Parker down with him after he'd punched Jeff to try and calm him down. And then, Mayor Milkowski and Margaret Jackson had been sitting together, chatting all evening, and they stayed until closing. She had known all four of them for years, and she couldn't imagine any of them having anything to do with Bill's murder. Though upon reflection, it seemed more likely that a customer that night had killed him rather than someone who met him there outside. The bar was a way out of town, and the killer would likely have made a special trip. Sally's thoughts darkened at the idea.

But then again, she didn't know exactly when Bill left the bar, so perhaps the killer was another customer. The bar had been busy all night. Saturday was always their best night.

She had spent most of the evening behind the bar, preparing drinks or cleaning up, so she didn't get much of any conversations. Maybe Jay would know more. He had been on table duty that night, taking orders and clearing up after guests who had left.

Sally sipped her coffee, the main question hanging in her mind. Why would someone want to kill Bill? Everyone at the bar and in town loved him. He was from Berry Springs and his family had been there for almost 200 years—one of the earliest settler families after the Arkansas territory was admitted to the Union in 1836. Any pre-Civil War family had automatic importance and standing.

But then again, being so ingrained in the local community didn't necessarily mean everyone liked you. Perhaps someone or some family built a grudge against him over the years? Maybe that was the best place to start, Sally mused. Of course, that meant knocking on some doors. Though it was Sunday, she was sure she could figure out some excuse to drop by a few houses and see people. One of the advantages of a small town was that everyone was always dropping in on everyone else whenever they felt like it.

Thinking about small-town life brought back memories of how she had discovered Berry Springs almost twenty years ago on a short vacation with her then-husband, Bart. She'd loved the fact that everyone seemed to know everyone else.

The building where her bar was had been run-down and unused for years when she bought it. Originally, it had been a bakery called The Pastry Palace, though she had quickly determined its real calling was to be a bar—she was definitely not a baker—and christened it "Sally's Smasher." Unfortunately, the name seemed to have encouraged more bar fights than she needed, but whatever.

As she finished the dregs of her now cold coffee, she made a list of people to try to see that day. First, she would talk to the last four customers at the bar. Maybe they had seen something or at least what Bill had been doing that evening. Maybe they saw someone lurking outside in the parking lot.

She would start with Father O'Malley. He had been sitting with Zeke Parker after the big bar fight and also before with Jeff. Their table was close to Bill's vintage bike, where he and his biker buddies had been standing. Maybe the priest heard something.

She checked her watch. It was a little after eleven. Just enough time to make the late eleven-thirty church service at St. Elspeth's. Hopefully, she'd be forgiven that it would be her first service in quite some time.

Chapter Six

Sally breezed into St. Elspeth's a few minutes late, though the organ was still playing. She found a spot in the last pew, which gave her a great vantage point to see who was there. Though there couldn't have been twenty or thirty parishioners there that Sunday morning, churchgoing wasn't what it used to be.

Although it was still September, she had put on a long coat and brought a scarf. The old stone church was never that warm. Father O'Malley was also quite tight with money, and his assistant, Diane, was always trying to get him to upgrade the heating. Sally wondered whether more people would come if the church were warmer. It would be a weird reason to come to church, she thought, but these days, who knew?

She scanned the people to see if she recognized anyone. Three pews up to the right, she grinned when she spotted the mayor. *Oh great, maybe I can get a chance to chat with her too*, Sally thought.

While Sally wasn't that religious, her parents had sent her to Sunday school, and she did enjoy the hymns and organ music. However, Bill had been a member of St. Elspeth's, though the rest of his family went to St. Luke's, the Methodist church on the other side of town. This was always a bone of contention with his family. They were not fond of the Catholic Church. Sally always thought this was due to being tainted by the anti-Catholic sentiment that had come to the fore during JFK's presidency, but in reality, she really had no clue. Knowing Bill, it was more of a rebellious act to annoy his mother.

Oh, Bill. A larger part of her was so sad, but another part of her was itching to solve his death. She owed it to Bill.

It was only when her retired neighbor, Mr. Sanford, tapped her on the shoulder that she stood up for the first hymn. The service took her away from the town and the events of the night before. And she relished in the serenity.

Father O'Malley liked to talk, so his sermons were always long-winded, significantly different from the very short sermons in her hometown church her mother took her to on occasion. She listened to every word today, though, because she thought he might mention Bill's death.

The lesson that day was on the second commandment: "Love thy neighbor as thyself."

Sally sat up straight. This seemed an odd coincidence after one of his "neighbors" had killed Bill. Well, assuming it was someone from the town.

The priest reviewed all the passages in the New Testament where Jesus talks about this commandment, but throughout the forty-five-minute sermon, there wasn't a single mention of Bill at all. This was odd, because Berry Springs, like any small town, was a breeding ground for gossip and information to spread rapidly. However, it was still just Sunday morning, so perhaps it was still too early for even the most ardent of the loose-lipped to have heard the news. Or if they had, they just hadn't got around to sharing it yet. Maybe Father O'Malley's sermon was a hint to everyone about supporting each other and not hurting each other. Or to the murderer.

Sally dismissed that thought. There weren't that many people in the church, and how would Father O'Malley know it was one of his parishioners?

Wait a minute, she thought, he might not even know Bill is dead. Although Bill was a member of the church, Father O'Malley might not have been informed yet. She would have to be extra discrete with her approach to him after the service at coffee hour.

She breathed a sigh of relief when Father O'Malley finally finished speaking and continued the service. The rest was a blur to her. She was anxious to get a cup of coffee and start digging.

* * *

Since she was at the back of the church, she was one of the first people out into the hall for the coffee hour. The entrance hall was large enough for a table of coffee and a table of cakes to be set up in one corner. The church did have a large hall in the basement, but it didn't make sense to heat it up and make everyone walk down the stairs—particularly with many of the parishioners being over seventy and rather frail. And anyway, there were never that many people there, even for a late Sunday service.

Sally walked over and poured herself a cup. It was usually help-yourself here. Sometimes, someone offered to pour, but only on Christmas and Easter when the church tended to be full.

Hot beverage in hand, she crossed to the opposite corner to watch everyone leaving the service and get a better look at who was there.

She saw the mayor leaving the service, and as she walked through the chapel doors, she happened to turn in Sally's direction, recognized her, and smiled. Mayor Milkowski was always full of grins, though Sally assumed most were fake. For a small-town mayor, she had a big-city political ego. The mayor was small, round, and had overly coiffed red hair. She walked rapidly in spite of her size. She always wore black and had a different pin on her blouse every day. She was a widow, and she now considered herself a definitive fixture at the town hall.

It took a while for Father O'Malley to appear. He was popular, and often, many people wanted to greet him right after the service. He was getting on in age and walked slowly out of the service into the hall, smiling at as many people as possible. His hair was white, and his clean-shaven face was full of wrinkles and age spots. The diocese had been trying to get him to retire for years, but he fought back, though Sally was a little worried he didn't have long for this world himself.

She let him have a few minutes to himself as he grabbed a cup of coffee and chatted with his assistant, Diane. She looked a lot like an older Gillian Arnold. In fact, sometimes Sally couldn't tell them apart. The only difference was Diane was a bit heavier and usually wore bright colors. She had small, round glasses, which she took off at every opportunity. Vanity, thy name is Diane.

Diane had come to the town years before Sally had. She also had no kids and wasn't married. While the mayor seemed married to the town, Diane seemed married to the church.

Sally was glad when she saw Diane move away to talk to a parishioner, so she could make her move. Even then, she only just managed to pull the priest aside before he was sucked into a long conversation with Mrs. Saunders, who loved to talk.

"Good morning, Father. What a nice sermon," Sally said.

"Thank you, Sally. Nice to see you here this morning. You don't often come to Sunday service."

"I needed the service this morning after what happened last night."

The priest's face was grim.

"So you heard?" Sally said. "I wasn't sure if news would have reached you yet."

"Yes, well, Bill was one of our flock, as you know, so Detective Finnegan notified me just before this service, but I wasn't sure if the Arnold family wanted me announcing his death from the pulpit, so I kept quiet. He's in our prayers, of course. I knew he was a close friend..."

Sally teared up but quickly wiped them away. She needed to stay focused on Bill. "I miss him so much," she said.

"It must have been horrible for you, finding him like that," Father O'Malley said. "If you need to talk, I'm always there for you."

"Thank you. That is very kind. It will take me a while to get over it, but what will help is finding his murderer, a task I've undertaken with a passion."

"Find his murderer? I know you like solving puzzles and little mysteries, Sally, but isn't solving a murder something completely different? And very dangerous."

In spite of his age and frailty, the priest was really working himself up.

"It isn't something I've done before, but I owe it to Bill. I owe it to his family."

"I think you should leave the detecting to the police, Sally," he replied, gently tapping her shoulder.

"I just can't, Father," she replied, a bit too sharply.

29

Luckily, the chatter in the hall was loud enough that no one heard the tone in her voice.

Sally felt bad about her harsh response. She watched the priest for a moment. He seemed to be considering whether it was time to give up trying to convince her otherwise. And she knew he certainly wouldn't want a scene at church.

"Well, I will help if I can," he said finally.

Sally breathed a sigh of relief.

"Thank you, Father. Could I ask you a couple of questions? You were one of our last customers last night."

With this, the priest's eyes darted left and right. Sally laughed to herself. He acted as if everyone had no clue what he did almost every Saturday night.

"A couple of questions, okay. Then I have to head to my office to prepare for the afternoon service."

"Thank you. Did Detective Finnegan ask you any questions when he notified you of Bill's death? I gave him the names of everyone still at the bar until closing, and you were one of them."

"Um, yes, he wanted to know if I had seen or heard anything. And if I had seen Bill leave."

"What did you say?"

He shrugged. "Unfortunately, I didn't really notice anything. I was having a long chat with Jeff about a difficult student we both were counseling. Magda served us our drinks a couple of times. And with all that liquid, I had to go to the restroom once."

"Did you see anyone else moving about?"

"It's a bar, Sally. A lot of people do that."

"You're right." She couldn't hide the disappointment in her voice. She was hoping to get all the clues she needed from the priest to solve Bill's murder right then and there, but that was ridiculous, she knew.

The priest thought for a minute.

"Well, Margaret Jackson and the mayor were sitting next to us. I think one or both did leave their table at some point. Probably to use the restroom like I had to. Otherwise, Jeff and I were engrossed in our conversation."

"Well, until Jeff got into the fight."

"Yes, that was awful. He needs to learn to keep his temper in check."

"I saw that you talked to Zeke Parker afterwards."

"Yes, I wanted to calm him down. I don't like seeing my Berry Springs friends hurting each other. "

"Did Zeke say anything to you about Bill or Jeff?"

"He was upset that Bill had broken up the fight. He had been ready to do more damage to Jeff for some reason—probably all that drink the boys had."

Sally was amused by the irony of that statement.

"Was there something between Jeff and Zeke?"

"Well, they know each other, of course. Zeke's son is one of Jeff's students. Maybe Zeke was upset about something Jeff did during one of the basketball games."

Jeff was the high school coach, among other duties.

"Thank you, Father. This is really helpful. If you think of anything else, please let me know."

Sally now had a few leads to follow up.

"I wish I had seen or heard something more, Sally. I was just saying to Diane that I have been racking my brain since Detective Finnegan called to try to remember something important. Bill's death is a blow to our community and even worse for Bill's family."

Sally nodded in silence.

Sally hadn't really had time to grieve, and the emotions were still raw, but she was pushing herself into her detective work to keep her mind off her sadness. It would come at some point. But for now, she had to bury it and get justice for Bill.

"Sally, again, if you need someone to talk to, please do stop by. You know I'm always here for you."

"Thanks, Father."

She excused herself to head back home. She needed to talk to the other customers, but she didn't want to question the mayor at the church as she would have her public-facing mask on. If Sally caught her at home, she might be able to have a more open conversation.

Once she had tackled all the customers, she would head over to the police station on Monday morning. Finnegan would hopefully have more details on the circumstances surrounding Bill's death. It was just a case of whether he would share them.

Chapter Seven

Sally's ancient blue Datsun 210, Gladys, looked like she would fall apart at any minute, but she hadn't let her down since Sally bought her new, the year she graduated high school in 1982. As usual, it took three tries to get her started. The huge puff of blue smoke meant the engine was leaking oil, but Sally was going to put off that repair as long as she could. It probably meant a new engine and that would probably be the end of the old girl.

Sally pulled out of her driveway and headed down Queen Street then took a right onto Route 55, heading north toward Mayor Jennifer Milkowski's place. Every road leading out of town was tree-lined and hilly, and the gorgeous foliage covering everything was a sight of beauty. Even though she'd been living there for years, she still relished the landscape. Every time she went out, she found new hiking and walking trails to explore. Though she had to make sure she kept her eyes on the road. With the hills and narrow roads, it would be easy to have an accident or miss a car coming the other way.

The warm September air meant she could roll down her window and breathe in the wonderful fresh air. *If* she could get the window to go down. One more problem with old Gladys, but she hadn't failed Sally yet.

Jennifer Milkowski had been mayor for the last fifteen years, the first Republican mayor in decades. She had been running against the Democratic incumbent, Mayor Tom Saunders, who should have retired years before. The town had been securely Democratic in a very Republican state, but Milkowski had promised a lot of improvements to the town and she pulled off a narrow win. Once in office, it became apparent she loved the ceremonial parts of the job and the prestige more than actually helping her constituents. The first thing she had done was redecorate the mayor's office, tripling it in size. Then she had used town funds to buy an expensive Cadillac as her "official" car. To keep citizens placated, she had fixed a few streets, built a new community hall, and bought the police and fire departments new computer equipment and new uniforms, but otherwise, she claimed there was little to no budget to do anything else. Somehow, though, she kept being re-elected. She was now on her fourth term, with the next election a year away. Sally wondered how she managed it each year. Maybe she'd ask her about it at some point. Or maybe she didn't really want to know. At this rate, with no term limit, as few states have for mayoral office, she'd probably be mayor until she keeled over.

Despite the wider public opinion, Sally actually really liked Jennifer. Like Sally, she didn't take any crap, and she was razor-focused on her goals. Of course, she agreed that Jennifer seemed more interested in helping herself than the town, but better the devil you know.

Sally pulled into the dirt road that led to Jennifer's cabin and parked behind her 4x4. The house was set about a hundred yards back from the road, with large pine trees on either side of the driveway. The place seemed a long way out of town for the home of the lead official, but the mayor loved her privacy. Though Sally wondered why she couldn't have privacy in one of the big mansions in town—it would certainly help the mayor's appearance of caring about the town. There were always several on the market, remnants of an era when Berry Springs was a spa town for the wealthy from Little Rock, the state capital. Most needed a lot of work, so you could get one cheap. Sally had thought about buying one herself—the thought of a ton of space really appealing to her—but instead, she had opted for her smaller Victorian, as it seemed a more manageable renovation alongside the bar. Saying that, she had spent so much time and money on turning the bakery into Sally's Smasher, it meant her house would probably remain half-finished forever. After the first few years in the house, she'd got used to the unfinished look and was in no rush to complete the job.

34

Looking at the mayor's house, she always thought it was odd that it was off-grid. It was a fancy log cabin, but water came from a well the previous occupant had dug, and power was from an old gasoline generator in the mayor's basement. The mayor had upgraded the septic tank when she moved in. The irony that the mayor didn't use any of the local authority's infrastructure wasn't lost on Sally, and it didn't seem to fit with the mayor's fancy remake of the town hall. She didn't talk much about her background, and Sally wondered whether a part of the mayor was still a rural farm girl and the off-grid house kept her rooted in her past. The mayor was definitely a puzzle she would never solve.

Sally walked to the front door on the side of the house and was just about to knock when the door flew open. Jennifer jumped back in surprise when she saw Sally. Her German shepherd, Oscar, was excited to see Sally and jumped all over her. Sally didn't visit the mayor at home that often, but the dog definitely remembered her. And she did love pets, even if she didn't have one of her own.

"Oh, Sally, you startled me. I just got back from church and was heading out to take Oscar for a walk."

Oscar was now huffing and puffing and jumping in front of her, straining on the leash. Sally gave him another pat on the head.

"I can see that. Sorry to bother you this morning, Jennifer."

Jennifer looked annoyed. Sally knew she didn't like surprises, though people did drop by other people's houses in this small town. And Sally had supported the mayor after her husband Sam passed away five years ago.

"I saw you at church. Why didn't you get my attention then rather than stopping by now?"

Sally debated how best to proceed. She had caught the mayor off guard, and her questioning might get a little awkward.

"Well, Jennifer. I guess you heard about Bill."

A tear emerged in Jennifer's eye. "Oh, tragic news. Chief Pulasky called me early this morning. I'm so sorry, Sally."

The mayor pulled her in for a bear hug, which was a bit difficult with Oscar pulling on the lead.

"Thanks, Jennifer. I've been trying to keep busy to not think about it. It's the reason I'm here, actually."

"Oh," Jennifer cocked her head.

Sally felt Jennifer was keen to take the dog for a walk as quickly as possible to not have to talk to Sally, but maybe just because the dog needed to get its exercise.

"Well, you were one of the last customers to leave, and I wanted to ask you if you had seen or heard anything."

"Sally, are you thinking about turning detective on me? Solving a murder should really be left to the police. It's what you pay your taxes for."

Jennifer was being evasive for some reason, and not just to warn Sally about the dangers of murder. Although Sally had to try not to laugh at Jennifer's comment about municipal funds.

"I owe it to Bill. If there is anything you may have seen last night at the bar that could be helpful, I would be so grateful. I know many people in town look up to your leadership." Sally was really laying it on thick, but she wanted to stay on the mayor's good side.

Jennifer paused. "Well, I was chattin' up a storm as I usually do. I briefly talked to Bill and had a long chat with Margaret about all the flooding in town we've been having."

"What did you talk to Bill about?" Sally asked.

"Hmm, just how things are going. He wanted to help fix the restrooms in the town hall. We were arranging a time for him to stop by."

"Why would Bill be helping to fix something in the town hall?"

Besides being part owner of Sally's Smasher, Bill worked for the Arnold family lumber company, in accounting. He wasn't really the Mr. Fixit type of guy.

"Somehow, we got talking about the restroom problem in the town hall. I was complaining how our repair service wasn't working out. And Margaret Jackson's team hadn't been very helpful either, and he offered to have a look."

Sally still thought this was strange. She'd have to look into that.

"And when was the last time you saw Bill?"

"Good question. We had that short chat…must have been a little after ten thirty. I remember you had just been talking to him yourself."

That made sense, as Sally remembered thanking Bill for breaking up the fight between Jeff Bartholomew and Zeke Parker.

"Was there anything about Bill that seemed odd?"

"Sally, I just had a short conversation with him about the bathroom. I'm not a psychiatrist or a detective," she said, clearly getting impatient as Oscar pulled hard on the leash, almost knocking Jennifer over. He was desperate to get outside and couldn't understand the wait, what with the door open.

"And after that?"

"I turned back to Margaret, and Bill walked away. Didn't see him after that. I really need to go now, Sally. Sorry, I can't be of more help."

Sally didn't want to press her luck and ask any more questions.

"OK, well, I'll leave you to your dog walking. Bye, Oscar!"

Jennifer let the leash loosen, and Oscar dragged her down the three stairs and down the path into the woods. Sally waved and jumped back in the Datsun.

She sat in her car a few minutes, going over what Jennifer had just told her. Jennifer had seemed evasive, and Sally didn't really buy her story about Bill wanting to help fix the restrooms at the town hall. She'd have to check with Margaret Jackson to see what she could tell Sally about the conversation she had with the mayor the night before.

Chapter Eight

Next stop: Betty Jo's Diner on Oak Street near the town square. Sally's breakfast had been meager and seemed hours ago. She needed to get some food inside her before she went to see Margaret Jackson, who the mayor had been chatting to all evening on Saturday night. Conveniently, Margaret's apartment was also on Oak Street, just across from the diner.

Betty Jo's Diner was one of her favorite greasy spoons. The bacon and eggs were dripping with fat, just as they should be, and the Southern buttermilk biscuits were heaven. Betty Jo's Diner was also a great place for her to relax, even if the staff did try to get you to eat and leave quickly. Like many diners, it was made to look like an old railroad car, but a small one. There were only a few tables and a small counter to sit at, so the staff liked to speed up customer turnover.

Sally pulled into the crowded lunchtime parking lot and managed to find a seat at the counter. Her favorite waitress, Belle, was standing behind it with a pot of coffee in her hand. Belle had been working there ever since it opened in 1960. She was now eighty, stooped low, and with severe arthritis in one arm. Sally hoped Belle would retire soon so that she could enjoy her golden years without risking pouring coffee down herself—or others—with her less-than-steady hand, though the diner wouldn't be the same without her.

"Hi, Sally, nice to see you. Coffee?"

The coffee wobbled in Belle's hand, the good one.

"Hi, Belle. You bet," Sally quickly responded. "That's why I come here, for the coffee. And the gourmet food."

They both laughed.

Sally sipped the coffee while she perused the paper menu, which also served as a placemat. Sally didn't know why she was bothering; she always ordered the same thing.

"What will you have today?" Belle asked.

"I'll have the all-day breakfast special, extra bacon and extra sausage."

"Same as always." She grinned. "You got it. Comin' right up."

Sally sat back and sipped her coffee. She glanced around at the other customers and was pleased when she caught sight of Detective Finnegan in the back, alone with his BLT.

He glanced up at that moment and waved half-heartedly. Then put his head back down. She debated whether she should bother him on a Sunday, but she needed all the information she could get if she was going to solve Bill's murder.

She motioned to Belle she was moving seats, picked up her coffee, and casually strolled down to Finnegan's booth.

"Mind if I join you, Detective?"

He looked up again. He was not smiling.

"Have a seat."

"Thanks."

She slid into the booth just as Belle came over with Sally's hot plate of greasy food.

"You enjoy, honey."

Sally dove right in. Everything was extra greasy, but extra good. It wasn't quite the good Southern breakfast she had grown up with in Savannah, but it did always hit the spot. She had moved to Atlanta for college and never left, until she moved to Berry Springs. She always regretted not moving back to Savannah after college. It was a charming old town and a wonderfully relaxing place to live. Maybe that is why she had quickly fallen in love with Berry Springs. It reminded her of home.

Finnegan broke the silence. "I heard you are detecting, Sally."

Up to that point, she had only talked to the mayor and Father O'Malley.

It wouldn't have been the priest, so Jennifer must have tipped him—or his boss—off. It wasn't surprising as although she had been helpful, the drop-in visit had obviously annoyed her.

"News travels fast," she said, nodding.

"Sure you're up to it?"

She could never figure out whether she liked the detective or vice versa, but she was going to interpret it as genuine care. For now. "I will be. I am determined to solve his murder."

"Me too, Sally. I'd like you to come down to the station when you're finished. I've got a few more questions I want to ask you."

"Sure. I was going to talk to Margaret Jackson next. You know she lives across the street. Could I stop by after that?"

Finnegan considered for a moment. He seemed about to object but just said, "Sure."

"Thanks. Have you talked to Margaret yet?" Sally asked.

"Yup, that's why I headed here for a sandwich afterwards."

That could be problematic. If she'd already spoken to the detective, she may not want to have to repeat the whole process again with Sally. She tried a different approach.

"Anything interesting from her?"

Finnegan ignored her probing and just replied, "I'm keeping an open mind."

Sally didn't want to press her luck with him, but any information he shared would be helpful. She wasn't sure what he meant by keeping an open mind, but maybe she could get something out of him when she meant him at the station to answer his questions.

"Great. Thanks."

He asked Belle for the bill, paid quickly, and left after a quick goodbye to Sally.

She shoveled the last bit of scrambled egg into her mouth and washed it down with the rest of the black coffee.

"Thanks, Belle. Top eating, as always." She put ten dollars on the counter and headed to Margaret Jackson's across the street.

Chapter Nine

S ally decided it would be best to give Margaret a little more time between interviews—she didn't want to start off on the wrong foot again, like with the mayor—so she sat in her car for a few minutes, going over what she knew so far.

Father O'Malley and the mayor hadn't seen much, though she couldn't have expected them to notice every detail that would help the investigation; like the other customers, they had been sitting in the middle of a large Saturday night crowd, seemingly engrossed in conversation.

However, Sally felt Father O'Malley had not been as forthcoming about his conversation with Jeff Smith. Maybe Father O'Malley treated it more like a confession, and at that, he would clam up, as he should. Sally wouldn't want him spilling the beans on what she told him at her occasional confession. Though the priest could also sometimes be forgetful, and he seemed a bit flushed by her questioning him at coffee hour. Maybe that hadn't been such a good idea. She could have been more discrete. She would have to visit him again when he was alone in his office.

Thinking back to her conversation with the mayor, Sally didn't think Jennifer Milkowski had had a good answer for why Bill would be coming to fix the restrooms at town hall. Having spoken to Bill before, Sally wasn't even sure Bill liked the mayor. His family didn't like big egos. But Bill did tend to be helpful, sometimes overly helpful, so perhaps Mayor Milkowski was telling the truth.

Sally glanced across the street at Margaret's building, another one of the beautiful sights in town. It was a beautiful structure in pale brick with several ornamental carved monkeys across the roof. She always admired it when she had food at Betty Jo's and had seen Margaret come out the side door a couple of times, which was what had made it so easy to know where she lived. Looking up now, she saw a movement on the second floor as Margaret appeared and opened a window. Great, she was home.

Gathering her thoughts, Sally climbed out of the car and headed across the street.

Margaret's building housed a café on the ground floor, so the entrance to the apartments was around the side. She was interested to hear what Margaret had to say about that night but also to hear about what she talked about with the mayor.

She had just gotten to the door and was about to buzz when she heard Margaret's voice from the open window above.

"…Yeah, I get it. Don't worry…" she heard Margaret say. Then silence.

Who could Margaret be speaking to? From her tone, it didn't sound like a pleasant conversation. Sally's detective brain immediately assumed it was the mayor on the phone, warning her about Sally's visit. The mayor was Margaret's boss and could be very dictatorial at times, though Sally couldn't figure out why she would be warning Margaret. One more topic to get out of her.

Sally pushed the buzzer next to *Jackson*.

"Yeah," Margaret barked through the intercom.

"Um, hey, Margaret. It's Sally. Can I come up?" Sally asked.

There was a long pause before the door buzzed. Sally pushed it open and walked up the two flights of stairs.

Margaret was standing in the open doorway with her hands on her hips. She had obviously not been expecting company on a Sunday. Her curly black hair was a mess. And she was wearing a gray tracksuit with the town logo on it. The tracksuit showed the fullness of her figure, but she didn't seem to care.

"Hi, Sally, come on in. Have a seat."

She led Sally to the living room, which was small and covered in piles of newspaper everywhere. The living room doubled as the dining room, and the small round table in the corner was also covered in newspapers. Sally wasn't sure where to sit.

"Oh, sorry," Margaret said as she chucked the newspapers onto the floor. "Coffee?"

"No, thanks, I just came from Betty Jo's."

"So what can I do for you?" Margaret asked after making herself a coffee and settling herself into the one other open chair in the room—a green armchair with worn arms and squeaky springs.

Sally was still debating how best to start and now wished she had asked for a coffee to sip and kill time with while she thought.

"I guess you heard about Bill."

"Yeah, Jennifer called me early this morning after she had heard from Chief Pulasky. And I just had a visit from Detective Finnegan."

"Well, I'm trying to find out if anyone saw anything that night. You know when Bill left or if someone saw someone lurking outside."

Margaret looked out the open window and sighed.

"Sally, I know you love solving puzzles, and you've helped a few people find lost jewelry and pets, but don't you think trying to solve a murder is a bit out of your league?"

Sally had jumped into the detective role without a thought, and she wasn't going to stop even if she had never investigated a murder before.

Though Sally understood how her visit must seem to Margaret. Getting questioned twice in one day could get annoying, and she hoped Margaret wouldn't ask her to leave right away.

She looked at Margaret and shrugged her shoulders.

Margaret stared at Sally and said nothing for several seconds.

"Ah, what the hell," she finally replied, "I like you."

Sally smiled a weird, toothy grin.

"I was talking to Jennifer, so I didn't see anything," Margaret explained.

"You never got up from the table?"

"Well, I did go to the restroom. Oh, and I had to go to the bar myself once to refill our drinks—you need to hire more staff."

Sally ignored the comment and pressed forward. "What were you talking to Jennifer about?"

"Town business. There have been problems with flooding recently with all the runoff from the rain. I was pushing her to invest in upgrading the sewer system."

Sally knew that wouldn't have gone over well. A new sewer system was not prestigious. And it would cost a lot of money.

"Did Jennifer ever leave the table?" Sally inquired.

"No, we talked the whole time. As I said, I just got up to get us drinks once and also went to the restroom."

"Did you see or talk to Bill?"

Margaret thought for a second.

"Um, I...no, he never came by. I saw him talking to his biker buddies and then, of course, breaking up the fight between Jeff and Zeke."

Sally frowned. The mayor had said she'd spoken to Bill about helping fix the restrooms at town hall. Why would Margaret forget that?

"You're sure he never came by the table?"

"Yes, I'm sure. Why would I lie?" Margaret replied, crossing her arms.

It was time to leave. Sally got up. "Margaret, thanks so much for your time. If you think of anything later, please call me."

Margaret just nodded and brought her to the door.

Sally walked downstairs, but waited outside the building door for a few moments under the open window. She thought there might be another conversation she didn't want to miss. It didn't take long for her to hear Margaret's voice.

"...Yeah, all set..." she heard Margaret say.

Sally would definitely have to find out what that was all about. Though, then again, it might be nothing.

Chapter Ten

J eff was the final person on Sally's list of last night's customers to interview. Besides recovering from the fight the night before, he would probably also have a terrific hangover from all the beer he had consumed. She wouldn't get any sense out of him until at least mid-afternoon, so she decided to wait until after following up on Detective Finnegan's request to come to the station before she headed over to his place.

The police station was on the far side of the town hall across the square from Margaret's apartment, so it only took Sally a few minutes to walk over. In the lobby, she found the detective waiting for her.

'Coffee?' he asked as they both headed to the elevator. Although she felt like she could sleep for a week, her veins were buzzing from her third cup already that day. She shook her head.

From the elevator, the walk down the hall to the interrogation room took a while due to Finnegan's bulk. Luckily, there were no stairs involved.

They sat across from each other at the cold metal table, Sally trying to find a comfortable way to sit on the steel-backed chair.

Finnegan put the blue folder he was carrying on the table between them. It was upside down, but Sally read the case number: *#3465*. A number Finnegan was probably hoping would make him police chief.

"Anything from Margaret?" he began.

Sally felt the conversation was friendly. Finnegan had given no indication this was an official interrogation. And at the moment, Sally was the one who found the body, nothing else. At least, that's what Sally kept telling herself. Finnegan seemed intent on getting 'justice' as quickly as possible.

So Sally debated what she should tell him. A part of her saw this investigation as a competition, though that made no sense. The main goal was solving Bill's murder. If that meant the police got there first, so be it. But still, Sally wanted to be the one to secure justice for her friend.

"Well, Detective, to be honest, I haven't gotten much beyond conflicting stories and little to no information at all. Father O'Malley, the mayor, and Margaret basically said they were all sitting at their respective tables most of the night and didn't really see anything unusual. Father O'Malley did think the fight between Jeff and Zeke might have something to do with Zeke's son. And the mayor told me some strange story about Bill offering to come and help fix the restrooms here at the town hall. When I pressed her, she brushed it off. Margaret, for some reason, didn't mention it at all. Only that she and the mayor had been talking about the town's flooding problems."

Finnegan opened his mouth in surprise.

"Well, you got a bit more than I did. And I haven't even had a chance to talk to the priest yet."

Sally glowed, but told herself to be more judicious with information for the police in the future. "What did they tell you?"

"Um, well, the mayor told me she hadn't seen anything."

"You didn't push for more?"

"Well, she is my boss's boss."

"And Margaret?"

"She just told me that she hadn't seen anything and the bit about the flooding discussion. Neither the mayor nor Margaret mentioned anything about Bill coming by to talk to them."

So Finnegan had nothing. She wasn't really surprised. Time to get some actual information from him.

"So, any news on how Bill was killed?"

"Now, now, Sally. As I said at the diner, I asked you here to answer a few more questions. Then I might be able to share some information."

Except I've just done your job for you? But she wasn't about to point that out and instead squirmed in her seat. She hoped the questioning would be worth it so she could get some information out of him.

"Sure, go ahead," she said.

With that, he turned on a tape recorder at the edge of the table and huffed a bit as he settled back down, his stomach touching the table.

"Well, the first question is, who do you think killed Bill? I mean, did he have any enemies?"

Sally raised her eyebrows, not expecting him to open with this. She had thought he would be more interested in time of death and what she might have seen that night.

She played nervously with her ponytail.

"Um, well, his family has been here a long time, so who knows who may have had a grudge against him. You knew him too, Detective. He was a big cuddly bear who helped everyone he could."

Finnegan shrugged. "But was there anything happening recently that might make someone want to kill him? You mentioned that fight just now."

Sally had told him about the fights at the bar when he had first questioned her.

"Yeah, well, it seems to me that Bill's death was planned, you know, because of the syringe. If it was to do with that fight between Jeff and Zeke, that seems more spontaneous, doesn't it?"

She threw up her hands. "Though I'm not a psychologist."

Or a cop, she thought to herself. Finnegan was nice enough not to blurt that out.

"But you think Zeke might have been mad at Jeff about something else?"

"Well, Jeff is the high-school basketball coach, and Zeke's son is on the team. Maybe he benched the son, and the beers the both men had resulted in the fight."

"And Bill broke up the fight?"

"Yeah, he doesn't like to see one of his biker buddies getting hurt."

"So Jeff might have been angry enough to kill him?"

Sally laughed. "Jeff? He's a well-loved teacher in town. You know that." She wasn't sure why she was defending him, because she also knew that alcohol and anger can make people do things they probably would never have done otherwise.

"You can think of no one else that might want Bill dead?"

"Not really. He was his regular happy self, like he was most nights at the bar. Otherwise, he had a really tight-knit family. You know how they all were when we went to see them."

"Right," Finnegan said.

"He's such a caring person. I have no idea who would want to kill him, but I've been racking my brain since I found him." Sally felt a couple of tears drip down her face, and she quickly wiped them away, hoping the detective didn't notice.

"Did you see anything unusual last night?"

She hadn't even thought about that. She had been running around questioning people, she forgot to ask herself. "That's a good question. It was really busy last night, though I was mainly behind the bar, helping Magda pour drinks. I went to the cellar a couple of times to restock the bar."

"You talk to Bill?"

"Just to thank him for breaking up the fight. We rarely had a chance to chat while I was working. And Bill always spent most of the time with his biker buddies and liked to be left alone, as if he were just a regular customer."

Sally had one question of her own that was burning in her mind. "What about the syringe, Detective? Did you find anything out?"

Finnegan had pushed his bulk up to lean over and turn off the tape recorder.

"The syringe?" he asked.

"Um, yeah, you found it last night under the dumpster."

Finnegan would be restricted with what information he could—or would want—to share with her, but he looked down at the blue folder he had open in front of him and pulled out the last page, sliding across to her without saying a word.

She scanned the paper, a good amount of which had been redacted, and the word *poison* jumped out at her.

"You think Bill was poisoned?"

"At the moment, I just know that the syringe contained the poison strychnine. We haven't ascertained if it killed Bill."

"But I saw blood on the side of his head."

"Looks like it's a bit more complicated than I hoped," Finnegan said, though he didn't seem too concerned.

She looked down at the page. "What about these blacked-out sections, Detective?"

"Police only, I'm afraid, Sally," he replied. He pulled the sheet back.

"And the time of death?" she asked.

Finnegan shook his head.

Boy, he was really playing hard to get.

"Well, thanks for sharing what you can, Detective."

He didn't respond to this but pushed himself up and reached across to shake her hand.

"Thanks for coming in, Sally. I'll let you know when we get the full forensics report. I'm sure I can share at least some of the information with you. You seem to have a good nose for detecting, but like I said before, please be careful and don't get yourself into any dangerous situations. If we want to solve Bill's murder, I can't be running around, getting you out of scrapes."

Sally shook his hand, which was moist. "Thanks, Detective. I'll be sure to be careful."

She turned to leave, then stopped.

"When can I reopen the bar, Detective?"

She wanted some time off to try and solve the murder, but she needed to keep the bar, and her income, moving along.

"I think we will be done by Tuesday, so you can reopen Wednesday."

She frowned. "Wednesday? Detective, this is my livelihood."

"You do want us to find Bill's killer, don't you? It's two days of lost revenue, no more. I've hurried up Forensics so you can open faster. It could have been later."

Sally wondered if the speed was to do more with his career aspirations than her income.

"Okay. All right."

He turned to head back to his office.

"Oh, one more thing, Detective. What about Bill's body? I know Momma Arnold will want to bury her son as soon as possible."

Finnegan was moving from one leg to another. She was pushing her luck and his patience.

"That's going to be a bit longer. I'm calling over to their place again later today."

Sally would love to have gone with him, but she was eager to get out of there to see if Jeff was available. Hopefully, he would be more forthcoming than Margaret, the mayor, or Father O'Malley.

On her way out, she looked around to see if Sergeant Soder was there, but no luck. He might be more helpful than Detective Finnegan had been, though she didn't want to get him into trouble.

Chapter Eleven

L eaving the town hall, Sally checked her watch. It was already 5 p.m.; maybe not the best time to visit Jeff. He would have to work the next day, and maybe it would be best if she called ahead and made sure he was in a mood to talk.

As she strolled down Oak Street, breathing in the fresh air and clearing her head, she thought it would be nice to invite Jay and Magda over for dinner so they could talk about what had happened, check they were okay.

Jay and Magda! She hadn't called them. And they would have probably heard about Bill.

Sally checked her phone. Five missed calls. All from Magda.

The poor kids.

* * *

Magda had been obviously crying for a while when Sally returned her calls, her voice cracked and raw. Magda had heard about Bill's death from her neighbor, and Sally apologized that it hadn't been her to break the news. It took a look of consoling and convincing for Magda to finally agree to come to dinner. Jay hadn't been available that evening. He had been shocked at hearing about Bill's death but said he had other plans. Sally thought the death may have hit him harder than he wanted to admit, and he didn't want Sally, or Magda to see that.

The two women sat across from each other at Sally's dining-room table. The sun had finally set, and it was starting to get chilly. Fall was almost upon them.

Sally had warmed up the beef stew she had made for lunch the day before and opened a new bottle of her favorite Chilean red wine. It wasn't much, but she hadn't exactly had time to shop or cook that day. And her mind was elsewhere. In the end, neither of them had been able to eat much.

What they had eaten had been consumed in silence. Sally wasn't going to push Magda. And she could tell Magda was still upset about not finding out about Bill directly from Sally.

"Can I get you some more wine?" Sally asked.

Magda pushed her plate away and took a sip of water. Her short brown hair bobbing. "No, thanks. I can't keep anything down. Some more water would be great, though."

"How about some herbal tea?"

Magda gagged.

Sally smiled. "No then, just the water." Sally cleared the plates and went into the kitchen to get Magda's water and pour herself another glass of wine.

Back in the dining room, she sat down next to Magda. "Magda, I'm so sorry I didn't call you earlier."

"How could you, Sally? Bill was our boss, but also our friend."

Magda took a deep breath.

"I know, but I was so upset myself and just got caught up in—"

"In trying to solve the crime before the police do," Magda said with a harrumph.

Sally nodded.

"I've never investigated a murder before, I know, but since Bill was killed, I feel like I have to do it and learn quickly in the process."

Magda laughed.

"Yeah, I kind of thought you might," she replied.

Sally was glad Magda had recognized this.

But she needed Magda and Jay, or the bar would be a mess, so she still had to be careful about questioning Magda too much at this point, but one of them must have seen something. "I just don't get how someone could kill him. The bar was so full last night. Who would do this? And so horrifying you had to find him."

Magda patted Sally's shoulder, and they hugged.

"Somehow, I'm glad it was me who found him," Sally said, surprising even herself.

"Why?"

"Well, maybe the murderer would have come back to get rid of his body, and then we would never know what happened to him."

Magda shuddered. "But who would want to kill him?"

"No idea. He seemed to be loved by all."

Magda looked away. What was that about?

"You were behind the bar like I was," Sally probed, "so I guess neither of us would have noticed something."

"It was so crazy last night. I felt like I spent the whole night just pouring drinks and washing glasses. Jay was on table duty, which is at least more varied. And then maybe I would have noticed something."

"You didn't serve anyone last night, did you?"

"No, why?"

Sally wasn't going to push it.

Magda checked her phone.

"It's late. I need to get home."

Sally led her to the door. "Detective Finnegan told me we should be able to reopen Wednesday, so take a couple days off and meet me Wednesday at three p.m. at the bar. I'll let Jay know."

Magda sniffled. "Sure."

Sally watched as Magda walked down toward her car in Sally's driveway. Magda had rented a one-room apartment south of town on Route 10, about halfway between Berry Springs center and Sally's Smasher. Her car wasn't very reliable, so she often walked to work, but at least it hadn't failed her tonight.

Chapter Twelve

T he next morning, Sally telephoned the school to talk to Jeff. She had thought of calling him before he got to work, but she wanted him to be on her good side if she was going to get any information out of him, and an early wake-up call would not have done her any favors.

Sally inwardly groaned when Bethany Wells answered the phone. Bethany was the school assistant but also the town gossip, and Sally knew it would be nearly impossible to keep the conversation short.

"Hi, Bethany. How are you doing? It's Sally."

"Oh, hi, Sally. I'm fine."

Sally wasn't going to try and probe how Bethany felt after having a bit too much to drink Saturday night. Who knows what Bethany the gossip would turn that into. Probably Sally harassing her for drinking so much. Then again, Sally did own a bar.

"I was hoping to talk to Jeff Bartholomew," she said sweetly.

"Really? What for? The school day has already started."

Sally ignored the question, though Bethany was her best (wine) customer, so she tried to be pleasant with her.

"Does he have a class right now?"

"You know I'm not supposed to give out that information. Security at the high school is tight, as, unfortunately, we have to be."

Sally nodded inwardly. Going to school these days wasn't as carefree as it used to be. School shootings were numerous in the country. And many schools tried to avoid that at all costs, even if that meant locking down like a prison. And not revealing any information to anyone not directly connected to the school.

So, Sally would have to take another tack. "It's about Saturday night at the bar. I just want to talk to him."

"Oh, I heard. Can you believe he got thrown out of the bar by Bill?"

Sally wondered why that was more important than Bill getting killed, but whatever.

"I just need to talk to him."

She could almost hear the cogs in Bethany's brain, wondering how much she should try and get out of Sally.

"Well, I will let him know you called. Give me your cell number, and I'll have him call you back."

Sally knew Jeff had her number, but she dictated it for some reason anyway, thanked Bethany, and hung up. She shook her head; Bethany was incorrigible.

* * *

Sally had just gotten out of the shower about an hour later when Jeff called her back. Apparently, everyone in town just assumed Sally was going to want to solve the murder, though Sally wondered why they all jumped to this conclusion.

Though actually, she knew why. She liked to solve puzzles, she liked to be in charge, and when something bad happened to someone close to her, she needed to be right in the middle of it.

That's why she felt he hadn't seemed surprised at all to hear from her, and they arranged to meet at his house after school broke up at five that afternoon. She had been vague about why she wanted to see him. She had told him she just wanted someone to talk to after Bill's death. Though she didn't think he quite believed her. She just hoped that Detective Finnegan hadn't already gotten to him and rubbed him the wrong way.

It was a long drive out to Jeff's place in Beaver Village on Silver Lake, and she didn't want to be late. She always wondered why Jeff lived so far from Berry Springs and Clinton High School, where he worked. She assumed it was to not bump into his students outside of work, though that was never completely avoidable since Berry Springs was the largest town in the area and was where most people went on a weekend.

She left her house, heading south on Route 10 toward Beaver Village. When she passed her bar, she cringed as she saw a large van parked out front. The Forensics team was still there. *I hope they aren't making too much of a mess.*

About five miles south of her bar, she turned right on Route 36. Still fifteen miles to go.

She had just passed the county hunting clubhouse when she heard a car backfire. Looking in her rearview mirror, she noticed a silver pickup truck following her closely. She hadn't seen or heard it before because she was tuned out thinking about Bill's murder. How long had it been behind her? They hadn't passed any turnoffs for a few miles.

She sped up, running her hands over the steering wheel. Gladys wasn't that fast, and she didn't want to push the old Datsun too much.

She looked in the mirror again, and the pickup had sped up too.

She wanted to go faster, but there were three hairpin curves coming up, about halfway to Beaver Village, and she didn't want to go flying off the road into a ditch or worse—some of the road followed an old mining gully, and if she went off there, it was a few hundred feet down to a nasty end.

Keeping her hands tightly gripped on the wheel, Sally maneuvered through the first curve much too fast. The right-hand bend caused the left rear tire to leave the road surface. She breathed heavily to stop herself from panicking and managed to steady the car. The pickup was getting closer, and the road was narrowing.

She slowed down at the next curve, and she felt a jolt from behind as the pickup collided with her rear bumper.

Now she panicked, sweat on her brow.

She quickly looked in the mirror to see the driver's face, but there was a glare on the windshield blocking her view. She slammed on the gas and saw an escape: one of the turnoffs toward the lake. She wasn't sure how she was going to make the turn without flipping the Datsun, but at this point, she just wanted to get away from the pickup. Just as she was slowing down to try the left-hand turn, the pickup went blasting by, honking at her.

She slowed down and pulled off the road to catch her breath, her heart in her throat. She sat for a few minutes to pull herself together.

People often follow closely, but hitting her bumper was obviously no case of simple road rage. Sally had just started her investigation, but could this already be a warning to back off? She debated heading home to clear her head, but she pushed on for the sake of Bill.

Reaching over to the passenger seat, she pulled out her phone and called Jeff to tell him she would be a little late.

"Hi, Sally. Not coming today?"

"No, Jeff, I'll be there in thirty minutes or so."

"What's wrong, Sally? You sound shaken."

He was stunned when he heard what happened to her and was glad she was okay.

Hanging up the phone, she collapsed over the wheel. She needed more time to catch her breath, and her mind was whirling with who that could have been in the pickup. There were too many pickups in Berry Springs for her to immediately say, "Oh, that was so-and-so's car," and she hadn't gotten the number plate.

She finally sat up and started the Datsun. Good old Gladys never let her down when she needed her most. Shifting into first and looking both ways, she pulled onto the road toward Beaver Village. She was wary the pickup might return, but she didn't pass any cars for the rest of the trip.

Chapter Thirteen

S ally stopped the car at the top of Jeff's gravel drive, took a breath of fresh air through the open window, and enjoyed the view of the lake as the cooling engine clicked over. The pine trees that lined the lake were beautiful, and only a few houses were built there. It was almost pristine, untouched country. Sights like this always reminded Sally of why she loved Berry Springs. The natural beauty helped calm her after the harrowing incident driving there. Her heart was still pounding a mile a minute.

She finally looked away and walked over to the front door. As she knocked, she heard loud barking from Jeff's Labrador retriever, Bacon. She could hear the dog scrambling toward the door. Sally loved that dog; her bark was definitely worse than her bite.

Jeff opened the door with a worried look on his face. "Are you really okay, Sally? That was quite a shock you had."

She looked down and saw her hands were shaking. She put them in the pockets of her jeans jacket to steady them. "Yeah, I'm fine."

He led her into the living room. "Would you like something to drink?"

She thought for a minute. "Rum and coke would be great." One wouldn't hurt. After the pickup incident, she needed more than a cup of coffee or tea.

Jeff went out to the kitchen to make the drinks.

Sally sat in the comfy armchair and scanned the room. Everything was just in its place and looked so cozy. She could imagine living in a wonderful house on the lake. Looking over at the table in the corner, she guessed Jeff hadn't been home that long when she had called. There was a backpack, a briefcase, and a small black leather folder piled on the table.

Settling into the comfy armchairs, Jeff sat watching her. "Do you think it was an accident?"

"What do you mean?"

"The pickup, you idiot," he said a bit louder.

"Why would someone want to hurt me?" she asked. Though she knew the answer already, even if she didn't want to fully admit it to herself.

"Good question, but it sounds more deliberate than anything else," Jeff replied.

Sally considered how she should start her questioning. She did want to get as much information out of him as possible, and she didn't want the business with the pickup distracting the question. On the other hand, they knew each other quite well—she and Jeff volunteered on the Fourth of July Committee each year, and they always got along—so she didn't want to jump right into an interrogation. On the phone, she had just told Jeff that she needed to get out of town after Bill's death and have someone to talk to. He was a good listener.

They remained silent for a minute.

"I'll miss Bill," he finally said.

"Yes. me too." Her voice cracked. "Why would someone do this to him? I hope the police find his killer soon."

"Well, they talked to me already."

"Really? I had no idea."

She wasn't a very good liar, but Jeff seemed to buy it.

"Yeah, well, after what happened at the bar Saturday night, I bet a few people thought I killed him."

Sally said nothing.

"I'm still ashamed about the fight," Jeff continued. "And I'll pay for that chair I damaged, Sally, no arguments. I'm still amazed I was able to bend wrought iron, but I fell pretty hard."

"Thanks, Jeff. That is kind. I was really worried on Saturday night—I thought you would all completely smash up my bar. Thought it would then really be Sally's Smasher." She grinned in spite of herself.

"Good point." Jeff laughed.

Then his face went grim. "I'm glad Bill broke up the fight. Zeke's a good guy, even if his son is a little brat."

"Is that why you two got into the fight?"

Jeff shook his head. "I was drunk and really annoyed at the loud bikers. Zeke just happened to be standing closest to our table."

Sally wasn't sure that was the full truth, but she let it go. For now.

"How did you get home that night?" Sally asked.

"I called a cab from outside the bar."

She frowned. "Geez, Jeff. I'm sorry. It was so busy that night, I should have had Jay or Magda or someone else give you a ride home."

"Well, at least I made it home. Unlike Bill…"

Now was the time to start questioning, though she had to be careful about it.

"Did you happen to see anybody strange outside that night?"

Okay, so there was no being careful about it there.

Jeff looked up at her, his eyes wide.

"Are you investigating, Sally Witherspoon?"

"I owe it to Bill."

"You owe it to yourself to not get killed."

"Well, yeah, but you know me, the inquisitive type," Sally offered.

"Be careful, Sally."

He raised his voice and leaned forward in his chair.

Gee, that's what everyone was telling her. But if they really knew her, they would know that she couldn't just let it be. And the suggestions were really getting on her nerves. She wasn't a child.

"Well, I can't tell you much. I was sitting chatting with Father O'Malley. He was worrying about the lower numbers of parishioners every Sunday and wondered if I had any ideas to boost attendance at mass."

Sally looked at him. Father O'Malley had said they'd been discussing a student they'd been concerned about. This was the second time the stories didn't match up. The mayor had told her Bill was going to help fix the restroom, but Margaret never mentioned it. And now Jeff was telling her a different tale to Father O'Malley at church the day before. This was bizarre.

Maybe just bad memories from all the alcohol the people had consumed. Or something worse. Much worse.

"Did you talk about any students?" Sally inquired.

"No, why?" His furrowed brow showed confusion.

"Just wondering."

"Sorry I can't be of more help," Jeff replied.

"I know you want to help. And thanks for letting me stop by."

She sipped her rum and coke and began feeling a little light-headed. She hadn't had anything to eat for a while.

"Would you like something to eat or maybe some water?"

Jeff must have noticed her unsteadiness in the chair.

"Food would be good. I don't think I can drive home yet," she admitted.

Jeff got up to go to the kitchen. "Won't be a minute."

Chapter Fourteen

Sally was glad to get some food and coffee in her. That rum and coke Jeff had mixed for her had been much too strong.

In spite of her feeling much better, she was still a bit wary of driving home. She took it slowly. This was partly due to the drink she had had, but also because she was worried she would be tailgated again. If she drove slowly, she could more easily pull over, hoping the pursuer would simply drive by again.

Except this wasn't a movie or book, and, of course, there was no pursuer, and she made it the twenty miles in safety. She'd probably just misinterpreted the whole thing, and the pickup had never bumped her. It might have been driving too close, but maybe she'd gone over a pothole or something.

Pulling into her short driveway and under the carport, she was surprised to see Mark Soder standing on her porch. The automatic sensor had done its job, and he was bathed in white light. He looked quite different out of uniform, dressed in a white skin-tight T-shirt, his arms bulging, and jeans. The typical jeans jacket of the area was over his arm, along with a black backpack.

The front light went off automatically after five minutes, so he couldn't have been there long.

She grabbed her backpack and checked her phone. 11 p.m. on a Monday night. It was a bit late to be making inquiries about Bill's case. What was he doing there?

"What's up, Mark?" she said as she approached the porch.

In spite of the pickup trying to push her off the road and the drink she had had at Jeff's, she tried to maintain a semblance of normality. If Finnegan got word that something had happened, he would block her from the case, and without any details from him, she would probably never solve it.

Soder was probably just checking in on her.

"Hey, Sally. Can I come in?" His eyes darted about.

Well, that was a bit shifty. She ushered him into the kitchen without saying another word.

They sat down at the kitchen table. She didn't think of offering him a drink. She certainly didn't need one at this point.

From the black backpack, he pulled out a familiar blue folder, which seemed to be the Berry Springs Police standard. His hands shook as he passed it across the table for Sally to look at.

Opening the folder, she quickly read through the page that was in it. It looked identical to the page Detective Finnegan had shown her the day before, but now nothing was blacked out.

About halfway through reading the report, she raised her eyebrows.

"Cause of death—strychnine poisoning," she read out loud. "So he was poisoned. And his head was bashed in?" She stared at Mark.

"Yeah, that's what it looked like. But apparently, that was just to cover up the real murder. And Dr. Wiggams, our medical examiner, also found strychnine in the syringe Detective Finnegan discovered underneath the dumpster."

"Yeah, Finnegan told me about the syringe yesterday. Though the page was mainly blacked out, so why are you showing this to me?"

"Well, I know Finnegan wanted to give you some information. But when he got the full report, he decided to only tell you about the poison in the syringe, not about whether it was used to kill Bill or the actual time of death."

She frowned.

"Why not?"

"Isn't it obvious, Sally? He sees you as the competition. He's keeping you on a short leash, feeding you just enough to keep you occupied, so you can reveal to him anything you find out."

"Wow, Mark. Thanks for this. I really appreciate it."

Mark swallowed and played with the collar of his shirt. "I could get fired for this."

She nodded knowingly and looked back down to finish the report. Again reading out loud, she said, "Time of death between midnight and one a.m."

He must have just been leaving when he was killed. Since she had felt the warmth from the motorcycle, it must have been closer to 1 a.m. than midnight. Though maybe he'd come back for some reason.

When she was done, she pushed the report back across the table. A part of her was stunned, but her financial analyst brain went into high gear, in spite of the current condition of her stomach. "Anything else you can tell me?" she asked Mark.

"We talked to Dr. Wiggams. As you saw in the report, the head bashing was post-mortem, which explains the small amount of blood you saw on the side of his head.

"How was he poisoned?"

"Dr. Wiggams surmises he was either injected sometime in the evening with a very small, very thin needle—matching the syringe found at the scene. Either that or the poison was in something he drank. There was a small puncture wound on his right forearm, but it could have been a bug bite. Dr. Wiggams couldn't be one hundred percent sure, but he believes it was injected."

It wasn't hard to imagine that. Dr. Wiggams was already over seventy and should have retired years ago. His hands shook when he talked to you. He was tall, although stooped from his years of hunching over bodies, and had a rather disconcerting habit of playing with his glasses.

"How long does strychnine take to act?"

"Well, he told us the symptoms usually start showing up within a half hour, but as Bill was a big, hefty man, it could have taken longer, maybe an hour or so. Probably longer to work if it was ingested. Though Dr. Wiggams isn't one hundred percent, I tend to agree with the doctor that it was the puncture wound that got him."

"Yeah, that seems to make sense. And if that is what Dr. Wiggams tends toward, then let's run with that."

Her words sounded so matter-of-fact, but inside, she was trying not to think about what Bill must have gone through in his last hours. She got up and poured herself a glass of water before proceeding.

She looked over at Mark, but he shook his head.

"The report says the estimated time of death is between midnight and one a.m. So that means that the strychnine must have entered his system no earlier than eleven?" Sally surmised.

That narrowed down the list of suspects to those last four customers at the bar from 11 pm-Zeke, Father O'Malley, Margaret, and the mayor. Her intuition had been right. Though she couldn't see a motive for any of the last customers, even if Zeke or Jeff were mad about Bill breaking up the fight, would they kill him? And anyway, if it was strychnine poison from that syringe, that would make Bill's murder premeditated. Who would carry around a poisoned syringe with them, just in case they feel the need to kill someone? She laughed out loud.

"What's so funny?"

"Nothing, just a thought."

Mark pulled another folder out of his bag. "This is the other really interesting piece of information. We took fingerprint samples of all your final customers when we questioned them yesterday and today."

"And…?"

"See for yourself."

When she saw the report, her hand went to her mouth. "The fingerprints on the syringe match those of Jeff Bartholomew." How could they? She'd only just come from his house…

Then she remembered Jeff had diabetes and used insulin. But the results showed strychnine in the syringe. How was that possible?

"We're bringing him in for questioning tomorrow morning. Promise you won't warn him. I don't think he's a flight risk, but I also don't want Finnegan finding out I gave you this information."

Sally nodded.

"No, I won't tell him, but I do have to admit that I just came from his house," she said.

65

Mark Soder smiled, "You seem to be on top of everything in this case."

"Well, actually…"

Her hands began to shake as she remembered the scary drive over to Jeff's.

"What is it, Sally?" Soder asked.

She took a deep breath.

"Well, I was over at Jeff's just now, but on the way, someone tried to run me off the road," she told him casually, as if she had just talked about a movie she wanted to see.

"What?" Soder said, jumping up.

"I'm okay. It's okay," Sally replied, motioning him to sit again, though she was acting calmer than she felt.

Soder was red in the face.

"I'm obviously on the right trail," Sally said.

"Yeah, you could say that. Be careful," Soder replied.

She could take care of herself, but tracking murderers was dangerous business she was learning, perhaps a bit too slowly. And she had only just started.

"I will, Mark," she said, yawning and getting up from her chair.

Mark got the signal and stood up himself.

"Okay, time for me to go," he said, smiling.

Sally led him to the door. When she shut it behind him, her head was spinning.

Chapter Fifteen

Sally woke up on Tuesday morning with a new sense of purpose. The details she had gotten from Mark Soder were going to help her solve the crime. She was sure of it.

The weather had turned colder, so she was seated with her morning coffee in the living room, the breakfasts on the patio over now for another year.

With all the information she had gotten, she needed to organize her thoughts. She pulled out her bright orange notebook to make some notes. She needed to figure out the timeline of what she knew so far. And thinking about the syringe, she wondered how Jeff fit into all of this. Why would his fingerprints be on the syringe? That was the thing that was bothering her the most, the damning fingerprint evidence against Jeff. She had known him for years and just couldn't believe he had anything to do with Bill's murder. There must be another reason for the fingerprints.

She opened her laptop and did a quick internet search. Hmm, strychnine is used in rat poison. Okay, so that could be anyone on this list. And the time it took to act seemed to fit with what Soder had told her.

At this point, she had a lot of information, a good list of suspects, but no motive. At least, no motive she could think of. She had read way too many detective novels over the years, and murderers usually had two motives: love or money.

Thinking about Bill, she couldn't figure out if one or both of these fit. The Arnolds had tons of money, and she assumed Bill's part of the Arnold family fortune would now be distributed among the family. And he had always promised her he would leave her his share of the bar, so she would own it

100 percent herself. She had always wanted to be the full owner, but she thought she would be able to buy Bill out at some point. Of course, Sally hadn't wanted to see him killed to get the share. Although, to others, she realized, this would give *her* a viable motive.

She would have to see what she could find out about his will. Maybe the Arnolds would help, or she could try to talk to his lawyer, Randall Wentworth. Of course, neither of them may be willing to talk, but as Sally was a client of Mr. Wentworth's too—Bill had recommended him—maybe she could persuade him to part with what he knew.

As for the other motive, love, Sally had no idea how this could fit in. As far as Sally knew, Bill wasn't seeing anyone. There were rumors around town that he was currently having an affair with Annette, Zeke's wife, but Sally just couldn't believe this was true. But if she were going to be thorough, she would look into this as well.

The ultimate motive might even be something she hadn't even thought of yet.

* * *

Randall Wentworth had agreed to meet her at eleven thirty that morning. His office was across the street from the town hall, so driving didn't make sense. And the fresh air would do her good. She still had a bit of a hangover from the rum and coke the previous day.

The receptionist led her into the expansive conference room. In spite of being a small-time law office, Wentworth, Shilling & Barnesworth had a big-city name with a big-city look. The room was dominated by a cherry-wood table with twelve leather swivel chairs around it. In the center of the table was a fancy teleconference speaker. In the corner was a matching sideboard covered with legal pads and golden ballpoint pens.

Sally wasn't so much impressed as reminded of her Atlanta job. That was why she tried to come here as little as possible. Everything felt a little too polished for Berry Springs. Sally much preferred it when Wentworth agreed to come to her house, but that wasn't often.

The receptionist brought in a plate of cookies, a large carafe of coffee, and two golden mugs. "Mr. Wentworth won't be long now," she said before tottering back to her desk.

Just as Sally was checking the time for the twelfth time, Randall Wentworth strode in, about twenty minutes late, and slid into the seat at the head of the table.

"Good morning," he said.

Only just, Sally thought.

He never apologized. And he was always late. This was another thing that reminded her of the bosses at her Atlanta job.

She leaned forward, feeling small compared to the massive table.

Randall Wentworth had steel-blue eyes and a well-groomed goatee that just oozed "powerful attorney." His black pinstripes completed the slightly cliché figure. This didn't quite fit with laid-back Berry Springs, but a lot of people were afraid of him, even his clients. So, the image must be working.

She didn't let people push her around, but even she was a little intimidated.

As long as he gets the job done, she thought. And in Berry Springs, it was better to have Randall Wentworth working for you than against you.

"Thank you for meeting me on such short notice." She smiled.

"What can I do for you, Ms. Witherspoon?"

She thought he already knew the answer to that, but she played along.

"As Bill Arnold's business partner, I wanted to find out about his will. I mean, he always promised to leave his share of the bar to me, so I was wondering…"

"If he did?"

"Well, yes."

Wentworth opened the leather-bound folder in front of him and pulled out a document.

Sally assumed this was Bill's will. She would love to get a copy of it, but she didn't think that was going to happen any time soon.

"I have here Bill's last will and testament, dated two months ago."

Sally raised her eyebrows.

Two months ago? Why would he have changed his will two months ago?

More importantly, what did he want to change in it? Now, she really needed to get her hands on a copy of the old will. But that was as likely to happen as Wentworth making copies of everything for her.

Wentworth began reading through it with solemnity—Sally didn't doubt he was enjoying the power. She sat on the edge of her slippery leather chair, waiting for him to speak.

"'I leave my forty percent share of Sally's Smasher bar to Sally Witherspoon...'" he read.

She beamed.

"...and Annette Parker."

"What the hell?" Sally blurted out.

The sadness of losing Bill went right out the window, at least for the moment.

Wentworth didn't react, however. He just kept staring at the paper.

Sally looked down at the floor and held back tears. Annette? Annette Parker? Zeke's wife? Why would she get part of the bar? Bill had always promised it to Sally—they were business partners, after all—not together with someone else in town. And what did Annette know about running a bar?

Apparently, the rumors Sally had been hearing about Annette and Bill were true. Sally was devastated.

She grabbed the arms of the chair until her knuckles turned white.

Wentworth continued, as if Sally had stayed quiet as a mouse the entire time.

"'I leave my precious Vincent Rapide bike to Sally Witherspoon so she can keep it in its proper place in the bar,'" he announced.

Sally tried to smile but became confused as Wentworth put the document back into the folder and closed it.

"What? That's it? What about the rest of his estate?"

Crossing his hands on the table, he smirked at her.

"I'm not at liberty to disclose that to you, I'm afraid, Ms. Witherspoon. And you know that."

Sally left the law office feeling sick and conflicted. Two months ago, Bill changed his will, but he had said nothing to her about it. Though she couldn't be sure, the previous version had been more generous to her, either. What had been going on with Bill? Had he ever had any intention of upholding his supposed promise of leaving the bar to her? She thought they had been so close, but then again, sometimes you don't really know someone.

Walking home, she planned her next move. She needed a bit of time to cool off, so she had a quick sandwich before calling the Arnolds. Momma Arnold rarely went out, and if Wentworth wasn't going to share the rest of the will with her, she hoped the Arnolds would.

Chapter Sixteen

"Thanks for seeing me so quickly, Momma Arnold," Sally began.

"Oh please, call me Carol, honey. We've known each other long enough, haven't we?"

Everyone in town called her Momma Arnold, so Sally had never thought otherwise.

"Oh, that is sweet of you," Sally beamed.

She and Momma Arnold were seated at the large kitchen table with a pot of tea and two mugs between them. Momma Arnold had just pulled a fresh batch of sugar cookies out of the oven, and they were cooling on the counter.

Sally's stomach growled at the smell.

Momma Arnold was dressed a bit differently than last time, with an old gray sweater over a pair of red slacks, but she was still wearing slippers.

"My pleasure. It's been such a hard few days since Bill left. I've been spending most of it baking, trying to get my mind off his death." She put her head down on the table and began weeping.

This brought tears to Sally's eyes. She hadn't really grieved for Bill yet; she wouldn't let herself. The time would come when she found his killer.

She let Momma Arnold cry, reaching over to rub her back, hoping she wouldn't be in too much of a state to tell Sally about the will. Maybe this wasn't the best time, but Sally had no time to waste.

Momma Arnold raised her head, brushing the tears and implicitly Sally's hand away. She took a strong sip of tea and looked over at Sally. "Sorry, I don't like people seeing me this way."

Momma Arnold smiled wanly. "You said you wanted to come over and talk about the will?"

Sally had called the house and was blunt about why she wanted to come over. There was no point wasting the journey if the Arnolds weren't willing to share straight out.

"I don't mean to intrude, and I know this is a bad time, but I just had some bad news from Randall Wentworth," Sally began.

"Ah, so you know about Annette."

So the family knew already? That was a surprise. She couldn't imagine that they'd be too pleased. "Well, I was speechless, to be honest, when I heard that Annette would be sharing Bill's part of the bar with me. I have no idea how that's going to work. Why Annette?"

Momma Arnold chuckled. "You had no idea, did you, honey?"

Sally's eyes widened. "About what?"

"Oh Sally, sometimes you really are naive. Annette was having an affair with Bill, of course."

"We all knew about it. I mean, we, in the family. I don't know who in town was aware. Or maybe a lot of people were just looking the other way."

Sally couldn't speak. There had been rumors she had heard, but a part of her just hadn't wanted to believe it. So she was shaken when Momma Arnold said it out loud.

Momma Arnold passed her the plate of sugar cookies, and she took two. Sipping her tea and dunking a cookie in it helped cushion the shock.

Momma Arnold stared out the window for a few seconds, and Sally wondered what was going on.

Finally, she pushed herself up and went over to the cabinet in the corner, opened a drawer, and pulled out a small envelope. She walked over to Sally and handed it to her.

"This is for you," Momma Arnold said, settling herself back down on her chair.

Sally stared at it, turning it over and over, scared to open it.

On the front it said 'To Sally,' in Bill's handwriting.

Momma Arnold stayed silent, though Sally felt she wanted to urge her to rip the envelope open. Sally didn't think it had been opened and resealed, so Momma Arnold must be as curious as she was.

Finally, Sally took a deep breath and ripped it open. Yes, she was impatient.

She opened the paper and read the handwritten note aloud.

'Dear Sally,' it began.

'If you are reading this, then I am in heaven (well, I hope so, lol). You have also found out that I left my share of the bar to you and Annette, and knowing you, you are very angry with me. So I'd like to explain why I did it. Sally, you are really my best friend in the whole world and Annette, well Annette, I love her so much. If I'm gone, I don't want you to have to run the bar on your own, and I thought if I leave a part of my share to Annette, this would bring you two together. I know she will want to help you now.'

Sally stopped reading as tears fell from her face. She glanced over at Momma Arnold, who was also crying.

"Go on," Momma Arnold croaked.

Sally finished reading: 'And if it doesn't work out with Annette, you can also buy her out. All my love from the grave, Bill.'

Momma Arnold laughed, "Always the businessman."

Sally put the letter down on the table and took another cookie, dipped it in her tea, and chewed on it.

She chased it down with a gulp of tea.

"I'm sad, but I'm glad I have an explanation from Bill. I guess a part of me is still angry, but life goes on," Sally said.

"It's a lot to digest for anyone, Sally," Momma Arnold said, patting her hand.

"You're right, of course," Sally replied, remembering her real reason to visit.

This helped her push the feelings about the bar out of her mind, at least temporarily.

"So what about the rest of Bill's estate?" Sally asked bluntly, probably too bluntly.

At this, Momma Arnold's face went dark.

"That is a matter for the courts," she said stiffly.

"What do you mean?"

Momma Arnold clenched her hands together before speaking through gritted teeth. "We found out yesterday from Randall Wentworth that Bill left most of the rest of his estate to Father O'Malley at St. Elspeth's. We, his family, only get ten thousand dollars."

"Father O'Malley? Why does he get Bill's money?"

Momma Arnold looked away. "I think I know," she finally said.

"What would the reason be?"

At this, Momma Arnold broke down in tears. "That's a family matter, Sally. I can't tell you."

Sally took the letter slipped it into her pocket, and got up. It was definitely time to leave.

"Thank you for the tea and cookies. And for the letter. I'm going to head out," she said.

Momma Arnold stopped crying and smiled.

"Thanks, hon, for stopping by. I hate you seeing me all emotional."

She got up and gave Sally a hug. They both walked together to the front door, and Sally headed out to her car.

Chapter Seventeen

Sally left the Arnold place and drove home. She debated going straight back to Randall Wentworth's office to get more on what Momma Arnold had told her. But she didn't think the lawyer would be forthcoming.

While money was a strong motive to kill, Sally couldn't believe an Arnold had killed one of their own. And anyway, Bill's will had already been changed. What good would that do now? Unless the killing was more out of anger over losing the money than any attempt to get it.

Anger was a bit what she was feeling now, too, if she were completely honest with herself. Knowing Annette and Bill had been having an affair and that resulted in Sally having to share her part of Bill's stake in the bar with Annette made her mad. She was certainly sad about Bill's death, but there was a lot of anger in there, too, at the moment.

Rather than immediately pursuing another line of questioning, like going over to St. Elspeth's to confront Father O'Malley, she went home to cool off.

She knew herself. If she went over there now, there might be words she would regret. Even if the anger she was feeling at the moment had nothing to do with the priest.

Back home, she made herself a cup of tea and sat in the living room with her notebook, reviewing what she had written that morning.

Father O'Malley

She couldn't imagine the elderly priest poisoning Bill, then dumping his body in the dumpster. And she didn't even know if he was aware of the legacy in Bill's will. On the other hand, if the Arnolds knew about it, Father

O'Malley probably did too.

Her head was spinning with the possibilities. Why would the priest kill Bill to get the money? He was a Catholic priest and had taken a vow of poverty. Speaking of poverty, could he even accept the money? She knew nothing about church law. Maybe her lawyer friend in Little Rock could help.

If money was a motive, then the mayor and Margaret Jackson seemed to be off the hook. Sally didn't see how they would benefit from Bill's death.

Zeke Parker.

Well, he certainly benefited. Or at least his wife did. Though he would probably be more angry at her affair than happy about her inheriting Bill's share of Sally's Smasher bar. Though from what Momma Arnold said, he probably knew about the affair already and kept quiet because Bill was kind of the head of their biker club and could be quite domineering if he wanted to be.

But he was a big bear at heart.

Sally sighed.

Finishing her cup of tea, she decided the next step really was to talk to Father O'Malley. That was the last lead she had from Momma Arnold, and she might as well do things in proper order. That was the accountant in her peeking its head out, she realized, smiling.

Sally lived close to the church, so she could just walk it. The fresh air would do wonders for her creative mind, and maybe the solution to the murder would come to her while she strolled.

The air was chilly, and she wished she had brought a scarf. She pulled her coat around her tightly and crossed her arms to keep in the heat.

It didn't take her too long to get to the church. It was only a couple of blocks away.

She turned into the church parking lot and was glad to see the priest's Toyota hatchback parked in his spot next to the parish house. Diane's pickup was parked right next to the hatchback. Sally always wondered why Diane drove to the church. She only lived a block away. But then, this was America, where people loved their cars. Even if only to drive it a few hundred yards.

Just as she was getting to the walkway that led to the front door of the church, the door burst open, and Diane came running out with a look of terror on her face.

Sally ran to her. "What is it, Diane?"

Diane turned over her hands and pointed to her pink skirt. She was covered in what looked like blood.

"It's Father O'Malley. He's been stabbed. I just found him near the back door on my way out. Do something." She was in hysterics.

Sally took her firmly by the shoulders and led her back inside to sit down. There were papers strewn all over the floor, and the women had to pick their way over them to the bench in the hallway.

Sally saw the priest lying in a pool of blood and rushed over to him. Her mother's nurse's training always came in handy. She had taught Sally the key things you do in an emergency.

Sally felt for a pulse, but there was none. This wasn't surprising, considering the amount of blood on and under the priest. She saw a large knife sticking out of his chest where his heart was. Sally hoped he had died instantly. She felt sick to her stomach but knew she had to pull herself together.

Diane was watching the entire time from the bench in the hallway, moaning and sniffling.

Sally pulled out her phone and called the police to tell them what had happened. Mark Soder answered and told her they and an ambulance would be over in minutes.

When the police arrived, Sally led Finnegan into Diane's office. Diane was sitting at her desk with her head in her hands, her petite body curled up even smaller. Her curly dark hair went every which way. There was already a pile of used tissues on the desk.

Diane raised her head when she heard footsteps in the office.

"Diane, I'm so sorry about Father O'Malley," Finnegan said.

Sally went over to Diane and sat with her. Diane sobbed.

"I know it's a difficult time, but I do have a few questions for you," the detective continued.

Diane sniffled. "Okay."

Sally patted her arm.

"First, could you tell us what happened this afternoon? I mean, how did you find him?"

Sally wanted to interrupt him. He wasn't being very diplomatic, but now that he had two murders to solve, he was hot on the trail.

"Oh, it's just a blur. First, Bill, now Father O'Malley. I'm so scared," Diane sobbed.

Sally had just learned about the will from Momma Arnold, so she immediately connected the two deaths. If someone was upset, Father O'Malley was now a beneficiary of Bill's will, that might definitely be a motive to kill the priest. That seemed to point to one of the Arnolds. She didn't think a serial killer was on the loose in Berry Springs. Then again, Sally was also a beneficiary. She would have to be even more careful. And someone had already tried to run her off the road.

"Just take your time. Were you here all day?"

Diane blew her nose and took a deep breath. "Well, I only work mornings, so I left about noon," she explained slowly as she smoothed her hair.

"And what brought you back here this afternoon?" he asked.

"I, um... Well, he called me to come in at three to type up some notes."

"What time did he call?"

"I don't know. I can't remember," she replied, grabbing another tissue.

Sally was glad that Finnegan didn't push this point.

"Was it normal that he would call you back in?" Finnegan asked.

Diane looked at the floor. "Well, sometimes, but not often."

"You're sure it was Father O'Malley who called you?" Soder asked.

"Oh yes," she replied quickly. She gathered up the tissues and threw them in the wicker basket under her desk. Apparently, her sense of organization was coming back.

"Can you tell us what happened when you arrived at the church?" Finnegan asked.

Diane pulled herself up and straightened her blouse.

"Well, I got to the church around three, I guess. I found Father O'Malley in his office. He gave me a pile of notes to type up, and I went down the hall to my office here."

"Okay, so you were working here. Did you hear anything?"

"I was typing away at my computer with the door closed. It gets so cold in the church—the heating doesn't work so well—so we try to keep the draft out and what little heat we have in." She pointed to the small space heater under her desk.

"And then…"

"Well, I had a couple of questions for Father O'Malley when I was finished. I opened the door to my office and started to walk down the hall toward his office when I saw him lying there at the end of the hall near the back door. I dropped the stack of papers I was carrying and ran as fast as I could and saw blood everywhere. There was a knife sticking out of his chest." Her voice was now a whisper.

"Did you check for a pulse? Was he still alive?" Finnegan asked.

Diane shook her head, "He wasn't moving, and there was all that blood." She began to shake.

"You're sure he was already dead?" Finnegan pushed, leaning over her.

"I guess. I didn't…I couldn't check," she sobbed, staring up at Finnegan's bulk.

"What time was this?" Soder asked calmly, getting a glare from his boss.

"Um, well, I guess about 4:45. It took me almost two hours to do all the work for Father O'Malley," she explained.

Sally had gotten there at five p.m., so that could make sense. Though 4:45 seemed a precise time considering how upset Diane was. Then again, as everyone knew, Diane was very efficient and organized.

"Are there any security cameras at the church?" Finnegan asked.

"No, why? This is Berry Springs. We never needed them, no break-ins, nothing. Until now." Diane suddenly wailed. "Oh, why, Father O'Malley?"

Sally turned to hug her. Finnegan seemed to know that was enough for now.

"Diane, we'll let you know if we have any more questions. Is there someone who you could stay with?" Finnegan asked.

"I just want to go home, if that's okay."

"We can drive you there if you want?" Soder offered.

"No, that's okay. I don't want to leave my car here," Diane replied, her manner suddenly matter-of-fact. She got up, gathered her things, and put on her brown leather coat.

"Are you sure, Diane? You've had quite a shock." Sally touched her arm.

Diane shook her off. "I'm not a child. I can handle it."

Sally looked at Finnegan and Soder. Both shrugged their shoulders.

"If you're really sure. At least let me walk you out," Sally offered.

"Fine."

Sally walked her out to her car. She wanted to give Diane a big hug, but Diane just jumped into her car and started it as fast as she could. Finding Father O'Malley seemed to have really shaken her. As she watched Diane pull out of the parking lot, Sally hoped she would make it home all right.

By the time Sally was back inside, she saw Dr. Wiggams dressed in his crime scene coveralls, bent over the body, having already started his initial assessment of the scene. Finnegan and Soder were standing over him. Hearing Sally approach, he looked up at her with his glasses down his nose, the typical pose.

Before speaking, he looked to check with Finnegan. Finnegan nodded.

"Stabbed three times, with this large knife sticking in him, and it hit the aorta. That explains all the blood. Father O'Malley would have died in minutes. I can give you more details when I get him back to my lab."

"Time of death?" Finnegan asked.

"I would say between one and two hours ago, so between four and five p.m.," Wiggams replied.

"Well, that seems to fit with what Diane told us. She got there at three and was working away with the door closed. And she said she found Father O'Malley a little before five."

So, it could have been Diane, Sally thought. On the other hand, she was small and probably not that strong. That knife looked unwieldy, but Diane could have done it. Adrenaline can give almost anybody superpowers. And if Diane had done it, why should she have typed up all those notes first?

Finnegan motioned for Soder to escort her out. That was obviously all the information she was going to get, but she was glad to have gotten that much out of the police.

When they reached the end of the driveway, Soder was about to go back inside when Sally grabbed his arm. "Mark, what did Jeff tell you this morning?"

He hesitated and kept checking the church door, apparently worried that Finnegan might appear any moment. "He admitted it looked like one of his syringes for his diabetes, but said he always had them at school and usually left them in his car, so he claims anyone could have taken one."

So that was the black medical bag Sally had seen Jeff take into the kitchen. Of course, Sally had forgotten about Jeff's diabetes. She should have thought of that immediately. During their many meetings together, Jeff had usually had to check his blood sugar at least once. He had mentioned once or twice to Sally how annoying that was for him to have to do.

"In the end, Finnegan decided afterwards to let him go for lack of motive. We're still keeping a close eye on him."

"What about the bar fight?" Sally asked.

"Finnegan doesn't think that would be enough reason to kill Bill. And the syringe shows premeditation, as we both know. Killing Bill after breaking up the fight would have been spontaneous."

"True," Sally agreed. "Anything else?"

"You're going to have to ask Jeff. I don't want to get into any trouble."

She could see in his eyes that he had probably told her too much already. She let go of his arm, and he turned to go back inside.

"Oh, one more thing, Sally. We've decided to put out a call for any witness who saw someone near the dumpster Saturday night. We've got to be cautious. You know Berry Springs—people will get upset if we are accusing a neighbor, but we need more leads."

Sally nodded.

"I agree, but it's definitely a good idea. I'll keep an ear out."

Soder turned to leave when Sally grabbed his arm.

"What's up?"

"I have some information about the will. I'm just going to tell you everything to be completely open and honest, even if part of this information points to me as a possible suspect," Sally began.

"Be quick. Finnegan may be out here any second."

Sally quickly related what she had learned from the lawyer and from Momma Arnold.

"Geez, that complicates things. And now Father O'Malley is murdered too."

Sally nodded, "I know. Somehow, this is all related."

She stopped talking, and Soder looked at her.

"You really need to stay out of this before something happens to you," he said.

"Sure, yeah, of course," Sally replied.

He shook his head and walked toward the church.

As she watched Soder walk back inside, she decided to head straight to Jeff's house. She was hot on the trail, so to speak. Jeff's fingerprints on the syringe and what he must have told the police that morning would be key to solving the whole thing. Well, she told herself that it would. She jogged home quickly to get her car.

She was desperate to find the killer. And now she had Father O'Malley's murder to solve as well.

Chapter Eighteen

I t wasn't until after seven, with the sun sitting low in the sky over the lake, that Sally made it to Jeff's. The nature-lover in her admired the beauty and the colors, but the detective in her pushed that aside almost immediately; there was no time for sunset-watching now.

Knocking on the door, she received no answer.

His truck was parked outside, so he must be home. But what was more strange was that what looked like Magda's car was sitting next to it. What was she doing here?

Sally went to knock again, noticing the vegetable garden on the far side of the house. Somehow, she had missed this the last few times she had been there, though it was almost out of sight from the front porch and protected by a wooden fence. If the circumstances had been different, she might have asked if he had any produce to spare.

As she rounded the corner, she found Jeff chatting with Magda on the small back porch overlooking the lake. They were sitting quite close to each other and talking in muted tones. They hadn't noticed they now had company.

Sally coughed.

Jeff jumped up. "Oh, uh, hi, Sally. What are you doing here again?"

Magda turned, her face red. She stood up. "Uh, hi Sally. I was just leaving."

"Hi, Magda. No worries. See you tomorrow at three."

Sally didn't want to make a scene. She would see Magda the next day when they reopened the bar anyway. And her first goal was to talk to Jeff.

Magda began walking quickly around the house, waving as she went.

"Sorry to startle you. I knocked hard a couple of times, but you didn't answer the door," Sally explained.

"Yeah, you can't hear anything back here."

Jeff led Sally inside. With the sun setting, the September air was turning chilly.

"Thirsty?" Jeff asked as they settled themselves in the living room area.

"A beer would be great."

When they were settled, Sally broke the news about Father O'Malley.

Jeff's reaction was solemn. "What is happening to this town?"

"That is what I am trying to find out, Jeff."

He nodded.

"What was Magda doing here, by the way?"

Jeff blushed, just as Magda had, and didn't answer.

"I uh, well, uh, it's complicated."

Sally was going to push it, but his answer had been so definitive there was no point. So she would ask Magda about it at the bar the next night. It was interesting, but wasn't really why she had come.

"Well, I'm not going to beat around the bush. I know the police questioned you this morning about the syringe they found underneath the dumpster at my bar."

"Oh," Jeff said. He looked down at his hands and clasped them together tightly when he saw they shook. But not before Sally had noticed the tremor.

"What were your fingerprints doing on that syringe?"

"Uh, wha?" Jeff stammered.

"When did you put it there?"

Sally wasn't even trying to be subtle.

"Um, I..."

"Jeff, I'm your friend. And I'm trying to find out what happened to Bill. The police don't think you have a real motive for killing him, and I don't either, but it's pretty damning evidence with your fingerprints on the syringe. It would help if we—I mean *I*—could understand what happened."

Jeff looked out the back window, his fingers tapping his beer bottle. His hands were shaking again.

85

"Well, I have boxes of those syringes and needles for my diabetes," Jeff explained. "I recognized it when the police showed me this morning. I keep them in that bag over there."

"There must be many people with diabetes or other diseases who need to give themselves a shot in Berry Springs," Sally said. "Why would you think it is yours?"

"I hate needles, so my cousin, who is a doctor, gets me these special syringes. They are very small and very thin, so the injection hurts as little as possible. You usually can't get them that easily as they are very expensive and reserved for hospital use only," he confessed.

Sally didn't quite know what to think of that. Jeff always seemed the uber-macho type to her. He played a lot of sports and must get hurt all the time. But maybe the not liking needles part was just an excuse to try and explain away why he was getting his cousin to procure special needles. If that wasn't illegal, it was at least in a legal gray area.

"That still doesn't explain why one of those special syringes made its way underneath the dumpster at my bar." Sally had to make sure she didn't push him too hard, or he would clam up. But he seemed to want to confess to something. She wondered if she would get more out of him than the police did that morning.

Jeff slid down in his chair. "Anyone could have taken one from my car," he replied meekly.

"Yeah, I know that's what you said, but is that what really happened?"

Sally gulped when she realized she'd blurted out that part that could only have come from the police. She needed to be more careful.

Fortunately, Jeff was too nervous to notice. "Well, okay, I left the prepared syringe and needle in an envelope behind the dumpster for someone," Jeff admitted.

Now, she was getting somewhere.

"Why didn't you tell the police about this? You could be charged as an accessory to murder. Hiding this isn't going to help your case, Jeff." She stabbed her finger in his direction.

"I just got scared," Jeff replied.

"Scared of whom? Of what?"

"I don't know," Jeff replied.

"How is that possible?" Sally threw her arms up in exasperation.

Jeff clenched the arms of his chair.

Sally sipped her beer and let him think.

"Well..." Jeff started

Sally put down her beer and leaned forward.

"No one knows this, but I have a problem. Online gambling." Jeff looked sheepish. "At first, it was just the occasional flutter here and there, but over time, well, it's gotten a little out of hand. Someone found out I owe two hundred thousand dollars and can barely make the minimum payments."

Sally said nothing. If Sally learned anything from working in a bar for the past fifteen years, it's that if someone wants to tell you their story, they will. She knew Jeff would tell her everything without any further prompting on her part.

"Well, a couple of weeks ago—must have been the Monday before Bill's death—I found a typed letter in my mailbox from someone who said they knew about my debt and they would tell the school about it. Well, you know the principal, very conservative. I was worried he would fire me," Jeff explained.

"You don't necessarily know that," Sally offered.

"Well, I was worried. The letter said if I didn't prepare the syringe as instructed, all would come out." Jeff was close to tears.

"How did they know about the syringe?" Sally asked.

"Well, most people know I'm a diabetic, and also that I have a small garden here. I guess they put two and two together," Jeff suggested.

Ah, the strychnine. Used in rat poison and pesticides.

"So, what did the letter tell you to do with the syringe?" Sally asked.

"I was to prepare it and leave it in an envelope behind the dumpster at your bar on Saturday night," Jeff explained. "That's why I picked a fight while the bar was busy. I hoped I would get thrown out, and then I could plant the syringe while everyone was inside."

Everything worked as planned. Too well, unfortunately, for Bill.

"And you have no idea who wrote the letter?" Sally asked.

"No. It was just a piece of paper, typed up, folded in half, and slipped into my mailbox at the end of the driveway. Anyone could have driven here and put it in there. My driveway is long and secluded, so I would never have seen whoever it was from the house."

"It was anonymous, Jeff. How could you know that the person would actually do something to you?"

He rubbed the arms of his chair. "Well, they knew the exact amount of my debt. And I guess I just panicked. I wasn't thinking straight."

Sally wished he would pull himself together. "Do you still have the letter?" Sally asked.

"Yeah," Jeff replied.

He got up to go upstairs, returning a minute later with a piece of paper. He handed it to Sally.

It was printed, no signature. There was an odd black smudge at one edge, but otherwise, it was just a plain piece of white paper with a short message printed on it.

You are a bad boy, Jeff. That debt you owe is going to be the end of you if you don't pay it back.

$215,657

If you don't want your secret to come out, then do as follows:

Prepare one of your syringes with rat poison and leave it in an envelope behind the dumpster at Sally's Smasher bar.

"You have to tell Detective Finnegan about this. They will need to check for fingerprints, and it's evidence in a murder case," Sally told him.

"I know. I wasn't thinking straight this morning. I should have brought it to the police then."

"Does Randall Wentworth know about the letter?" Sally asked.

Sally knew that Randall represented Jeff and more than half the town.

"No, I didn't tell him either," Jeff replied.

"You need to tell him too, Jeff," Sally said.

"I know, I know," Jeff said, waving his hands and knocking the empty beer bottle onto the brown carpet.

"I think you should call Detective Finnegan right now and tell him everything."

"No, no..." Jeff began to protest.

"If you don't, I'm going to have to. You can't withhold information from the police in a murder investigation. They killed *Bill*, Jeff." Her voice got louder.

"You call him, Sally. I just can't."

Sally pulled out her phone and called the police station. Finnegan was still there and asked them both to come to the station immediately. Sally was glad he wanted them to come in rather than wait at Jeff's for a police cruiser to bring him in for further questioning. He didn't deserve that indignity.

Hopefully, Finnegan wouldn't be too upset that she got more out of Jeff than he did. But she wasn't going to mention it if he didn't.

Chapter Nineteen

Sally woke up Wednesday morning with a splitting headache. It had been a long night. On the drive into the station, Sally had also gotten Jeff to call his attorney, who made it to the station just after they did. Detective Finnegan then held Jeff pending investigation of his story and fingerprints on the anonymous note and envelope he received. He wasn't too happy about hearing it after Sally, but he appreciated she had called. Finnegan didn't get anything more out of Jeff than Sally did, but he let her stay and watch the interrogation from a room next door. He grudgingly admitted to her that her bartender perception skills might actually come in handy. He was a bit gruff about it, but Sally was glad he was sort of accepting he needed her help. Well, at least for now.

She had also used the opportunity to confirm with Detective Finnegan that she could reopen today. He gave the go-ahead. Now, she just had to get everything together to reopen the bar that night.

Sipping her coffee at the kitchen table, she made a list of topics she wanted to somehow weave into the conversation with Jay and Magda that afternoon.

Putting her pen down, she realized this was pretty heady stuff. She didn't want to interrogate them, but they would be upset if she didn't tell them what was going on. And both of them were witnesses the night of Bill's murder, not leaving the bar until gone midnight when Sally sent them home. She wasn't sure about the last point though; she didn't want to worry them.

Looking up at the kitchen clock, it read eleven thirty. Time to get ready and drive over. She had asked Jay and Magda to be there at three, but she always liked to get there earlier to do a pre-inspection and make a list of jobs for them. Her work in finance had made her the model of efficiency when it came to running a bar. Though, for some reason, it didn't mean she was most efficient with her own finances. Maybe that was a subtle reason why she had left that job.

At half past one, Sally pulled into the parking lot of Sally's Smasher. She knew it wasn't going to be easy to work tonight, what with it being the first opening after Bill's murder, but it was the place Bill loved, and he would have wanted them to carry on. She'd arrived early to take some time to herself to think about Bill and get things organized before Jay and Sarah showed up later.

She parked on the far side of the parking lot, got out, and walked around to the front door; she couldn't bring herself to go in the back door, where the dumpster was.

Looking up at the Sally's Smasher sign, she took a moment to collect herself before heading inside. She hadn't been there since the night of Bill's murder.

Staring at the sign reminded her of that day 15 years ago when she and Bill had put that signup and officially opened Sally's Smasher. At the time, it had seemed like a miracle that all had worked out, but looking back, she knew it was due to her hard work. And Bill's money, moral support, and friendship that had kept the bar going all those years. Bill was really part of the DNA of the place. It would be a different Sally's Smasher without him.

She took a deep breath, unlocked the front door, and stepped in.

Overall, the bar had a cool but comforting feel to it. She loved working there every day and basking in the atmosphere. It always gave her a sense of calm. *This is my bar.*

She poured herself a small glass of beer and dropped onto one of the bar stools to absorb the memory and peace. A tear dropped from one eye as she realized it would be the first night ever that Bill wasn't there. He had helped draw in customers with his belly laugh. As a member of one of the oldest families in town, he also knew a lot of people. Many came to see Bill and his motorcycle.

It was her bar now.

Then it hit her. No, it wasn't.

Her eyes were suddenly dry as she sat up.

She thought back to the conversation she had had with Randall Wentworth. It wasn't just her bar now. She had to share it with Annette.

She tried to push this thought out of her mind.

Her eyes swept around the bar again as she sighed and got up from the stool to get to work.

Sally spent the next hour doing a thorough cleaning with vacuum, mop, and sponge. The wooden bar and tables and chairs were shining when she was done. Just as she liked it.

Then, it was back to the office to get the cash drawer for the night. It was almost time for Jay and Magda to show up to help finalize everything for the reopening.

When she opened the safe, though, and pulled out the drawer, she stopped short. The drawer felt lighter than when she'd locked it away on Saturday night. Sally locked the safe up and turned, placing the drawer on her desk. She lifted it again, certain she had counted it right on Saturday night. She counted the bills and coins again and made a note of it, but couldn't find her paper from Saturday night to double-check the number against it. It still felt light for what was meant to be in there. It had been a great night, she remembered, and she'd been pleased with the takings. She tended to keep all these records on paper, and then at the end of the month, she'd enter them all into her spreadsheet.

Oh well, maybe I've misremembered after everything that happened that night, she thought.

At just before three, Sally sat down at one of the tables, glad to be off her feet for a few minutes before the door opened. She looked around the room; everything looked ready for opening. Except it wasn't. Bill would not be walking through those doors tonight. Nor would he ever walk through them again. She had been an independent person for a long time, even before she got divorced, but now she really felt the hole of Bill's absence. Sally's Smasher, and Berry Springs, wouldn't be the same without him.

Chapter Twenty

The chime above the door jingled, and Sally looked up to see Jay and Magda entering. She was glad they were on time.

"Hey, you two. Wow, you really got dressed up for tonight," Sally said, giving them a once-over. Jay was in a fancy cowboy outfit with a silver buckle and a huge brown cowboy hat over his wavy black hair. It fit him like a glove. While Magda wore a tight-fitting bright blue polka-dot dress. She had a red bow in her short brown hair.

"Jay's idea. We thought we should be extra special for our first night open after..." Magda said, choking up.

Sally walked over and gave them a big hug. This was going to be a hard night to open the bar.

When they released, all three looked across the room to Bill's vintage motorcycle. She motioned them to follow her over to it. "Let's have a moment of silence for Bill. He loved this bike," Sally said.

The three of them joined hands and stared at the bike for at least five minutes. Magda sobbed silently, putting her hand on the metal cage, while Sally and Jay had dry eyes. Their hands were white as they held each other tightly.

Looking up to the ceiling and around the bar, they said a last goodbye to Bill.

After a few minutes of silence, Sally released her hands. Jay and Magda did the same.

While walking over to the bar to start the final preparations, Magda grabbed Sally's arm. "Oh Sally, we heard about Father O'Malley. That poor old man."

News traveled fast.

Bill's death was bad enough for Sally. Now, the second tragedy hit her again as well.

"It's a blow to everyone. I happened to get to the church right after Diane found him. So sad. He was such a wonderful person."

"Who would do that to a priest?" Jay asked, shaking his head.

"It's a tragedy. Diane is still so upset. I'm going over to see her tomorrow," Sally replied.

With that, Sally straightened herself up. "Okay. I know this is a difficult time for all of us, but let's make this a great night in Bill's honor."

Jay and Magda nodded reluctantly. Sally hoped they would not fall apart that night. Actually, it was that she hoped *she* wouldn't fall apart, she reluctantly admitted to herself.

"So, what should we start with?" Magda asked.

"Why don't you two organize the tables? I didn't get around to doing that. And double-check the upstairs stock," Sally instructed.

"Let's hope we have customers tonight," Jay mused.

Sally was sure there would be people. And she already knew what the main topic of conversation would be. She would have to keep her eyes and ears open for any information. And somehow find time to pull Jay and Magda aside separately. Jay had been on table duty that night, and he must have seen something. And Sally was eager to ask Magda about finding her at Jeff's the day before. She decided to focus on questioning them about Saturday night rather than worry them about the fact that they had two bosses now, Sally and Annette. Every time Sally thought of that, her stomach went into knots.

Pushing that out of her mind, she debated the best way of talking to them. She decided to start with them together.

Sally moved to the middle of the room between Jay, who was wiping the table tops, and Magda, who was behind the bar doing a final inventory.

"Before we open, I wanted to ask you two if you saw anything Saturday night," Sally said.

Jay and Magda stopped what they were doing and exchanged a look.

"Do we really have to do this now? We just had a moment of silence in Bill's honor. I'd like to concentrate on getting the bar ready to open. And try to forget what happened, at least for a few minutes," Magda replied.

"Ah, but the boss is sleuthing, Magda." Jay grinned more jovially. "Are you sure you are smarter than whoever did this, Sally?"

She hated being called stupid. Or at least that's what she thought he was implying.

"Well, yes, I know I will figure it all out in the end. And don't you two want to know what happened?"

Maybe it wasn't being too tactful, starting right in with an interrogation. But she didn't have any time to waste. She had to find the killer or at least help Detective Finnegan find them.

"You're right. I'm sorry. Just be careful," Jay said.

Geez, everyone was telling her that. She wasn't twelve.

Magda sighed, and Sally knew she couldn't ignore the boss.

"Well, it was really busy Saturday night—well, until eleven, anyway—so I was running around making drinks," Magda explained.

"And I was waiting tables. Didn't have much of a chance to talk to anyone or see anything," Jay added.

"Did either of you talk to Bill?" Sally asked.

"No, not really. He spent most of the evening with his biker pals, though I did see him talk to the mayor briefly. Not sure when that was," Jay explained.

"Magda?" Sally asked.

"No, he never came over to the bar Saturday night. One of his pals always got the drinks. I think he was worried one of them would somehow try and steal his precious motorcycle," Sarah grinned.

They all had a laugh.

"Yeah, you're probably right," Sally said, "Okay, let's get to work."

Jay and Magda turned to finish doing their final prep.

"Oh, one more thing."

They stopped again and looked at Sally. This time, Sally saw a glint of annoyance in both their faces.

"When I took the cash drawer out of the safe earlier, it felt a little light. Do either of you know anything about that?" she asked.

"Is cash missing?" Jay asked.

"I don't know. Saturday night was a blur, and I can't find the paper I noted the numbers down on. I was going to enter everything in the computer this afternoon."

"I wouldn't worry, Sally. No one has access to the register except us, and you're the only one with the combination to the safe," Magda said.

"Yeah, I guess you're right," Sally said, shrugging her shoulders.

Sally had hoped they had seen something. But maybe it was just her imagination. If one of them had seen something, they might have been nervous about speaking out when they weren't alone with Sally. Or maybe they were still upset about Bill's death, and now Father O'Malley's to think straight. She would have to try again tomorrow when she could catch them separately, and her questioning might jog their memories.

Jay motioned that he was going to the basement to get some booze to fill up the shelves.

Maybe this was Sally's chance. "Could you also do a full inventory?" she asked.

"But that will take forever, and we open soon," he replied, whining a bit.

"Oh, you're quick. It won't take long at all."

Jay shrugged and sighed and went downstairs. After he had gone, Sally used this as an opportunity to corner Magda. She had an important question to ask her. And she got it out quickly.

"Oh, Magda, I was wondering what you were doing at Jeff's on Monday?"

Magda kept polishing the beer stein she was drying and kept her back to Sally.

"Magda?" Sally said a bit louder.

"Oh, what was that?" Magda finally responded.

"I was just wondering what you were doing at Jeff's on Monday?"

Magda turned red. "I can't say."

"Come on, it's me, Sally. Does it have anything to do with Bill's murder?"

Magda turned away from her sniffling. "Well, I..."

"Just tell me. You know I'm trying to solve Bill's murder. And if it's about Jeff and the syringe, I already know about that."

Magda whirled around, her brown hair swirling with her.

"Jeff told me."

Magda stared at her with her mouth open.

"Wow, he told me I was the only one that knew."

Sally shrugged. "Well, the last time you talked to him, I guess you were. So what were you doing at his place on Monday?"

Sally decided not to mention to Magda that Jeff had spilled the beans to the cops the night before. It might just upset Magda more.

Magda sighed. "He just needed someone to talk to."

Sally stared at her. "Why you, Magda?"

"Well, we dated briefly five years ago, and I guess he thought he could trust me. And he was trying to figure out what you knew, well, since I work for you."

"You and Jeff dated then? But you were barely out of high school. Wasn't he your teacher? I didn't know anything about this."

"Well, yeah. He was over thirty, and I was nineteen. You can understand why we kept it quiet. And anyway, it didn't last that long."

Sally was amazed how, even in the tiny town of Berry Springs, people could somehow still keep things secret. She had been here a long time, but the small town still surprised her.

"Okay. What did you tell him about what I knew?"

"Well, not that much. You didn't seem to have much yourself when we talked on Sunday."

This was true. Though, maybe Jeff was trying to influence what Magda thought before everything came out. Who knew?

At that point, Jay came back upstairs, huffing. "Inventory done," he said coldly.

Sally was going to ask him why he was being so short with her when they heard a knock at the door.

"Wow, five-thirty already. Time to open," Jay said.

Chapter Twenty-One

As expected, the bar wasn't that crowded for a Wednesday night. Also, as expected, everyone was talking about the two murders in Berry Springs. Both Bill and Father O'Malley had been beloved and long-time neighbors. Sally had gotten a lot of questions, as most now knew she had turned from problem-solving to murder-solving.

Diane had also turned up. She had told Sally she didn't feel like being alone. They had only had a brief conversation, as in spite of the smaller crowd, they were all quite busy serving a lot of drinks. Sally had had to make a couple trips to the cellar storage to get more rum and vodka.

Diane had told her that the church would hold a double funeral that Saturday at 3 p.m. They both agreed that would help the healing. But it now meant that Sally's goal had a deadline; she needed to find the killer or killers in the next three days so that her friends could be laid to rest in peace, justice secure. It didn't seem realistic—she barely had anything to go on at the moment—but she had to try.

With the last customers leaving fairly promptly, Sally had been glad when she was able to fall into bed at 2 a.m. However, at four a.m., she was tossing and turning with the two murders preying on her mind. Nothing made sense. Bill was poisoned, and his head was bashed in. Father O'Malley was stabbed. To Sally, Bill's murder seemed premeditated, while Father O'Malley's seemed spontaneous. Though who would have a knife of that size with them at all times? And as both she and Detective Finnegan agreed, what was the motive?

Wait a minute. She thought back to her talk with Randall Wentworth, her lawyer, and Momma Arnold. Bill's will was at the center of this. If Bill died, Father O'Malley would get a large chunk of the estate. She couldn't imagine the priest killing Bill for the money. He was a man of the church, after all.

But he still stood to gain a large inheritance as a result of Bill's death. Perhaps Father O'Malley had been killed by a member of the Arnold family, whose portion of the estate was far smaller than they'd anticipated. If the priest died, would the money revert to the family or the church? She would have to check up on this. And find out if Father O'Malley himself had left a will.

With sleep seemingly not forthcoming, she finally pushed herself up at six a.m., and went downstairs to make coffee. She sat at the kitchen counter and sadly realized that now that the bar had reopened, she would have to talk to Annette about the business. The thought had kept popping in her mind the night before, but the crowds had helped push it away. Now that she was home alone, there was nothing to distract her from the inevitable. Part of her still couldn't believe how Bill had gone back on his promise, after all the work they'd put into the place. Sally had been the one who'd come up with the idea of the bar, she had put in most of the hard work, and she was the one in the bar every night. Yes, Bill had helped with an investment and did help out, hence the 40 percent share, but everyone knew it was Sally's bar. It had her name on it!

But Annette, of all people. She still was in shock she hadn't seen that Annette and Bill had something on the side, but that was different than changing your will and leaving something to your on-the-sly girlfriend. What did Annette know about running a bar? More to the point, Zeke must be furious, that's if he even knows yet.

She sipped her coffee, but it made her nauseous. She dumped the rest in the sink.

Sally was just about to sit back down at the kitchen table when the doorbell rang. At that early hour, the sound was deafening. Who would be bothering her at seven in the morning? Most people knew she worked late.

The bell rang again.

"Ugh, all right, I'm coming," she yelled as she walked to the door.

DEATH IN THE OZARKS

She looked through the glass and saw Annette standing on the doorstep. It was like Sally's thoughts had summoned her. Annette smiled faintly and waved. She had on a blue coat over her jeans and red sweater. Her long blonde hair was a mess, and her drawn face suggested she hadn't slept for days.

Sally slowly opened the door. "Annette, what are you doing here?"

"Um, Sally, hi."

Sally scowled. Of all the people...

"Isn't it a bit early to be dropping by?" Sally replied in a monotone.

"I'm sorry, I have been thinking about the will, and I really wanted to talk to you," Annette asked.

Sally remained silent. Yes, she had just been thinking about talking to Annette, but she liked to do things on her terms. Now she felt steamrollered. She didn't want to be cruel, though.

"So you know?" Sally asked.

Annette just nodded.

Apparently, Wentworth had already informed the people named in the will.

Sally was still tired from the late night at the bar, and Annette was the last person she wanted to see that morning, but she was brought up to be polite. And somehow Sally would have to work with her.

Sally waved her in.

"Come on in. I don't have that much time, though. I have to get ready to open my bar later."

Oops. She had meant to say *the bar*. Her subconscious was definitely taking over this morning, saying the inside words out loud.

Annette followed Sally to the kitchen.

"Would you like a coffee?"

Annette nodded. "With a shot of rum if you have any. It's been a difficult few days."

At just seven in the morning? She was a little worried about Annette's request but went to the living room to get the rum anyway.

Seated at the table, Annette sipped her warm drink and got right to the point.

"Oh, Sally, I didn't know about Bill's will. Well, until Wentworth told me."

Sally didn't quite believe her. She clenched her hands together.

"I was as surprised as you were when I heard Bill wanted us to share his part of the bar. I think everyone knows he and I were an item, but—" Annette said.

"What about Zeke? Didn't it bother him that you were carrying on with one of his biker-club buddies?" Sally hadn't meant that to be as direct as it was, but she had hoped to have more time to prepare for the conversation with Annette.

Annette rubbed her hands on her coffee cup and took a sip before responding. Sally noticed her cheeks were turning red. "He hated it. But in his Catholic family, divorce is not an option. And he loves me and wants me to be happy."

Sally couldn't imagine Zeke wanting to stay with her, in spite of his Catholic family. Having the biker club head sleeping with his wife must have made him very angry.

Mad enough to kill Bill?

Sally admitted to herself that she didn't know Zeke that well, but she did usually chat with Annette when she accompanied him to the bar. While she ran a bar many bikers frequented, she wasn't a motorcyclist herself. That was Bill's part of the bar.

"I came here to tell you that I never asked Bill for this. I loved him, and he loved me, and that was enough for the both of us."

Sally took a few moments before responding. She was holding in her anger and didn't want to take it out on Annette. She was mad at Bill right now for not following through with his promise.

She reached across to take Annette's hand. "I don't blame you, Annette."

Sally's walls began to crumble as her grief started to bubble up, overtaking the anger, but she couldn't show either weakness.

"I am just upset because when we opened the bar, Bill told me I would get his share if anything ever happened to him. Sally's Smasher was my idea and built mainly from my hard work."

"I know, Sally." Annette grabbed another tissue from her purse and blew her nose.

Sally was close to tears herself, but she told herself to be strong. She wanted to keep control of this difficult conversation.

"Do you want to leave everything like it is?" Sally asked.

"What do you mean?"

"Well, wouldn't it make sense for both of us if I bought out your share?" Sally wasn't sure how she would manage that financially, but it seemed like the best way to move on.

Annette looked up from her mug.

"Oh, well, I hadn't thought about that."

"What had you been thinking? Wouldn't it help us both move on?"

Annette shook her head. "I'm not so sure, Sally. I will need to think about it. And talk to Zeke."

Really? Sally couldn't imagine how that conversation would go.

Both women stayed silent for a few minutes. Sally didn't want to push her.

"Well, Sally, I just want you to know that it is your bar. You run it as you see fit. I don't want to interfere. I'm just the silent partner. I can't help out at the bar like Bill did because of my teaching job, but do let me know if you get in a jam," Annette offered.

"Thanks, Annette," Sally replied, her voice breaking as she thought of Bill.

"Do you have any leads on Bill's killer?" Annette asked.

The emotion of talking to Annette had almost made her forget the investigation.

"I have a few ideas, but it's been difficult. And now Father O'Malley is also dead."

Sally waited for Annette to say something about Father O'Malley being named in the will, but she remained silent. Maybe she knew nothing about it. Perhaps she could use the early-morning interruption to her advantage.

"Um, Annette, did Zeke say anything about Saturday night at the bar?"

"Is he a suspect?" she replied, her voice raised.

"Well, he was there Saturday night and got into a fight with Jeff. I just thought he might have mentioned something to you."

"Zeke wouldn't kill Bill."

Hmm, maybe she should have left out the questions about Zeke. It definitely wasn't the right time. "I'm sorry, Annette. I didn't mean to upset you."

Annette took a deep breath.

"I'm sorry, too. I didn't mean to snap at you. I know you are just trying to find Bill's killer. And Zeke was already questioned by the police."

Sally let her think for a minute.

"He told me he didn't know why Jeff had been so upset. Though he admitted to me that it seemed that Jeff had had too much to drink."

Sally thought back to what Jeff had told her. Maybe he and Zeke had made up the fight to get Jeff out of the bar. But no, Sally couldn't imagine Zeke would be involved. Even if his wife was having an affair with Bill.

Apparently, the talk was over as Annette put down her mug and got up. She hung her coat over her arm and walked to the front door with Sally right behind her.

"Thanks for the chat, Sally. I'm sorry I bothered you so early in the morning."

Sally was going to say something petty; she still wasn't sure how to best deal with Annette. Instead, she swallowed and just said, "I'm glad we talked." And she meant it.

As she went upstairs, her cell phone rang. It was Detective Finnegan with a lead.

Finally.

Chapter Twenty-Two

"I didn't expect to hear from you so early, Detective," Sally began. It seemed she was very popular this morning.

"Yeah, well, I thought I should share this with you. You seem to be getting information much faster than we can, so maybe this will help us both solve the two murders more quickly."

There was a definite tone of bitterness in that final sentence. But she almost wanted to jump through the phone to get at whatever he had to say as quickly as possible.

"We put out a call for witnesses who may have seen something behind the bar Saturday night, and we finally got a bite, two to be exact."

"Wow, who called you?" Sally said, biting her lip.

"First, Margaret Jackson. She told us she had seen someone in jeans, a long coat, and a baseball cap pull out an envelope from behind the dumpster."

Well, she hadn't mentioned that when Sally went to speak to her. Why would she hold that back? But then Sally had overheard those strange phone conversations that Margaret had made just before and after her visit. But if she was covering for someone, why would she tell the police she saw someone?

"Did she see what they did or where they went?"

"Unfortunately, no. She said they walked away either toward the back door or the bar or maybe around the side."

Not very helpful.

"Did she say whether it was a man or woman?"

"No, she had been in the restroom and happened to look out the window.

It was pretty dark, so she only got a brief look."

"Then how did she know what they were wearing?"

Finnegan laughed. "Actually, that might explain the second witness statement we got."

Sally had to sit down on the stairs. Her legs were shaking with excitement.

"Mike Watkins from the diner next to your bar was out back smoking at around ten on Saturday, and he claims he saw Margaret Jackson near the dumpster."

Sally shook her head.

"If it was so dark, how would he know who it was?" she asked.

"Good question, but if it was Margaret, that would explain her call to try and deflect the blame if someone came forward," the detective countered.

Sally didn't think Margaret was that clever. The calls she had overheard sounded more like she was taking orders from someone than planning anything herself. Though why would Margaret have anything to do with Bill's death, or Father O'Malley's death, for that matter? Sally had a hunch the two were related—two murders in almost as many days in this small town had to be linked—but she still wasn't sure of anything at the moment.

"What will you do now, Detective?"

"We're going to bring Margaret in for questioning."

"Thanks so much, Detective, for the info. I really appreciate it." She was genuinely glad he had called, and what luck to finally have a lead.

"Oh, one more thing." She heard the rustling of papers.

"No fingerprints found on the letter Jeff received."

"Kind of what I thought," Sally replied.

"Yeah, me too."

Chapter Twenty-Three

As Sally showered and got dressed, she decided to tackle Mike, the witness from the diner.

Since Mike worked at the diner next door to Sally's Smasher, she often saw him in the evenings when she got to work or took out the trash. This was more often than not, so she assumed he worked the late shift, meaning he should be home. His boss was a member of the local chamber of commerce as she was, and they had often been at chamber meetings. She thought he would help her with Mike's address. She texted him, and he luckily got right back to her.

She still had a bit of time before she needed to get to the bar. And fortunately, Mike lived on the way, just off Route 10, not too far from Magda.

She drove to his house and knocked on the door. It took a few minutes for him to open up.

"Hi. Can I help you?" he asked, rubbing red eyes.

He was wearing a white T-shirt and blue boxers, which Sally could partly see through his bathrobe, pushed out by his large stomach. His feet were bare. She had obviously woken him up.

"Hi, Mike. It's me, Sally, from Sally's Smasher."

His eyes slowly showed recognition as he rubbed his triple chin.

"Oh, Sally, hi. What are you doing here?"

"Um, well, I'm helping the police with their investigation of Bill's murder."

He looked surprised. "I didn't have anything to do with it," he cried, trying to shut the door in her face.

She got her foot in fast enough to block him. "Mike, I'm just here to ask a couple of questions, not accuse you of murder. I thought if you worked at the diner next door, you might have seen something Saturday night. I've seen you outside some nights smoking or taking out the trash."

She didn't think it was a good idea to reveal that Finnegan had told her about Mike's witness statement.

Mike stood up tall and puffed out his chest.

"Actually, I did see something, and I went right to the police yesterday to tell them," Mike said proudly.

"Wow, really? Can I come in?" she asked.

"Well, I have to get ready soon, but I guess I have a few minutes."

His minor "celebrity" had clearly gotten the better of his time management.

"Great, thanks. I have to get to the bar soon, anyway."

They sat in the kitchen.

"Want something to drink?"

"Coffee would be great," she replied.

Caffeine kept her going most days.

Mike poured her a mug of coffee and handed it to her. He then poured himself a mug.

When he sat down, she turned back to him.

"So what did you see exactly?" she began, sipping her coffee and smiling.

Bill took a sip of his coffee and sighed.

"Well, I happened to be taking out the trash that night and saw someone crawling behind your dumpster. I didn't think anything of it at the time. I thought it was one of you picking up some trash you'd dropped, but after Bill was found and the police started looking into it, I began thinking maybe I saw something stranger than that."

Sally was glad he was opening up. Mike tended to be a gruff person of few words, spending most of his time flipping pancakes at the diner the few times she had stopped there for food before her shift at the diner. Sally much preferred Belle's kind-hearted, albeit slightly shaky, service at Betty Jo's.

"So you first thought it was one of us at the bar?"

"Right, but only because I glanced at the person. But looking back, it seemed odd. The person was medium-sized with dark, curly hair, though I didn't see their face directly, just from the side."

"Did you think it was a man or a woman?"

Mike looked confused. "Actually, come to think of it, I'm not sure."

"So, who did you think it was?"

"Well, Margaret Jackson's was the first name that popped into my head when I saw the figure, and it just seemed to fit."

"Margaret?"

"To be honest, your bright lights overlook the back of the building, but not near the dumpster. And the person was crouching in the shadows, so I could be mistaken."

A big mistake to wrongfully accuse someone of murder...

"Who else do you think it could have been?" Sally prompted, hoping for a clue.

"I've been trying to figure that out. The other person I thought of was Gillian Arnold, but that doesn't make any sense."

Sally was surprised at first, but thinking about it, Gillian looked like a younger version of Margaret, and of Diane.

"Um, Gillian does have dark curly hair, but she isn't that short, and she's more athletic."

"Well, yeah, it's true."

"Thanks, Mike. I really appreciate you telling me about this."

"I'm glad to help you. That's good enough for me. Maybe I'll be famous, he grinned."

She hoped he had actually seen something and wasn't making it up to get attention. She didn't know him that well to be able to tell either way.

He left her to get to the door herself as he nursed his drink.

As she walked to her car, she contemplated the thought of Margaret, Diane, or Gillian being involved in Bill's murder.

Diane. She had told Magda and Jay the day before that she had wanted to stop in on Thursday to see Diane she was doing after Father O'Malley's death. Checking her phone, Sally realized it was time to head to the bar. She would have to tackle Diane Friday morning instead.

And speed up her investigation if she was going to solve both murders by Saturday. Though her goal of solving everything before Saturday's double funeral was looking more remote than ever.

Chapter Twenty-Four

On her way to the bar, Sally planned how she would question Magda and Jay to hopefully finally get something out of them. The most important detail was to have enough time with each of them alone. One of them must have seen something or noticed something out of place. They knew the people who came to the bar as well as Sally did.

Someone in the bar had used the syringe to poison Bill at the earliest 11 p.m. If only she'd been paying attention at that time. She wished she had walked around more that night, but hindsight is always twenty-twenty, isn't it?

Sally headed down to the cellar. Jay was sitting at the small table in the corner, finishing up the inventory. She glanced around the shelves and it looked like almost everything was in order, though she had hoped he would have done more of the shelves in the time she was chatting to Magda.

"Hey, Jay, how's it going?" Sally asked.

"Fine, just doing the last few shelves," he replied, not looking up.

"That's great. I brought the list of what we need upstairs."

She handed him one sheet and a crate and began packing the other crate.

"So, I wanted to talk to you about the Saturday night Bill was killed," Sally said.

Jay stopped moving bottles. He stood up slowly and turned to stare at her. He brushed his dark locks back and wiped the sweat from his brow. "So that's why you called us in early. We were trying to figure it out. Time for my interrogation."

He seemed a bit annoyed, which, if she were honest with herself, Sally could understand.

She didn't want to pressure them, but if anyone saw something unusual that night, it would have been one of them. "I don't want to interrogate you, Jay, but I was hoping you might have thought of something weird that happened. You know, I thought our chat yesterday might have jogged your memory. We are all still mourning Bill, but I'm determined to find out who did it, for Bill, for his family, for all of us," Sally replied.

"I know," Jay said in a monotone. "Of course you are."

"You had table duty that night. Anything you noticed that you haven't already told me?" Sally asked.

"It was such a busy night, I didn't have time to stop and chat with everyone," Jay explained.

"Sure, but maybe something caught your eye?" Sally asked.

"Well, I think I told you about Bill talking to the mayor," Jay continued.

She nodded. Same story as Magda had told her.

"I did walk by the table where Jeff and Father O'Malley were sitting, and they seemed to be arguing about something. I didn't quite get what it was about, but Jeff, in particular, seemed really angry," Jay described.

Sally frowned. There had been a discrepancy in the two men's statements, sure. Father O'Malley said they had been talking about a mutual student, while Jeff had told her Father O'Malley had been worried about low church attendance. However, neither of them mentioned it getting heated. She wasn't sure this meant anything. It might have just been Jeff embarrassed he had difficulty handling a student.

"Really? Why didn't you mention this before?" Sally asked.

"Well, I guess when you first asked me yesterday, I was thinking more about what Bill was doing that night and who he was talking to," Jay explained.

"Sure, that makes sense," Sally replied. "Did you notice anything with the biker club?"

"Didn't really go over to that part of the bar, mainly the tables in front," Jay answered.

"But you must have cleared their glasses," Sally said.

"No, Zeke did that mainly," Jay answered.

"So you saw him go to the bar?" Sally asked.

"Yeah, a couple of times. I glanced over at his table and saw him clearing their glasses himself," Jay explained.

"Well, wasn't that helpful of him," Sally said with a smirk.

"Yeah," Jay laughed.

"Did you notice Bill acting strangely?" Sally asked.

"No, he was his jolly, happy self, though he did mention a headache, or at least I heard him mention a headache when I passed by on the way to the restroom," Jay told her.

"What time was that?" Sally asked.

"Hmm, lots of people still here. I think around ten thirty or so, though it might have been a bit later. Saturday really was busy—I barely had time to think," Jay replied.

The timings all seemed to fit with what she knew from the police.

But while the connection between Bill's and Father O'Malley's death seemed to be Bill's will, she didn't yet see why the same person would kill both of them. If it was, indeed, the same person. Of that, she wasn't sure either.

Chapter Twenty-Five

Friday morning, Sally decided to stop by Diane's and talk to her. Since Father O'Malley's murder, she didn't think the church would be reopened. And she couldn't imagine Diane wanting to go there after what she had found. Even so, she decided to leave early enough to catch her before she left her house.

Sally had grabbed her backpack and was about to head out the door when her cell phone rang. Mark Soder from the police station.

"Mark, what's up? I'm just about to head out."

"Glad I caught you," he said.

"We found something strange about Father O'Malley's murder," he said.

She went into the living room to take notes. It was hard to hold the phone and make notes at the same time while standing in the hall, even if she put the phone on speaker mode.

"What is it?" she replied, sitting down on the couch.

She pulled her notebook and pen out of her backpack.

"Well, you remember Diane told us that Father O'Malley had called her to come back in to type up his notes?"

Sally nodded, "Yes, she said that. I remember."

"Well, there weren't any calls made from either the church, his cell phone, or the parish house that afternoon."

Sally put down her pen.

"That's odd. Why would she lie?"

Now, she picked up the pen and tapped it on the table.

"Well, maybe he did call her, but from another phone."

"Or maybe it was someone pretending to be Father O'Malley," Sally suggested. It was a possibility that she herself wasn't quite sure of. Diane had worked for the priest for years and should have been able to recognize his voice.

"Yeah, we'll have to look into that," Mark replied.

Sally debated whether she should tell him she was actually headed out to see Diane at that very moment. Since he had been keeping her up-to-date with information, some of which Detective Finnegan probably didn't want her to know, she went with honesty.

"Actually, Mark, I was just about to go over to Diane's to see how she is doing. I could somehow bring this up with her."

Mark laughed loudly. "Um, you mean go to her house to pump her for information?"

Sally grinned. "Um, yeah, I guess so. I'll keep you posted."

Diane lived between Sally's home and St. Elspeth's, so it wasn't too far for Sally to walk. It was a windy day, so Sally had put on a scarf to ward off the chill. The days were getting shorter, and the cool air was picking up. It never got Arctic cold in Arkansas, but it certainly got chilly in the mountains, especially when the sun went down.

Sally walked slowly. She felt like she was getting somewhere, but it had been almost a week. She really hoped she would have been able to solve the crimes already. What with the funerals tomorrow, she was really feeling the pressure. But then, Detective Finnegan didn't seem to be doing much better than she was, so there was that, she thought. She was glad that Mark Soder was keeping her informed, and now she had an important question to ask Diane about the supposed phone call. Though she wasn't sure how she would ask her without overtly accusing Diane of lying.

Sally walked up the short stone path to Diane's front door and rang the doorbell. Rather than the normal ring, classical music started playing. Sally chuckled. Diane did love her classical music. Sally thought it was something by Bach, but she wasn't sure. You could buy doorbells with all sorts of sounds these days.

The door opened, and Diane was in a blue sweatshirt and black running pants. Her eyes were puffy and red.

"Sally, what are you doing here?" Diane said, a look of surprise on her face.

They knew each other quite well from the church but were never the best of friends.

"Hi, Diane. I just wanted to check and see how you were doing. You know, after Tuesday."

Diane sniffled. "Oh, that's nice," she said weakly.

Diane led her to the spacious kitchen and offered her a comfy chair at the expansive wooden table.

"Would you like some coffee?" Diane asked.

"Coffee would be great, thank you."

Diane made a coffee for Sally and poured herself a glass of water.

"Hungry?"

Sally realized she had gotten up so early she had only had a coffee at home. The murders had taken up most of her brain capacity, it seemed.

"Sure."

Diane offered Sally some cheese and crackers to go with the drinks. Diane was always an expert entertainer.

"So, how have you been?" Sally asked.

She reached across the table to hold Diane's hand.

Diane looked down and pulled her hand away. "I've had so many wonderful sympathy calls and letters this week about Sean's—um, about Father O'Malley's death. It's really helped me get through the week." She sniffled and grabbed a tissue from the box in front of her.

Sally waited a bit before starting to ask some questions. She sipped the coffee and chewed on a delicious oat cracker with cheddar cheese. "These oat cakes are delicious," she said.

"Thank you. I made them myself. I love to bake. And it's helped keep my mind off the events this past week."

"Very impressive," Sally replied.

"My little hobby, I always call it," Diane said, trying to smile.

Sally grinned and waited a moment before cracking on with the real reason she had gone to visit Diane that morning.

"Do you know of anyone who would want to harm Father O'Malley?" Sally asked.

"Everyone loved him. I don't understand why he was killed. He was so excited about the inheritance from Bill, and he was thinking about plans of how to use the money to improve the church and expand the services we offer our members, particularly those in need," Diane explained.

"Were you surprised by Bill's will?" Sally asked.

Diane looked out the back window without answering right away. She had both hands firmly on her glass of wine. "I had no idea Bill cared for the church. He always seemed so close to his family."

She blew her nose and finished the glass of water in front of her. Sally noticed she nearly knocked the glass over when she tried to put it down. Sally would have to be quick with her questioning. Father O'Malley's death seemed to be hitting her hard.

"Did you see anyone else in the church or passageway when you returned to St. Elspeth's on Tuesday?"

"No one. I wish I had. The place seemed deserted, except for the light coming from Father O'Malley's office. He always left the door open into the hallway, even though it was freezing."

"And was the outer door locked?"

Diane looked confused.

"Actually, I didn't need to use my key to get in."

Well, there was something.

"So anyone could have come in when Father O'Malley was by himself?"

Diane nodded. "Oh yes, it must have been an intruder."

"Do you remember when you got there exactly?"

"Well, like I told you all on Tuesday, it was just about three," she replied.

"And when did he call you?" Sally asked.

"I guess sometime around one."

Diane was wringing her hands and looking over to the fridge.

Sally realized Diane had told them on Tuesday she couldn't remember what time he had called her to come back in. A couple days later, her memory had returned. It was strange, but on Tuesday, it may have just been the blow of finding his body masking her memory.

"And you are sure it was him?" Sally asked delicately.

Diane turned red. "Of course, it was him. Why wouldn't it be?"

She got up and began pacing in the kitchen.

Sally had to make a decision now to ask her about the phone call or not. Soder and Finnegan seemed certain no call was made. But if it was Father O'Malley, where did he call her from?

"Well, it seems no call was made from the church," Sally began, hoping Diane wouldn't question her about how she knew that. Sally was making it up as she went along.

Apparently, her emotions meant Diane ignored it.

"Well, he called me from his cell phone," Diane offered, finally sitting down again at the kitchen table.

"Now that I think about it, I just assumed it was his cell phone. The connection wasn't as good as the landline, and the number was blocked. Yes, that is strange."

"So maybe it wasn't Father O'Malley?" Sally offered.

"It sounded like him. It definitely sounded like him," Diane responded.

"But it could have been someone else?" Sally asked.

Diane stayed silent and got up to go to the fridge. She sat back down, her glass full of iced tea this time. She grabbed a piece of cheese and stuffed it into her mouth, washing it down with a big gulp.

"Well, I don't know. It must have been Sean. Who else could it have been?"

"If it wasn't him, maybe it was his killer," Sally surmised out loud.

"Terrible, terrible," Diane replied, grabbing a tissue.

Diane now had her head down sobbing on the table, so Sally let herself out.

Heading home, Sally wondered whether Diane might actually have an idea who it could have been who called her. But if it wasn't Father O'Malley, and she knew it, why would she have returned to the church that day just to find the body?

Chapter Twenty-Six

The more Sally thought about it, the more she had to admit to herself that Diane seemed to be lying about getting the phone call from Father O'Malley that brought her back to the church on Tuesday. She had known Diane for years, and she'd always come across as an honest and earnest sort of person, so Sally couldn't help but wonder why she would lie. But then again, Sally didn't know that much about her, apart from their meetings through church events. Maybe a background check on Diane would give her a clue. She wasn't sure though what she was looking for, but somehow she knew she would recognize it when she found it. She needed to find out more about Diane's family, where she came from, any connections she could have, etc. Diane wasn't from Berry Springs, of that Sally was sure. She could go to the Berry Springs records office, but she wanted to be a bit more discreet, so she called her friend, Nancy, at the registry in the state capital, Little Rock.

She definitely wasn't going to mention this to Detective Finnegan. This was her line of questioning at the moment, she told herself. And anyway, Sally was only going to talk to her friend, so he didn't need to be told that.

She tried Nancy via video chat. It didn't take long for her to answer.

She beamed when she saw Sally's face. "Oh Sally, this is a surprise," Nancy said.

Her bushy red hair took up most of the screen, and she was wearing one of her bright print dresses with a purple scarf.

Sally got right to the point and explained why she was calling. Nancy had already heard about the two murders. While there were, of course, murders in Arkansas, there hadn't ever been two murders in one week in a small town in the Ozarks.

"Hmm, Sally, that's a big ask. I could get into trouble for this."

Sally waited to respond. She didn't want to pressure her, but she knew if she let Nancy think about it for a second, she would probably come around. Sally just smiled into the camera.

"Is this really important?" Nancy asked.

"I think someone is hiding something important, and I want to find out what that is. I thought a background check would help. And you do have access to a lot of records."

Nancy thought for a minute, looking away from the camera.

"Okay, Sally, as it's for you."

"Thanks so much for the help. I know this is semi-illegal, but it's a great help."

Sally was relieved she had agreed to help her. Otherwise, she'd had no idea how she would have gotten this information without alerting someone in Berry Springs. And that person might include the killer. Sally was tough, but she wanted to make it out of this investigation alive.

"No worries. Since it's for your double-murder investigation, I can live with myself for helping on this. I have access to a nationwide database, so we should be able to find something. Who are you looking for?"

"Her name is Diane Gregory."

"Do you have her birth date?"

"Hmm, good question. She must be about fifty-five."

Nancy shared her screen so Sally could watch. She saw her type in the name, select all databases, and estimate a birth date, give or take five years either side.

"Is she originally from Arkansas?"

"Another good question. From her accent, I would guess at least from the South, though maybe from Arkansas. I do know that she is not from Berry Springs originally."

Nancy selected all the Southern states and began the search query.

A second later, the results showed twenty Diane Gregorys with a rough birth date of fifty-five years earlier and from Southern states. About half showed a picture, but none of them were the Diane Sally knew, so they quickly discarded them. The other ten they ran through, but none of them were Diane from the church.

"That's odd," Sally began, "She must be in there somewhere."

"Was she married?" Nancy asked, raising her eyebrows in the little window in the corner of the screen.

"I don't think so."

"Well, if she changed her name at any point, good luck trying to find her."

Sally hadn't expected Diane to be so difficult to find, but Diane must be in there somewhere.

"Can we try someone else?" Sally asked. While she had Nancy on the line, she might as well make the most of it.

"Sure, what's the name and birth date?"

"Gillian Arnold. She is thirty-five. Born and raised in Berry Springs."

As Nancy had been searching for Diane, Sally had been thinking about what Mike Watkins had said about who he could have seen behind the bar. And if the murders did have something to do with Bill's will, Gillian was closest to Bill. She also looked very similar to Margaret Jackson, who Bill had instinctively thought it was. Though why would she kill her own brother? And Sally hadn't seen her at the bar that night. But it was worth a try.

Nancy typed the information in quickly, and the results were much easier to follow. "Let's see, birth certificate, baptism, deed to property, arrest record—"

"Arrest record?" Sally interrupted.

Nancy pulled up the record.

"Yup, arrested about three years ago for assault. Some fight she had with her boyfriend outside a bar in Little Rock. She put him in the hospital for a week. And for some reason, the arrest record is marked sealed, not available through the normal channels without a court order."

Sally did remember Gillian had had a boyfriend at one point where it ended badly, though she hadn't ever met him. But she hadn't known about a fight. Bill usually shared everything with her about his family, but maybe this was a bit too embarrassing. And as it happened in Little Rock, it would have been easier to keep it to themselves.

Nancy continued reading.

"Seems the boyfriend didn't want to press charges, so she was fined five hundred dollars for disturbing the peace, and that was it."

"Is there a name for the boyfriend?"

"Yup, Jay Carstairs."

Sally was stunned. "Jay Carstairs? Are you sure? He works in my bar. What's the birth date?"

"June 5, 1986."

"Yup, that must be Jay. He dated Gillian Arnold. Wow. Did not know that."

"And got beat up by her," Nancy added.

"Wow, that's a weird connection I never expected. I'm not sure it gets me anywhere, but at least I have something to ask them both about."

"Any idea of how we can find Diane?"

"You said she works at St. Elspeth's Catholic Church?"

"Right."

"Well, they must have done a background check on her when she was hired. I can contact the diocese and see what I can get out of them. One of their clerks owes me a favor. I should have something for you tonight. I'll call you when I get it."

"Oh, wow, that would be great, Nancy."

"No problem. I'm glad to help. I remember meeting Bill a couple of times. A great guy."

"Thanks so much, Nancy."

"My pleasure. Let me know when you've solved the case." Nancy grinned.

"Will do."

Sally ended the video link and sat back on the sofa. She was feeling excited but apprehensive. Gillian had beaten up Jay. But what did this have to do with Bill's murder or Father O'Malley's murder? And Diane Gregory seems to have appeared from thin air all those years ago. What did that mean? And how was Jeff mixed up in all this?

Chapter Twenty-Seven

To clear her head and gather her thoughts, Sally headed into town to her favorite café, The Nutmeg. It was on Oak Street on the far side of the square, so that gave her time to walk and think.

By the time she got to the café, she was ready to pull out her notepad and plan her next moves.

"Hey, Sally," Joanna, the cheery café owner, greeted Sally as she walked through the door.

Joanna was quite petite, but a barrel of energy and power. Her café was always in perfect running order. Sally sometimes wished she was as organized as Joanna, though Sally's Smasher was pretty successful.

"Hi, Joanna." Sally dropped her coat and backpack on a chair at a table in the corner near the window.

"What can I get you?" Joanna asked.

"A large cup of your strongest coffee and a blueberry muffin, please."

"Sure, I'll bring that right over."

Sally had barely settled herself in the corner when her order arrived. She sipped her still very hot coffee and sorted through all the information she had gathered up to this point. The one thing nagging her mind was the fact that Bill had changed his will two months ago. This was the connection between Bill and Father O'Malley. The change had obviously upset Momma Arnold and the rest of the family. And it had caused a very difficult situation for Sally now that she had to share Bill's part of the bar with Annette. But why would Bill have changed his will so recently? And change it so the people he loved were partly disinherited. It made no sense.

Maybe she should have asked Nancy to get her a copy of Bill's old will as well, if at all possible. No, she didn't want to push Nancy. She was already going out on a limb for Sally as it was. Having the details of both testaments, though, would help narrow down the pool of suspects. If this business was all to do with the will. Sally took a bite of muffin, washing it down with some more of the delicious coffee.

She thought about the family. There were Bill's brothers, Steve and Jack. They were both as big and strong as Bill. They were both angry and could definitely have done it, but she didn't know of a connection between either of them and Jeff. The Arnold family was well known, but they tended to keep to themselves. Bill was the only one who really had a lot of friends in town.

Then there was Bill's sister, Gillian. She had been arrested for beating up Jay. So that showed she had a violent side. But she and Bill were so close, and she wasn't a parishioner of St. Elspeth's.

Jeff.

While Jeff claimed to have been blackmailed into preparing the syringe, he could have easily injected Bill when Bill threw him out of the bar. The timing would be at the far end of what Dr. Wiggams had thought on time of death, but possible. And maybe he wasn't as drunk as he pretended to be when he got in the fight with Zeke.

Annette

She wasn't even at the bar that night, though her husband Zeke was. And he had gotten into a fight with Jeff, which Bill had broken up. When Annette had come to see Sally, she had seemed genuinely upset about Bill's death, and Sally knew of no connection between her and Father O'Malley.

Father O'Malley

He did inherit a lot of money as a result of Bill's death, but she had known him for years, and she just couldn't bring herself to think he had killed Bill, only to get himself killed. Though he was at the bar until closing that night and could easily have injected Bill, as they were not seated too far from each other. She was continuing to go with injection, as that's what Dr. Wiggams felt was more likely.

Diane?

While Diane wasn't named in the will, the money would certainly help the church, which she was always trying to improve. Though was that motive enough to murder Bill?

Holding her pen over her paper, Sally realized in the eyes of the law there was one more suspect: herself.

They were going to be logical and thorough about it; she was named in the will, though not quite the way she expected. Up to now, neither Detective Finnegan nor Mark Soder had made any indication that she was on the list of suspects. She decided to hope for the best and not ask them about it unless they decided to pull her in at some point for a real interrogation.

She shuddered at the thought and pushed it out of her mind.

Father O'Malley's murder also had to be solved. Who would the suspects be here?

Definitely one of the Arnolds. Momma Arnold seemed very upset about the terms of Bill's changed will. Maybe one of Bill's brothers decided to take care of the priest? Though where would the money go then? Sally realized she needed to find out more details of Bill's will.

As if he knew she was thinking about him, the door chime rang, and Randall Wentworth walked in. She let him make it to the counter and place his order, a takeout coffee, before waving in his direction. He happened to wave back.

When he had paid for his coffee, he walked over to her table.

"Good morning, Ms. Witherspoon."

"Hi, Randall. I was just thinking about you."

He frowned.

"Really? What for?"

Sally thought he knew exactly what she wanted.

"I was going to come over and see you."

"Ah, most intriguing," he said.

Sometimes, she thought Randall was just weird.

"Well, I do have some time now if you would like to follow me back to my office."

Sally didn't know why he suddenly seemed more cooperative. Maybe it was the fact that Father O'Malley had also been killed that had made him lighten up. Although this didn't dispense with attorney-client privilege, she knew.

Sally didn't want Randall to change his mind. She quickly paid Joanna and got the rest of her coffee in a to-go cup. She then followed Randall out.

He remained silent as they walked across the street and up the stairs to his second-floor office. He led her to the conference room and, this time, sat close to her.

"I was so sorry to hear about Father O'Malley," he began.

"Yes, Bill is dead, and now Father O'Malley."

Wentworth went strangely silent.

"Well, thank you for agreeing to see me. I know you are very busy." She thought buttering him up would help get her the details she needed ASAP.

Randall looked down at his hands. "Yes, well, I would like to help you find Father O'Malley's killer...and Bill's, of course," he added quickly.

"Why the change of heart?" Sally asked, intrigued by Randall's thawing.

He didn't look her in the face. "Well, I didn't attend St. Elspeth's, as you probably know, but I have known Father O'Malley for years."

Another unknown connection was revealed. It was a small town, but somehow, some people were connected in ways no one would have suspected.

There was an awkward moment between them. It seemed Randall was about to reveal something personal. Sally's bartender skills told her to stay silent and let him speak when ready.

He remained silent for a few moments before continuing. "Well, you know my son, James."

Sally nodded. Actually, she had met him only once when Randall's wife had stopped in at the office with their son one day when Sally was signing some legal paperwork.

"When my wife died a few years ago, James went through a very difficult time."

If Sally wasn't mistaken, Randall was choking up. She hadn't known he had a human side to himself.

"Oh, I'm sorry to hear that."

"It's been difficult for both of us."

Sally squirmed in her seat and hoped Wentworth didn't notice. She felt for him, but she was also eager to get to the point of her visit.

"Well, Father O'Malley leads the town youth group, as you know. James has been a member there since he was five. When my wife died, Father O'Malley took him under his wing and really helped him work through the pain of his mother's death. This brought him out of his misery and helped him prepare for college. I'm proud to say he is now attending the local community college and plans to study law at the University of Arkansas in Fayetteville. And that is why I want to help you find Father O'Malley's killer."

This outpouring of emotion from Randall Wentworth was almost too much for Sally. The town knew him as the robot. Apparently, this was just a facade for the very emotional man behind it.

Sally noticed his eyes welling up, but he quickly pulled himself together, drying them with a handkerchief he pulled out of his pocket.

Facade back in place, he looked over at Sally. "So, what did you want to know?"

"Well, I want to find out the terms of Bill's old will," Sally explained.

"Yes, I thought that would be of interest to you."

"But I guess my first question is what happens to the money Father O'Malley was supposed to inherit. Now he's dead, too. Does it go to the church? Revert back to the estate or go to someone else?" Sally asked.

"That is a very good question," Wentworth replied. "The Catholic Church does love its money, but it's a bit more complicated here, as Bill's will specifically mentioned Father O'Malley and not the church."

"Interesting," Sally replied.

"Once I heard of Father O'Malley's death, I reached the legal aspects of this. Apparently, Father O'Malley did leave a will for his personal property, which wasn't much until the inheritance from Bill. He left his personal possessions to his brother in Little Rock, but any money would actually go to Diane, his assistant."

Sally whistled. "Wow, so Diane gets all that money."

"Looks like it. I imagine the Arnold family will go to court about that as well," Wentworth replied.

"What about the old will? I mean, Bill's old will. Do you know why he changed it?" Sally continued.

"He didn't say, unfortunately," Wentworth replied. "I was also surprised he wanted to change it, particularly the part about leaving the bulk of the estate to Father O'Malley and the church. But I was his lawyer, not his financial advisor. It was his money, and he could do with it as he pleased."

"Can you give me any clues about what the old one said? Without breaking any laws, of course," Sally asked, smiling as delicately as possible across the table.

"Well, let's see," he said. "I can tell you that Father O'Malley wasn't in the last will, and that there were only two beneficiaries, both sharing fifty-fifty."

"Aha, and these were who?" Sally asked hopefully.

"Nice try. I can't reveal that, but I can tell you that one of the people was a family member and one was not," Wentworth replied.

"Was Bill's share in my bar part of the family member or non-family member legacy in the old will?" she asked.

Randall Wentworth smiled coldly.

"Nice try, Ms. Witherspoon," he said.

Yup, the blank lawyer face was back.

Sally sipped her coffee and wondered whether she could squeeze anything else out of him. But the robot Randall Wentworth was here to stay, it seemed. Sally didn't think she would ever see an outpouring of emotion from him ever again. And she had the notion that he was feeling guilty about more or less blurting out what he did to her just now.

"Thanks, Randall, this has been very helpful," Sally said.

He led her to the office door and shut it quickly behind her.

* * *

Sally walked home, her head swirling.

Diane would get the money. Wow. She knew from her conversation with Momma Arnold that the Arnolds were suing anyway, but they would double down if they knew it went to Diane.

The Arnolds were wealthy themselves and didn't really need Bill's share. But what was once an Arnold's was always an Arnold's, she had heard Bill say numerous times. And what was worse, Arnold money couldn't go to an outsider.

As she turned left onto her street, her phone buzzed. It was a text message from Nancy telling her she wouldn't have more on Diane until Monday.

Sorry, I'm still digging.

Chapter Twenty-Eight

Sally didn't sleep well Friday night. She sat up most of the night thinking about her investigation. It also didn't help that the next day was the double funeral.

She finally pushed herself out of bed at nine and went downstairs to make breakfast. She wasn't very hungry, but she needed something to keep her going for the emotions the day would bring. She brewed a big pot of coffee and put two English muffins in the toaster oven.

Smearing the warm muffins with tons of salted butter, she reminded herself that she had wanted to solve both murders by today. So much for that. She did have more information, particularly that on the wills and on Gillian and Jay, but none of it helped her put a definitive finger on the killer or killers.

She decided to give Detective Finnegan a call and update him on what she had found. Maybe he would have something for her. She assumed he would be at the funeral later, but she didn't think that was the best place to discuss a murder investigation. Though she was hoping to get a quiet word with Gillian and Jay, and maybe Diane if she could.

She called his cell phone and found him at home.

"Well, good morning. How is my favorite amateur sleuth?" His tone reeked of sarcasm.

"Good morning, Detective. Sorry to bother you at home. I wanted to check in with some information I've been gathering."

"Hopefully, all legally," he replied.

Sally didn't answer that. Instead, she filled him in on what she had found out from Mike, the witness behind the bar, from Diane, and from Wentworth about the will. Finnegan was genuinely impressed. Then she told him about Gillian and her arrest record and Diane's seemingly murky past.

"Well, haven't we been busy? That information on the will and Gillian's arrest record would have taken us a while to get. Judge Jenkins isn't too pleased when we want to unseal information from a lawyer or doctor or get information from another jurisdiction."

Sally beamed, though the detective couldn't see that. He didn't seem to be having as much luck—or questioning and listening skills, for that matter—as she did.

"Puts a new twist on things. I'll have to bring Jay, Gillian, and Diane in for questioning."

"What about Jeff?" Sally asked. "Have you charged him?"

"Not yet. We're hoping he will lead us to the killer, who we don't want to scare off. We've been having him followed for the past few days."

"Any luck?"

Finnegan coughed loudly. "Nothing. He's been following a regular routine, and we haven't seen him meet with anyone."

"What about at school?"

"Sure, but you can't just waltz into a school these days if you don't belong there."

Sally agreed this would be difficult.

"Yeah. Well, thanks for updating me, Sally. If you find something else, let me know. Since we have a few more, ahem, restraints, shall we say, we can't get information as fast as you can."

Sally wasn't sure whether to take this as a threat or a compliment, but it was another one of his statements she just ignored.

"Anything else on your side?" she inquired.

"Not really, we're following a few leads."

Of course, he'd say that. He didn't seem very forthcoming, but maybe he was trying to sound important for her sake. She seemed to be getting further than he was.

"I guess I'll see you at the funeral later?" she replied.

"Of course."

Conversation over.

* * *

Sally arrived at St. Elspeth's around 1 p.m. She wanted to be early to comfort Momma Arnold and the rest of the family when they got to the church. However, upon her arrival, she only found a few people that she didn't know milling about. She assumed they were from out of town. She said hi to them as she passed and made her way into the church.

She took a seat in the second row on the left. There was a sign pointing to the left side for Bill's family and friends, while the right side was designated for Father O'Malley's friends and family.

As she sat down, she noticed Bishop Billingsley at the front speaking to Pastor Johnson. Johnson was the minister at the Arnold's Methodist church, St. Luke's. The bishop waved to her. Sally waved back and then continued reviewing the service booklet she had picked up at the back of the church.

Slowly, the church filled with most of the town. Bill and Father O'Malley were popular people in Berry Springs. Sally turned to see Jay and Magda looking for a seat. She waved them over to her pew. Zeke and Annette Parker appeared and slid in next to Jay. Sally was glad she didn't have to sit next to Annette; she still hadn't gotten used to the fact that Annette had part of her bar. But she couldn't even begin to imagine how Zeke must be feeling, attending the funeral of the man he had considered a friend, but was also sleeping with his wife.

Sally continued to peoplewatch, nodding to Detective Finnegan and Sergeant Soder as they sat down in the back. She was not too surprised to see Chief Pulasky with them. Right after that, Mayor Milkowski came in with Margaret Jackson. Sally raised her eyebrows, because they seemed to be holding each other very closely, though they pulled away quickly as they walked up the aisle. They both sat next to the chief of police.

Diane came in from a side door and sat in the front on the right. She looked straight ahead, but surprisingly, was not crying, at least as far as Sally could tell. This must be hard on her. She was accompanied by an elderly couple. Sally guessed this was Father O'Malley's sister and brother-in-law. The sister was blubbering, and her husband could barely get her to walk the few steps to the front pew.

Several people from town knew both of the deceased and weren't sure where to sit down. They looked left and right, most then settling to sit on the right as it was a bit emptier than Bill's side.

Bill's family didn't get there until just before the service started. Gillian led a weeping Momma Arnold up the aisle to the front row. Steve and Jack followed behind them, their heads bowed, their steps slow.

Jeff Bartholomew was noticeably absent.

* * *

After the funeral, the Bishop and Pastor hosted a coffee hour in the church hall in the basement. Almost everyone that had attended the funeral joined the coffee, and the room was quite crowded. At the back, a long set of tables had been set up with three large coffee urns and plates and plates of cookies and cakes. The Nutmeg Café had donated all the food, and Joanna herself was behind the table serving people, handing out coffee, plates, and napkins. It was all finger food. In the middle of the room, ten small round tables had been set up for people to stand at, chat, and enjoy the coffee and treats.

Since she was at the front of the church, she had been one of the last people to leave the service. There had been a long receiving line with the Arnolds and Father O'Malley's sister and brother-in-law.

Sally walked downstairs with Jay and Magda, and all three waited in line together.

"It was a beautiful service," Magda said, tears drying on her face.

"Yes, a great tribute to two wonderful people," Sally replied.

It really had been a wonderful sendoff, the beginning of healing for the town.

"I feel so bad for Bill's family," Magda said. All three looked over at Momma Arnold at one of the tables in the center, being comforted by the bishop and

Gillian at a table on the far side of the buffet. Diane was near them, chatting with Father O'Malley's sister. Sally wasn't sure where the brother-in-law was.

"So great that the bishop came," Jay said.

"Well, Bill was a long-time member of his diocese," Sally reminded them.

As she talked to them, she was scanning the room to see who was talking to whom. Her eyebrows raised when she saw Randall Wentworth talking to Steve Arnold. Steve was waving his hands at him, and Randall was only able to free himself from the conversation when Gillian Arnold came over and pulled Steve with her. Arnold business would stay Arnold business, would be what she must be thinking.

When she saw Margaret Jackson chatting with the mayor near where Momma Arnold and the family were standing, that reminded her she wanted to follow up with the mayor on the confusion about fixing the restrooms. In spite of Mike's statement that he thought it was Margaret picking up the envelope with the syringe, though then later not being sure, Sally didn't think the mayor or Margaret had anything to do with the murders. However, the discrepancy in the topics they claimed to be talking about last Saturday night still bore investigation. It had been a week, and there was still so much to do.

Sally, Jay, and Magda found a table in the middle of the room. There was just enough space for them to squeeze together. They said hello to the two people standing there, whom they didn't recognize. Though the priestly collars gave away their profession.

Sally sipped her coffee and only partially listened to Jay and Magda chatting about Bill. She was eager to continue her investigation, but with all the people there, it wouldn't be very easy to pull anyone aside for a conversation. And a funeral was probably not the most appropriate place either. Though the day before, she had thought catching people at the funeral was a good idea.

She bit into the carrot cake and only partially heard Jay and Magda say they were going back for seconds. *Those kids can really eat fast.*

She finished her coffee and chatted with the elderly priests at their table.

They told her that they had gone to seminary with Father O'Malley in Atlanta so many years ago.

Sally was surprised to hear them say Atlanta, where she used to live, and they reminisced together about the best museums, best parks for a walk, and how the city had grown over the years. She had never loved Atlanta, but it brought memories of good times there with her ex-husband, of which there were sadly only a few.

She looked around to see if Jay and Magda had returned, but they were still in the buffet line. She wanted to go over and have a word with the Arnolds and give her condolences. The line upstairs had been like an assembly line, and she felt she should say more to them than she had upstairs, even if she had seen them during the week. Though that had been for her investigation.

She was about to go over by herself when she heard loud noises and a commotion coming from that part of the room. She ran to see what was going on and was stunned to see Gillian Arnold lying on the floor with Momma Arnold over her in tears. Gillian had foam around her mouth and didn't seem to be breathing.

At that moment, the three police in attendance, as well as Dr. Wiggams, came running over. They all stopped when they saw what was going on.

"All right, Soder, call an ambulance and get back up here," Finnegan yelled while still huffing and puffing. Sally had never seen him move so quickly.

Soder made the call. Then ran out of the hall to flag down the ambulance. Sally saw him speak to the cop waiting outside the hall, who was also the chief's driver. The cop positioned himself at the door of the hall, seemingly to keep anyone from leaving.

The chief of police pulled Finnegan aside to confer. The mayor joined them, both men trying to ignore her presence.

Sally helped Momma Arnold up, who was now beside herself.

"Oh, Sally, my babies are dying," Momma Arnold wailed.

Dr. Wiggams worked on Gillian, but Sally didn't think she had a chance. He leaned down to her mouth and stopped, turning to look up at Sally.

Sally understood the look and nodded. As Sally moved closer to Momma Arnold, she noticed a distinct aroma of bitter almonds.

CHAPTER TWENTY-EIGHT

Cyanide. And everyone in the room was a suspect.

Chapter Twenty-Nine

Confusion reigned as the news of Gillian's murder, right under their noses, rippled across the room. Many people had seen her collapse but had thought it was due to the sadness of losing Bill.

Sally moved Momma Arnold to the other side of the room so they wouldn't all be standing near Gillian's body, while Dr. Wiggams stayed with Gillian until the ambulance arrived.

The rest of the family, the bishop, Jay, and Magda had followed them. Sally held Momma Arnold, who could barely speak. Magda found a chair in a nearby room and brought it over for Momma Arnold to sit. Sally and the bishop helped her into the chair.

"Oh, who would do this?" Momma Arnold asked both of them.

Sally didn't say anything but squeezed her shoulder.

"Tragic, tragic," the bishop responded not very helpfully.

Sally looked up at the family and could think of a few people who might want Gillian dead if it meant increasing their own share in the will. But maybe the will was just a red herring. She still wasn't 100 percent sure that was the motive for the deaths.

The paramedics swooped in at that moment, although everyone knew it was already too late. Momma Arnold saw them, too, and continued weeping. Dr. Wiggams had a quick word with them while Soder questioned each table on whether they had seen anything.

Sally was anxious to listen in on all the conversations, but she felt more of an obligation to comfort Momma Arnold. Her two sons, Steve and Jack, were standing next to her, their bodies frozen in place, and would be of no help. Gillian had been the baby in the family, and Sally could feel their loss, especially after losing Bill only a week ago.

Jay and Magda were standing next to Sally, not sure what to do. Magda teared up.

In spite of the shock, Sally's eyes were dry as she ran through the possible suspects in her mind: the people standing near Gillian. Anyone of them could have slipped the cyanide in her drink as they passed to say a word of comfort to the Arnolds. Then again, it could be anyone in the room, as the Arnolds had been standing near the buffet. And was Gillian really the target?

Sally thought back to who she had seen near them. Margaret, the mayor, Diane, Father O'Malley's sister, and the bishop.

Well, Margaret may have been seen behind the dumpster last Saturday night, though Mike had said he wasn't sure it was her.

The mayor told a story about Bill helping to fix the restroom at town hall, which was definitely a fib.

And Diane? Well, she had a murky past, which Nancy in Little Rock was researching.

As for Father O'Malley's sister and the bishop, Sally doubted they had anything to do with it.

But why Gillian? That made no sense.

At that point, Finnegan came over to interview the Arnolds, who had been at the center of it all. Sally appreciated his seeming empathy to not tackle the Arnolds immediately after Gillian had collapsed.

As he came over, the paramedics removed Gillian's body from the room. That was a relief. Sally had seen enough corpses this week for a lifetime.

"Momma Arnold, I am so sorry for your loss," Finnegan said. Noticeably, as always, he took charge of the questioning of these people, not Soder.

"Who is doing this, Detective?" Momma Arnold asked, razor sharp. She stood up slowly, and Sally feared she would collapse again.

"Well, that's what we are going to find out."

"Like you are doing with Bill's death?" Momma Arnold retorted.

Sally felt that sting as if it had been aimed at her. Whereas Finnegan smartly ignored it.

"Did you see anyone near Gillian besides yourselves?" he asked.

"Well, we were all standing together with Bishop Billingsley," she replied, nodding at the bishop, who was standing next to her.

"You weren't too far from the buffet," Finnegan continued.

"That's true, but we had many people come by and offer words of comfort. I was focused more on them than on what my kids were drinking," she responded. "There was a fair bit of jostling and hugging. There are a lot of people here."

Finnegan had hoped for a quick answer, Sally felt. Well, she did as well.

She hadn't been standing too far from the Arnolds, but Momma Arnold had been right, most of the crowd had stopped by to talk to the family and with Diane and Father O'Malley's sister.

"Anyone else see anything?" he asked as he scanned the rest of the family. They all shook their heads. It was clear they were all in a daze.

"Okay, well, if you think of anything, please call me," he said as he motioned for Sally to follow him to a quiet corner.

Sally looked down at Momma Arnold, who nodded, and she joined Finnegan.

"So, Sally, what do you think?"

Momma Arnold's comment had clearly gotten to him, if he was starting with asking Sally what she thought.

"I really don't know, Detective. I was standing not too far from the Arnolds, but so many people came by."

He nodded. "Yeah, now we have three murders and probably three methods of killing."

"You smelled the bitter almonds too?"

"Yes, but we'll have to wait for the lab results for a definitive answer."

"What's your next step, Detective?"

She was enjoying the conversation, feeling like the police were finally including her in their investigation as opposed to humoring what they thought was a hobby.

"Well, as I said this morning on the phone, I'll pull Jay and Diane in for questioning. And I am going to tackle Randall Wentworth again. We need to know the details of the original will. There may be a motive within those pages."

While the list of suspects hadn't really narrowed, there didn't seem to be a real motive for Jay, Diane, or Margaret to have had anything to do with the deaths. Or at least a motive that jumped right out at her. Oh, wait, except for the will. Diane was now a very wealthy woman. But she would have to have known about Bill's will and Father O'Malley's will to plan this. And then how would she kill all three? The only murder that Sally could see her doing was the one that just happened.

"Sally?" Finnegan asked.

"Oh, sorry, yes, sounds good," she replied.

Finnegan moved off, and Sally headed back to the Arnolds.

"Momma Arnold, how about I stay with you tonight?"

The older woman's face broke into a weak smile of relief. "Oh, that would be so helpful, Sally."

Steve and Jack didn't seem too happy about this, but then again, they tended to keep to themselves, unlike Bill and Gillian. However, they uttered no protest, so Sally led Momma Arnold out and took her home in her old Datsun.

Chapter Thirty

For some reason, Sally slept soundly in one of the Arnolds' guest rooms. Each bedroom had its own attached en suite, and she felt like she was in a hotel. She stretched cozily and pushed herself up. The sun streamed in the window and the clock on the bedside table told her it was already past nine. Time to get up.

What a week this had been. She was still mourning Bill's loss, and it hit her every morning when she woke up to reality. She took a moment to remember him and all he had done for her. But her trip down memory lane turned sour when she thought about Gillian. Why had Gillian been murdered? She hadn't been at the bar the night Bill was killed. And she didn't attend St. Elspeth's.

Sally smoothed her hair, tied it into a ponytail, and slipped on the bathrobe and slippers Momma Arnold had provided her the night before. The bathrobe was an old one of Momma Arnold's, and it was in a bright seventies print. The elbows were worn, but it was fluffy and comfy.

Sally padded downstairs to find the family having breakfast in the kitchen.

She felt a bit guilty about sleeping so late. It was her idea to stay over and help Momma Arnold, but she hadn't done much supporting so far. She should have gotten up early to make breakfast. Although knowing Momma Arnold, that would have meant getting up in the middle of the night to be up before she was.

"Oh, good morning, Sally. I hope you slept well," Momma Arnold said quietly. She was wearing a similar print bathrobe, and her hair was every which way. It was obvious they all had been crying.

140

"Good morning. I did. That bed is so comfortable."

Steve held a chair for her, and she sat down. Jack brought her a cup of coffee. She helped herself to the scrambled eggs, bacon, and buttermilk biscuits that were already on the table.

She opened a warm biscuit and buttered it. But as Sally looked down at her plate, she realized she wasn't that hungry. So she merely sipped her coffee and nibbled on a biscuit.

Momma Arnold motioned for Jack and Steve to leave them alone.

"Well, thanks for staying over, Sally," both said in unison as they headed out of the kitchen. Sally had never really liked either of them, but the loss of their brother and now their sister seemed to have mellowed them a bit, at least for now.

Sally looked across the table at Momma Arnold.

"Sally, I've been up all night thinking."

This sounded like the beginning of some kind of confession, and she perked up her ears.

"Oh, I can imagine. What a horrible loss for you. It's been such a difficult week."

Momma Arnold nodded. "Well, actually, I've been thinking about something else," she admitted.

"What is it?" Sally asked, her detective brain now at full speed, but she tried to not seem too anxious to get the information Momma Arnold was about to share with her.

"Well, you remember when you were here on Tuesday, I mentioned I might know why Bill changed his will, but I told you that the memories were too painful?"

Sally just nodded, saying nothing.

"I did something when I was young and first married that I'm not proud of."

Momma Arnold rubbed her wrinkled hands together and pulled on her graying locks. The whole time, she had her head down. "Well, you see, when I was still in high school, I had a sweetheart. I won't give you his name, but just that he was not Mr. Arnold."

Sally was surprised. She had always thought Hank Arnold had been her one and only love. Apparently not. Sally had been about to grab a piece of biscuit, her stomach was growling after all, but she stopped her movement and just stared across the table.

"We broke up just before I graduated. I met Hank Arnold then and knew he was the man I was going to marry. However, just after graduation, I learned I was pregnant. And I knew Hank Arnold was not the father."

Sally was stunned.

"While I was in my delicate condition, I stayed hidden at my grandparents' farm just outside Little Rock, where no one would know me. I am so sorry to say that my Daddy Fletcher made me give that baby up for adoption all those years ago. Just after that, Hank and I were married in the spring of 1963." Momma Arnold looked up at Sally.

Sally reached across the table and took her hands.

"Momma Arnold, I'm touched you shared that with me. It couldn't have been easy. But why tell me now?"

She patted Sally's hands. "The more I think about it, the more I think it could have something to do with Bill's murder."

"Why do you think that?"

"Well, over the past few months, I've been getting threatening letters from someone in town who claims to be the daughter I gave up for adoption all those years ago."

"How do you know they are genuine? These letters, I mean."

"The birth date is correct, and the person knows they were born in Little Rock to a single mother. Apparently, she has been searching for her birth mother for years, and as my grandfather had the record sealed, she wasn't having too much luck until she somehow found me here in Berry Springs. Records can be found, even if they are sealed."

"What was this person threatening to do?" Sally asked.

"Tell my family and tell the town about my shame."

"Why would you feel ashamed about it?" Sally asked.

"Oh, Sally, I know these days, it's not something to be ashamed of. But in my time, you just didn't have a child out of wedlock."

Well, if Momma Arnold really was worried about people finding out, that would be a good reason for Momma Arnold to kill someone, but with the victims being two of her children and another unrelated man, it didn't make sense that she was the murderer in this case.

"And how does Bill's death fit in with all of this?" Sally asked as delicately as possible.

This was apparently the reason Momma Arnold was laying this confession out for her. "I think he found out somehow. And he had become so Catholic over the years, he was a bit disgusted."

At this, she put her head in her hands and began sobbing. Sally debated between comforting her or just letting her get the tears out. She chose the latter.

After a few minutes, she looked up, her eyes soaked. "You see why I am so upset? That is why Bill changed his will. And if my long-lost daughter turns out to be a killer. Oh, what a family."

Sally had never seen or heard Momma Arnold so open about family business.

"I really appreciate you telling me this," Sally said, "But I wouldn't jump to conclusions."

"Sally, I want you to take this information and use it to find who is doing this to us. If it is my daughter, I want her brought to justice. I really do."

"I promise you. I will."

Sally needed to shower and get dressed and out of there quickly. She wanted to get home and sort her thoughts before making her next move. And the next one could be quite dangerous.

Chapter Thirty-One

Back home, Sally's head was abuzz. She made herself a pot of coffee and sat down at the kitchen table.

The last week had been a whirl of information, murders, and confessions. Unfortunately, no confession for the murders of Bill, Father O'Malley, and now Gillian, but Sally knew she was getting close.

After Momma Arnold told her about her giving up a baby for adoption, she finally had some idea of who was behind all of this. Well, at least approximately. The only women in town that could fit the age of Momma Arnold's firstborn were Mayor Jennifer Milkowski, Diane, or Margaret. Why did everything keep coming back to these three women? Sally wasn't that close to any of them. Sally hoped Nancy's background check would turn up something useful.

Sally pulled out her notebook where she had made notes at the café about the deaths. She crossed off Gillian as a suspect.

Oh, Gillian. The double funeral the day before should have been the start of healing, instead, there was one more horrific death to deal with. This time, there were so many people in the room, and the poison was so quick it would be difficult to point the finger at one person and have proof to back it up.

If everything hinged on the daughter Momma Arnold gave up all those years ago, Sally would have to start there.

The Mayor, Diane or Margaret.

Who would she talk to first?

Since Mike had initially thought he had seen Margaret Jackson picking up the envelope with the syringe near the dumpster and she had overheard two strange conversations Margaret had had with someone, Sally would start with her.

As she sipped her coffee, shaking a bit from all the caffeine she had already had that day, she contemplated how best to tackle Margaret. Before heading to her apartment, she would call her and not surprise her, which could put her on her guard. Sally would make it look like a friendly visit as much as she could.

She reached for her cell phone and dialed Margaret's number. Luckily, she had saved the number when Margaret had answered a sewage emergency they had had in the bar a few months earlier. Although Margaret was the head of the sanitation department, she liked to assess situations first herself. Sally had called the main number, and Margaret had shown up. After that, Margaret had given her her personal number for future emergencies.

It rang a few times before Margaret picked up. "Hi Sally, another emergency?"

Always on the job, it seemed.

Sally had thought Margaret might mention Gillian's death the day before or the disastrous week they had all been having, but apparently, her first thoughts were always about her job.

Sally took a deep breath. "Not exactly. I was wondering if I could come over and talk to you this afternoon?"

Margaret gave a cough. "What for?"

"Well, I wanted to follow up on our conversation from a week ago. I've had a breakthrough and thought you might be able to help."

"Well, like I told you before. I didn't see anything Saturday night. And I certainly don't know anything about Father O'Malley's or Gillian's death. Awful for the town, to be sure," Margaret said, clearly unhappy with the line of questioning.

But Sally felt she knew more than she was letting on, so she pressed anyway. "It would be really helpful for me if I could come over. Just for a chat."

Margaret was silent for a few moments. Sally wished she had gotten to know her better over the years so she would have a better idea of how to connect with her.

Margaret finally spoke. "Why don't you stop by for a late lunch? I'm making my spicy chicken salad," Margaret said.

Lunch? Well, she hadn't been expecting that, but it might be a more relaxing setting to ask Margaret some delicate questions about her past. And what she was doing behind the dumpster Saturday night.

"That sounds great. I'll be over in thirty. Work for you?

"Sure, see you then."

* * *

The walk over to Margaret's was refreshing after the events of the day before.

Sally debated texting or calling Mark Soder before she left the house, but decided to just see where the conversation would lead. She had known Margaret for years, and she felt confident she could handle her.

Margaret buzzed her up and led her into the kitchen. She was wearing jeans and a sweatshirt, her usual ultra-casual outfit. Sally had never seen her in anything else.

"Thanks for the invite, Margaret. I love chicken salad."

She hadn't been hungry that morning, but by the time she had walked over to Margaret's, she was famished.

"My pleasure, Sally. I realized when you called that it really has been a weird, strange week, and I could use some company."

The chicken salad was in the center of the table with a basket of bread and a plate of butter next to it. Margaret handed Sally a plate. The napkin and flatware were already at each place. Then, taking two chilled frosted beer mugs from the fridge, Margaret poured them each a beer.

Sally dug right in, and it was delicious. Everything was perfectly moist, and there were several interesting spices that Margaret had added to the chicken salad. Washed down with a strong German Bock beer, Sally felt it was one of the best meals she had had in a while.

"Wow, Margaret, thanks. It really hits the spot."

"Oh, that is so sweet, Sally. I do like to cook, but rarely have someone to share it with."

Sally helped herself to another scoop of chicken salad and a piece of bread and butter. She was even keeping up with Margaret on the beer, who opened a second bottle for each of them.

"So, what have you found out so far?" Margaret had asked as Sally was chewing, so it took well a few seconds for her to respond.

"I now think that all three murders are connected."

Margaret put down her fork and leaned across the table. "Interesting, why?"

"It all seems to have something to do with Bill's will and the Arnold family."

Sally tried to be as careful as possible with her questioning, but she couldn't avoid the most important subjects.

"Why would an Arnold kill two of their own and a priest?"

Sally sipped her beer, contemplating how best to respond.

"What if one of them thought they were being disowned?"

Margaret was ruddy-cheeked and obviously enjoying the effects of the beer, but she was still bright-eyed. "That would definitely be a reason to kill someone," Margaret agreed. She put a hold on Sally's questioning by suggesting they have dessert in the living room.

"Would you like a coffee with your cake?"

Sally felt full from all the food, and the heavy Bock beer was going straight to her head. She took a sip of water to help balance the mix.

"Sure, shall I help you clean up?"

"Oh no, you head into the living room. I'll clean up and prepare the dessert."

Sally got up from the table and felt a little woozy. She wasn't used to drinking in the middle of the day, but everything had been so yummy.

Margaret came in a few minutes later with two mugs of coffee and two plates of German chocolate cake.

Sally thought she must have German roots, what with the beer and cake she was serving. Would that discount her as Momma Arnold's firstborn? Either way, she hoped the coffee would help to settle her thoughts and counteract the effects of the alcohol. Her head was spinning. That beer must have been stronger than she thought.

"So you were thinking someone might have been disowned?" Margaret asked. "Who might that have been?"

Sally didn't have time to respond before she tipped over and crashed to the floor.

Chapter Thirty-Two

Sally woke with a splitting headache. She tried to speak, but no sound came out. She couldn't even move.

Her hands and legs were tied tightly to the small bed she lay on. Her throat was parched. Every muscle in her body ached. She lifted her head a few inches, blinked her eyes, and tried to look around the room she was in. The room was dark, with only a slit of light through the heavy curtains covering the one window across from the bed. She saw the outline from a few pieces of furniture, but the headache made her drop back after only a few seconds.

Margaret, she suddenly remembered. She had been at Margaret's for lunch. What had Margaret slipped into her drink?

Why would Margaret drug her, and where was she? Had Margaret kidnapped her? Maybe she had found the killer or just one of the killer's henchmen. Margaret had always seemed more like a follower, not a leader. Sally regretted not texting Mark Soder before going over there. She wasn't sure how she was going to get out of there. She sobbed and shook with fear. She didn't want to die.

Sally tried to croak out a weak "Help." But apart from her own feeble voice, she didn't hear a peep. So Margaret must have taken her somewhere. Otherwise, she would have heard the noise of the traffic on Oak Street.

She tugged on the ropes holding her hands and discovered they weren't that tight. She wriggled her arms to try and loosen them further, but they just got tighter as she moved, digging painfully into her wrists. Then she tried to move her legs, which were twisted toward her chest, but she couldn't budge them an inch. A rusted chain and old padlock ran from her legs over the side of the bed. It must be locked to a hook on the floor. She groaned and lay back.

It was the first time in her life she thought she might actually die. She instantly regretted wanting to get involved in solving the murders. Look where it had gotten her.

Pull yourself together, Sally. You owe it to Bill to get out of here.

She took several deep breaths to calm herself and think clearly, but she was so thirsty.

Sally raised her head again to try to see what was in the room. Through the slit of light between the curtains, she noticed a low dresser with drawers and the door to a small closet on the far side of the room. On the chest of drawers was an old lamp with a broken shade hanging to one side. This seemed to be a child's room or had been one at some point. There was a child's rocking horse in the corner, and the small metal bed she was on must have been a child's bed as Sally barely fit on it.

Well, she definitely wasn't at Margaret's. Margaret had never had children. Neither did Diane come to think of it. Nor the mayor.

Her mind wavered from trying to get out of this scary situation to figuring out what this all had to do with the three deaths. Sally decided she should really concentrate on getting out of the place she was in at the moment, because if she didn't, she may not have a chance to investigate the deaths at all.

She was deciding on what she should do next when she heard footsteps coming up what sounded like stairs. The door opened, and Margaret walked in.

Sally hollered at her as she came into the room. "Margaret, what the hell did you do to me?"

It came out like a croak; her throat was so dry.

"Shut up, bitch."

Sally was stunned into silence. She bit her lip.

Margaret carried a square wooden tray with a sandwich and a small bottle of water. She put the tray on the bed next to Sally. Then she pulled out a gun and pointed it at Sally.

Sally tried to move back on the bed to get away from the weapon. Tears came to her eyes.

"Okay, I'm going to untie you so you can eat. But don't think of trying anything. I have no problem shooting you," Margaret said. "Do you understand?"

"Yes," Sally replied in a whisper.

"What did you say?" Margaret asked, waving the gun.

Sally used all her willpower and strength to say *yes* in a normal voice.

"Good girl."

Margaret held the gun in one hand and used the other to untie Sally's hands.

Sally thought of trying to attack her, but she was so weak. She was also worried Margaret would make good on her threat to shoot her. Sally would try to get her strength back first and then attempt to overpower Margaret at the next meal. If there was one.

Sally reached for the sandwich and devoured it in two minutes. Washing it down with the water felt so good. She wasn't sure what day it was or how long she had been tied up, but at least she now had some food and drink in her.

When she had finished, Margaret quickly tied her hands back up, pulling them extra tight. Sally winced, but Margaret ignored her. She took the tray and its contents with her and headed out the door and back downstairs.

Sally heard several voices, but they weren't that loud, and she didn't recognize any of them. Geez, how was Margaret involved in all of this? Was Margaret Momma Arnold's long-lost daughter?

While she was thinking about this, she noticed a sharp edge on the metal bed near her chest.

If she could twist herself and rub the ropes tying her hands against, they might come free. While the metal chain and padlock looked secure, the ropes tying her hands weren't that thick, even though they dug into her wrists every time she moved them.

She took a deep breath to steel herself for the pain that she would feel while twisting herself toward the edge of the bed.

She lifted herself slightly and bit on her tongue to stop herself from crying out and bringing Margaret and her gun back up the stairs. Moving her upper body as much as she could, she managed to get her hands close to the metal.

She rubbed the ropes slowly and as hard as she could against the metal again and again, and one of the strands of the rope finally snapped after what felt like an hour. She fell back on the bed, the sweat dripping from her brow. This was going to take a while, and hopefully, she had enough strength for it. Though she didn't have anything else to do at that moment, she tried to humor herself. Was anyone out looking for her?

Pushing all thoughts from her mind except getting away from her kidnappers, she rested for a few moments to gather her strength for the next move toward freedom. Positioning her hands again required a lot of pushing, grunting, and wincing.

Finally, she rubbed the ropes against the sharp metal again and again, and slowly but surely, another strand popped open. She wriggled her wrists, trying to get the rest to rip, but all they did was dig into her skin. The pain made her tear up.

She fell back in exhaustion. Her shirt was soaked, and her face was dripping from all the sweat. Her long hair fell into her eyes, and she tried to sling it away from her face.

While she was lying there, she realized the voices downstairs had stopped. To be on the safe side, she waited a few minutes before continuing to make sure Margaret wasn't coming up the stairs again.

She took a deep breath and pushed herself up for a third time. She barely had the strength left to do it. She was running on only adrenaline at this point. Leaning over again, she rubbed the ropes against the metal edge, pushing down as hard as she could. She slid the ropes back and forth and slowly felt them tearing. She silently yelped for joy.

Finally, the rope split open and fell on the bed. She didn't know how long this had taken her, but her hands were free. She rubbed her raw wrists, trying to get the circulation going, and fell back on the bed, breathless. She wiped her face on the pillow in an effort to dry herself. The sweat was making it hard for her to see.

She hoped Margaret wasn't going to be coming back up the stairs. She kept listening closely for a sound on the stairs, but only heard the distant voices from the ground floor that had started up again.

She looked down at the padlock. While it was locked securely, it was old, so she figured she could maybe try to jimmy it open.

She felt in her pockets for her keys or something, but Margaret had emptied them.

She thought of trying to rip the zipper off her jeans and use that, but she knew that was useless.

Then her eyes fell on the broken lampshade on the chest of drawers. If she could knock it off the dresser, she might be able to reach it on the floor and then use one of the metal ends to get the padlock open.

But how would she get it off the dresser?

She slowly twisted herself toward the lamp and cried out in pain from the chain digging into her ankles. She cursed herself silently and held her breath, listening for any change in the voices downstairs.

She waited a few minutes, and the conversation continued. Luckily, they hadn't heard her.

She looked around the room again and felt the lumps of the blanket under her.

Of course. She could use the blanket like a lasso to knock the lamp toward her. But that would cause a lot of racket and bring Margaret upstairs. But it would be her only chance to get the padlock open and out of the room. Then she would have to somehow get out of the house—wherever that was—and to freedom.

One step at a time, Sally.

Pushing herself off the blanket, she managed to get it all out from under her. It was awfully dusty, and that almost made her sneeze. Pulling most of the blanket toward her, she whipped the end toward the chest of drawers and just missed the lamp. This would be harder than she thought.

Pulling the blanket end back toward her, she twisted it tighter and tied the end to try and make a hook. The tied end would also be heavier than the normal loose end of the blanket.

Sally flung the end of the blanket toward the lamp, and it tipped over and hit the floor in front of the dresser. She listened for movement on the stairs. She knew if Margaret came in now, she might easily die. Sally shuddered at the thought and tried to push it out of her mind.

Whenever she rested, she remembered how scared she was. She had gotten this far with escaping, but she wasn't in the clear yet.

She leaned down toward the floor and used the hook end of the blanket to pull the lamp toward her. Reaching as far as she could, she pulled it up on the bed.

Pulling the shade off the lamp, there was a thin round metal end on the frame she could use to push into the padlock. It looked like it would fit in the lock, but she wasn't sure if the lock would open.

She pushed herself up and felt the pain in her bent legs.

Jamming the end of the lamp frame into the padlock, she twisted it around, but the lock stayed shut.

Chapter Thirty-Three

It felt like it had been hours since Margaret had brought Sally that sandwich, though in reality, Sally knew it must have been less. When was she going to come back? Her stomach was in knots, worrying Margaret would appear any second. The uncertainty was the hardest part. She took a few deep breaths to calm herself.

She examined the metal lamp frame and found she could bend it and crush it between her fingers. It was cheap brass that easily welded under her force, even if she wasn't up to full strength yet. She flattened one end of the frame to try and form a kind of key.

Taking a deep breath, she pushed it into the rusted padlock and wiggled it around, trying to get the lock to open. She heard a click, so she pulled the top of the padlock, and one end released, but the other stayed tightly locked.

She was so close, but the tension was giving her a headache. Or maybe it was from lack of water. She had only had that small bottle of water Margaret had brought, and she had been sweating for a while trying to get out of there. She tried her makeshift key in the lock again and moved it around while at the same time pulling on the side of the padlock that was still stuck. Slowly, she felt something give, so she pulled as hard as she could, grunting and straining, and the padlock opened.

She took another moment to catch her breath. Now that she was free, she wasn't sure she had enough strength left to make it out of the house and to freedom, but she had to try.

She removed the chains from around her legs and rubbed her ankles. She tried to swing her legs out from under her and almost cried out in pain. She held her breath and slowly moved her legs over and onto the floor. Pushing herself up, she sat there for a few minutes to gather her strength for the escape. She rubbed her legs, which had pins and needles, and slowly the circulation returned.

It took a few minutes of massaging her legs before she felt ready to stand up. She only had one chance to get out of there. She took a deep breath and pushed herself off the bed. She almost toppled over but managed to grab one of the metal bed posts to stop her fall. She hobbled across to the dresser and closet to see if she could find a weapon to defend herself from Margaret and whoever else was downstairs, but the drawers and closet were both empty.

Then she remembered the lamp on the floor. The base was just wood, but if she swung it hard enough, it might knock somebody out.

As she was leaning over to pick it up, she heard a car start outside. Whoever was in the house must be leaving. That would make her escape a bit easier. It was probably just Margaret left, she assumed.

Then, there were footsteps on the stairs.

Sally quickly grabbed the lamp and stood behind the door, holding the lamp like a baseball bat over her shoulder.

The door slowly opened, and she saw a foot enter. Before the person could get a look inside the room, Sally swung the lamp around as hard as she could, bashing the person right in the stomach.

As Sally came around the corner, she saw it was Margaret.

The lamp had hit her hard, and she almost fell backward and down the stairs, but she managed to grab the banister just in time to stop her fall.

Sally threw the lamp at her as she raced past Margaret and down the stairs as fast as her sore legs would take her.

The stairs ended in the kitchen. She quickly looked around and saw Margaret's keys next to the sink, along with the gun. She grabbed both as she headed to the front door. This was it. She was going to make it. But then she tripped and fell. Looking down, she'd fallen over her own backpack. She just had time to grab it as she heard Margaret shouting right behind her.

Sally ran outside to Margaret's pickup that was parked next to a garage.

She pushed the button on the key, and it unlocked. She jumped inside and just managed to re-lock the door before Margaret was there banging on the window. Sally shrieked in fear, terrified by the look of hatred that stared back at her.

She put the pickup in reverse and slammed her foot on the accelerator. The pickup jumped backward, and she swung it around the large gravel driveway and floored it down the road. Pieces of gravel hit the windows, and she was worried they would break. Margaret had fallen backward when Sally had reversed the truck, but now Margaret was running after her, yelling and cussing up a storm.

Sally reached the end of the driveway. Not knowing where she was, she didn't even think and just turned right to get away from that house and Margaret as quickly as possible.

Chapter Thirty-Four

Sally held the accelerator to the floor and bolted down the narrow road. Her fear almost prevented her from noticing a hairpin bend that raced toward her, and she managed to brake just in time and navigate around the corner without spinning out or tipping over.

Her chest was heaving as she realized she had escaped. But where was she? The road didn't look familiar.

While keeping her eyes on the road, she managed to slowly open the zipper on her backpack.

Feeling inside, she was relieved to find Margaret hadn't taken her phone. That was because Margaret probably thought Sally would never need it, or the backpack ever again.

Sally was shaking. The adrenalin from the flight from the house was wearing off, and fear and panic were settling back in.

She grabbed the steering wheel and looked straight ahead while she took several deep breaths. She needed to stay as calm as possible to figure out where she was and how she was going to get back to town, to the police and safety.

Pulling the phone out of the backpack, she glanced down at it and saw there was no reception. She could be anywhere.

She drove another few miles before the road forked. There were still no road signs, so she took the left fork to see where it led her.

She debated trying to make a phone call, if there was ever service, but thought her best course of action was to get back to Berry Springs and go to the police department as soon as possible.

Checking her phone again, she saw it was almost six p.m. on Monday. She had lost a day and a half. Magda and Jay would have just started worrying, because the bar was closed on Sundays, and they would have just have turned up for their Monday shifts. She wondered if anyone else was missing her. But no one knew she had gone to Margaret's the day before. She certainly had a thing or two to learn about the investigation business. She would have to learn quickly, though, or the next time something like this happened, she might end up dead. She gripped the steering wheel like a vise while contemplating this.

That's when she heard a ding.

The gas gauge was almost empty.

Her heart jumped in her throat. She had no idea where she was, and there was no gas station in sight. If Margaret had another car in that garage, she could be coming after her. Running out of gas would be the last thing Sally needed, even if she had Margaret's gun on the passenger seat.

She prayed the gas would be enough to get her back to Berry Springs. If she was even headed in that direction.

She slowed down to conserve whatever was left in the tank and kept checking her rearview mirror for a sign of Margaret. No car was behind her. Maybe Margaret had taken the other fork in the road, or Sally had actually taken the only car at the house. Sally prayed this was the case.

At least she had Margaret's gun, so she couldn't shoot out one of Sally's tires. Then again, she might have had another gun with her. Sally shuddered at the thought.

Sally concentrated on the road in front of her. The road curved left, then right, then left, then right, but it seemed to never end. She just needed to get back to Berry Springs as soon as possible.

She felt like she had been on the road for hours when she finally came to the end of the highway she was on and saw a sign she recognized.

Route 10

The right arrow pointed north toward Berry Springs and indicated it was ten miles. That would take her right by Sally's Smasher. Since the bar should have opened already, she knew she couldn't just drive by and wave to Jay and Magda, who might be waiting there for her to show up with the key. She'd call the police from the bar.

After Sally had gone about halfway up Route 10, she began tipping in her seat. She could barely keep her eyes open, and the aches and pains were getting worse.

Hang on, Sally...

She opened the window and took in several deep breaths of cold air.

Her phone beeped. This meant she was getting close to the bar and town if there was a signal again. Were all these notifications missed calls? And if Detective Finnegan was one of them. She didn't have the strength to look at her phone. She just had to get to the bar.

It couldn't be that far, she hoped.

The red glare of the gas light was searing into her eyes. The truck started slowing down for some reason and began to sway on the road.

She jumped awake with a start and narrowly missed a deer that jumped across the road. Maybe she should pull over immediately and call for help. Otherwise, she might go right into a tree.

That's when she saw lights ahead and a familiar sign. She made it.

She slammed on the brakes and went squealing around the corner and into the parking lot of her bar. She saw a large crowd at the door as she came to a stop, the engine slowly dying from lack of fuel. Magda's wide eyes stared at her in the headlights while she saw Jay a ways off on the phone. When he saw her, he stopped talking and shoved his phone in his pocket.

Both of them reached the truck at the same time. Sally opened the door and collapsed into their arms.

Chapter Thirty-Five

S ally lay on the couch in her office while the paramedics examined her. They checked her pulse, checked her heart, and shone a light in her eyes, making her follow it slowly from left to right and back. Detective Finnegan and Sergeant Soder were perched on two chairs opposite the couch, leaning over anxiously.

After Sally had collapsed in Jay and Magda's arms, Magda had quickly called the police and the ambulance. It hadn't taken that long for both of them to get there. Sally hadn't had time to mention anything to either police officer, but just before the paramedics came in, she had whispered "kidnapped" to Finnegan.

"No sign of concussion," the taller of the two paramedics explained. "You're just a bit dehydrated. If any headache returns, go to the hospital or call an ambulance. There may be aftereffects of whatever you were given."

When the paramedics had first arrived, they had insisted she get in the ambulance and go to the county hospital right away, but she would have none of it. While she was glad to be alive, she didn't have time to waste in the hospital while the killers were still loose. Rest would come later when the murderer or murderers had been arrested.

"Thanks, guys," Finnegan said as the paramedics headed out. He then turned to Sally. "You know you could have been killed. Why didn't you let us know what you were doing? That was dangerous."

Sally looked across at him and nodded slowly.

"You just don't trust me, is that it?"

"Well, I..." she said and then started crying, dropping her glass of water in the process. Luckily it didn't break, but the liquid seeped across the carpet, wetting the police officers' shoes. Both moved their feet away from the soaked carpet.

"Okay. Okay. Just take a deep breath and tell us what happened," Soder said, glancing across at his boss and shaking his head.

Now that they were alone, she could tell her story. She related all that had happened since she talked to Detective Finnegan at the church after Gillian's death. It had only been two days, but a lot had happened.

Soder took out his notebook and followed her story by furiously taking notes.

She told them about Momma Arnold's confession about giving up a daughter for adoption, a daughter that seems to have reappeared in Berry Springs and was taunting her. How Sally guessed the long-lost daughter might be Margaret, both from her age and from Mike's initial witness statement.

"And you just decided to go to Margaret's without letting us know? If she is the killer, you could be dead right now," Finnegan said, raising his voice.

He seemed to really care.

"Well, to be honest, I did think of texting Mark, but then somehow thought I could handle it."

At that, Mark Soder blushed. Finnegan didn't seem to notice because his wide eyes were still on Sally.

"Thought you could handle it?" Finnegan replied even louder.

Soder grabbed his shoulder, which caused Finnegan's chair to creak loudly under his weight.

"Okay, it was stupid," Sally admitted.

She then told them about the lunch and the beer and how it seemed to hit her hard. The next thing she remembered was waking up in what she thought was a child's room somewhere.

"And you have no idea where the house is?" Finnegan asked.

She thought back to how she raced away from the house. Her hands trembled.

"Well, I know I ended up on Route Ten, south of town, so it's somewhere near there. But there were so many twists and turns in the road, I'm not sure I'd be able to find the driveway again."

"Well, we'll bring Margaret in for questioning," Finnegan said. "If she hasn't left town already."

Sally looked across at him and nodded. "Well, I don't think she is the killer, or the mastermind behind it. If she were the killer, she probably would have just gotten rid of me. And someone else was there in the house talking to her, probably giving her orders. They left a little before I escaped." She hadn't really thought about this in detail before now, but as she related her immediate thoughts to the officers, it all somehow made sense.

At this point, Jay came in. His dark, wavy hair was covering part of his face. He brushed it back, and Sally watched his muscles bulge under his skin-tight T-shirt.

"Sally, how are you? Can I get you anything?" he asked.

Sally could hear the ruckus of the bar through the open door from the back hallway to the front.

"Thanks, Jay. I'm feeling a bit better. Oh, and another water would be great." She pointed to the glass on the floor.

Jay picked it up. "Sure, right away, boss."

She watched him leave to get her drink. A part of Sally wanted to get out front and help them both. This Monday night was busier than she thought it would be. *Another murder in town will do that*, she suspected.

Berry Springs people were tough. Rather than locking themselves in their homes, they wanted to get out and gab about it with their friends and neighbors. No one would dare admit they were actually scared. Jay and Magda had wanted to keep the bar closed that night, but Sally insisted they open. She needed the revenue, and she knew the customers needed a place to chat about what was going on. And maybe comfort each other in the process.

But there was no way she would be able to walk around that night. And anyway, Finnegan and Soder wouldn't have let her.

"We'll send an officer over right away to pick Margaret up, if she's home. And Jeff. And Soder, ask Jay to come into the station when his shift here is over. I'd like to get his story about the fight he had with Gillian in Little Rock," Finnegan said, motioning to Soder, who walked out to the hallway to call it in and pull Jay aside.

"So you didn't talk to him already like you planned to?" Sally asked.

Finnegan frowned. "Unfortunately, no. I was going to quietly ask both him and Diane at the funeral to come to see me Monday morning, but then Gillian was killed, and we were busy with that."

Well, that would explain why Jay seemed his normal friendly self. If he had already been questioned, he might act differently around the police. And come to think of it, he hadn't seemed too upset at Gillian's death. Maybe her beating him up in Little Rock had something to do with it.

Obviously changing the subject, Finnegan turned to stare at Sally.

"Is there anything else you haven't told us? Like what you might do next," Finnegan asked.

Oops, caught.

Despite everything, Sally was ready to head home to plan her next move. Even if the smart next move would be to first get some rest. "I guess I'll just sleep."

Finnegan laughed. "Yeah, right. You need to be more careful now, Sally. Three people have been killed, and I don't want you to be next."

Sally thought for a moment before responding.

"I know, John."

At that point, Jay reappeared with her water.

He left quickly, calling out, "Real busy tonight," as he did.

Sally gulped down half the water before replying to Finnegan. "I guess the first thing to do is identify Momma Arnold's daughter."

"And how are you going to do that?" he asked.

"I'm still waiting for some information from a source."

"A source with access to government information, I assume," he said accusingly.

"Well, uh…"

He put his hand up to stop her. "I don't want to know."

"Margaret might be the one who blackmailed Jeff to plant the syringe."

"But you said before she didn't seem like the mastermind type."

Sally nodded. "I did, but she still could be the person tasked with getting him to prepare the syringe. If I were the killer, I'd want to stay away from as much of the prep work as possible and just do the deed."

Finnegan raised his eyebrows.

"Well, that's my thinking, anyway," she replied.

Soder walked back in. "Okay, an officer is headed to Margaret's now."

"Good," Finnegan replied. "All right, Sally, I'll take you home now so you can rest. We're going to post an officer outside your house for the next few days, just in case."

Sally yawned and got up.

"Come on, Sally, let's go," Finnegan said, a bit abruptly, she thought.

As they got up to leave, Magda popped her head in the doorway.

"Oh, you're leaving? Sally, can you give me the key to lock up later?" she asked.

Sally hesitated because she liked to be the one in control of access to her bar. After a few seconds, though, she realized that made no sense right now. She needed to get home, and one of the two working for her would have to lock up later. Sally reluctantly reached into her backpack and pulled out the bar keys, and handed them to Magda.

Magda gave her a bit of an over-the-top grin, seeming to know that this hadn't been easy for Sally. "Don't worry, Sally. All will be fine here."

"Right, thanks," Sally replied.

Finnegan motioned that they should finally be leaving.

He turned to Soder. "Mark, you head over to arrest Margaret, if she's actually home. I'll be over after I've escorted Sally home."

"Sure, boss."

The three of them walked out the back to avoid the bar crowd and any questions. As they trudged across the back parking lot, Sally caught a glimpse of the dumpster and froze.

Just over a week ago, she had found Bill's body there. How drastically their little world had changed since that night.

Chapter Thirty-Six

It took a while for Sally to convince Finnegan, but he finally gave in. "All right. It's against my better judgment, but maybe you can help," he said, turning slowly in his wooden desk chair.

They were sitting in Finnegan's office at police HQ the next morning. Sally's wrists and ankles were still sore, and she had a bit of a limp, but she was determined to push through and solve the murders, whatever it took. She was too far in to take a break now, even if a part of her realized that she should.

Sally had come in the next morning to see if Margaret and Jeff had been brought in, which they had. Either there was a car in the garage at that scary house, or Margaret had been driven home by the killer or another accomplice because when the officers drove over to the house, she was already home. Both Sally and Finnegan were glad Margaret had been caught. Sally didn't think she would try anything else on her, but still, she couldn't be sure.

Though Sally did wonder why Margaret hadn't made a run for it. Something or someone was keeping her in town, regardless of the consequences.

Sally had also wanted to listen in to Finnegan and Soder questioning Margaret and Jeff. That is where Finnegan had balked, but after some massaging and pleading from Sally, he had finally given in.

"Okay, let's go," Finnegan said as he pushed his bulk up from the chair. For once, it wasn't Finnegan who was struggling with his body as Sally took a few seconds to get back up from the chair she was sitting in, and every bone in her body cried out for rest.

They headed down the hall to the interrogation room, both walking slowly, Sally hobbling.

"You watch in here," Finnegan said as he stabbed a thumb at the door to the small room next to where he would question Margaret. The one-way mirror and speakers in there told Sally all she needed to know. Luckily, there was a small chair for her to sit on, because she knew she wouldn't have been able to stand the whole time.

She sat down and took out her trusty notebook and pen. Looking up, she was just in time to see an officer escort Margaret into the room. The officer motioned for Margaret to sit and then stood in the corner of the room, her arms crossed, keeping a close eye on Margaret.

Margaret sat down at the table and looked directly at Sally as if she knew she was in the next room. Sally got shivers down her spine and looked away.

Finnegan and Soder came in soon after. Finnegan sat down across from Margaret, while Soder stood behind him. Soder reached over to turn on the recording device at the edge of the table. Margaret didn't react to this. Sally wondered if she had asked for a lawyer.

Finnegan opened the blue folder he had in front of him and looked at it for a while, as if he were studying his notes and questions and evidence against her.

Margaret drummed her fingers on the table. She didn't seem to care that she had been picked up the night before and spent the night in jail. Sally assumed she thought she had some kind of protection, since she was a town employee.

"Margaret, haven't you been busy lately?" Finnegan said, finally looking up from his folder.

Margaret looked directly at him. "I have no idea what you're talking about, Detective."

Finnegan shook his head. "That's not going to do, Margaret. We know what you did to Sally."

At the mention of Sally's name, Margaret clenched her fists.

Sally was on the edge of her seat, wondering what she would say.

"I don't know what you're talking about," Margaret said, her voice level.

"I haven't seen Sally since the double funeral on Saturday." Her hands told another story.

"Really, then why do we have these?"

Finnegan reached into his pocket and pulled out the keys Sally had used to start Margaret's truck and make her getaway. He threw them across the table at her.

"Never saw them in my life."

Sally was a bit stunned by her audacity.

"Really?"

He reached down and showed her the *M* on the key chain.

She just stared at it silently.

"So you're telling me you have never seen these keys before?"

"Yes, that is what I am telling you," she replied, her voice tight.

"Well, then, how do you explain that the key on this chain starts the truck outside that is registered to you?"

"That's a lie," Margaret seethed, shaking in her chair.

Finnegan remained silent, though Sally saw Soder standing on one foot, then on the other, his upper body leaning toward the table, and Margaret. Finnegan gave him a look that kept him still.

"Margaret, we have your car. We have your keys. And we have your fingerprints all over the keys and the truck."

At this, Margaret froze.

Of course, Sally thought, all town employees have to be fingerprinted when they start working for the town. She wondered what Margaret would say next.

"I'm not saying anything else until my lawyer gets here."

She pulled out her wallet, took out a business card, and slid it across the table. Finnegan picked it up and handed it to Soder, who left the room to make the call.

"Why did you get Jeff into all this?" Finnegan asked.

Margaret shrugged her shoulders.

"He's an idiot," she replied, then realized she had spoken. She now crossed her arms in annoyance and stood up.

CHAPTER THIRTY-SIX

"Sit down!" Finnegan barked.

Margaret hesitated but then sighed and returned to her seat.

Finnegan continued: "We have Jeff here, and he's spilling the beans."

"No way," she replied, forgetting again she had told the detective she wouldn't talk.

Sally watched in awe at Finnegan's chutzpah. If he kept at it, Margaret might just tell all. Though if she were honest with herself, she didn't think that would happen so quickly.

"Are you protecting someone?" Finnegan continued.

He followed Sally's reasoning that Margaret couldn't be the planner behind all this, just the accomplice and henchman. The mastermind must have been the person Sally overheard Margaret talking to on the phone and at the house where Margaret held her tied up. She winced at the thought of the ropes and chains.

"No, what do you mean?" Margaret was screeching by this point. She sat down shaking and shivering.

With that, Finnegan got up and left the room while Margaret fumed. Sally watched as the police officer on watch got a bit closer to Margaret in case she tried anything. Maybe they should have chained Margaret's arms and feet to the table like she had done to Sally.

No, that just seemed revengeful and cruel. Although, it was tempting.

The door opened, and Finnegan joined Sally.

"Well, what do you think?" Finnegan asked.

"She seems to have so much pent-up anger," Sally replied. "My first thought was that she was pissed off about being caught, but also a bit scared of what she might say. There's someone controlling her."

"That was my thought too." Finnegan nodded. "She realizes she's screwed. We have a lot of direct evidence against her."

"If we could find the house where she kept me, you could really pin something on her. Her fingerprints and DNA would be all over the place," Sally said.

The door opened again, and Soder joined them.

"Randall Wentworth will be here in an hour," he told them.

Sally was always amused that Randall Wentworth was involved in so many different cases. Of course, he constituted half of the legal representation in town, but she wondered how he kept all his confidential information straight, since he knew so much about everybody.

* * *

The three of them headed upstairs, where Jeff had been brought for questioning. As with Margaret, Sally sat in the small anteroom to watch through the one-way mirror.

Sally settled herself in the hard wooden chair and kept crossing and uncrossing her legs to keep them from cramping. Maybe she should have gone to the hospital as the paramedics had suggested. She shook her head and tried to focus on the questioning going on next door.

Finnegan took a friendlier tack with Jeff. He had been pretty cooperative so far, but he still hadn't told them who was blackmailing him. He claimed the letter in his mailbox had been anonymous, but Sally was sure he knew who it was. And she felt Finnegan did as well.

"So, Jeff. I really want to help you," Finnegan began.

"You do?" Jeff replied, his eyes wide.

"Yes. I know you didn't really want to hurt anybody, but someone pressured you to help. Can you tell me who that person was?"

Finnegan grinned, something Sally hadn't seen him do very often. He had a reputation in town for being an old curmudgeon, so Sally wasn't sure if Jeff would buy his friendliness.

Jeff looked down at his hands and rubbed them together. His shoulders were shaking. Sally wished she could go in and comfort him, but she knew that wouldn't go over too well with Finnegan.

Jeff finally looked up. "I can't tell you."

"We know about your gambling debt, Jeff, so why don't you just tell us?"

"I'm scared. I don't want to get hurt."

Finnegan sighed. "We won't let anyone hurt you, Jeff."

Sally wasn't so sure he could really guarantee that, but hey, if it got Jeff to talk.

"Really?"

"Yes, Jeff. Just tell us what you know. It was Margaret, wasn't it?"

Jeff began to speak, then bit his tongue.

"We have her here now, and she is telling us everything. How you prepared the syringe and left it behind the dumpster. Just everything."

"She wouldn't…" he began, then fell silent.

Finnegan smirked in spite of himself. Sally noticed.

So Margaret was the blackmailer. But who was behind Margaret? Sally looked down at her notebook and realized she hadn't written a word. She had been on the edge of her seat the whole time.

Chapter Thirty-Seven

Randall Wentworth arrived and quickly tried to quash any additional questioning of Margaret. In spite of some of the words Margaret had said and the fact that Sally had identified her as her kidnapper, he threatened to sue the police department for harassment.

Finnegan stood up to him, explained the strong evidence against Margaret, and Wentworth reluctantly backed down. Sally watched Finnegan smile broadly as he watched Wentworth march out of the police station, without his client.

Sally assumed he was going to try and find a judge, but even in this county, getting Margaret out even on bail was going to be a challenge.

Back in Finnegan's office, he was seething.

"We are *this* close to getting the killer or killers, and now I have Randall Wentworth playing his typical games."

"You really think he's going to be able to do something quickly for his client? You did a great job today getting that info out of Margaret and Jeff."

Finnegan looked across at Sally. "Thanks, but I'm not feeling as positive about all this as you are," he admitted. "And I'm worried that you aren't as safe with whoever is the mastermind behind these murders still roaming the streets."

Sally shrugged. "Margaret only got me on Sunday because I was too naive. That won't happen again." While she said these words, she admitted to herself that she really didn't know what the murderer might try. But she was determined to put on a brave face in front of the detective.

"You be careful. I don't want another murder on my hands."

"Agreed."

Sally looked at her phone. She needed to get over to the bar soon to get ready to open. Her rational side told her that was probably not a good idea. But she couldn't sleep now, and working at the bar would help keep her busy. She stood up slowly.

"Where are you going?" Finnegan asked.

"I've got to get over to the bar and get ready to open it."

"Are you crazy? You need to rest and stay safe."

"John, I've got a bar to run, and we both have a killer to find. I can't just sit at home doing nothing. And the bar is my livelihood, in case you haven't forgotten."

Finnegan waved her out without saying a word.

* * *

When she pulled up to the bar, Sally was surprised to see Magda standing outside. She was bundled up in a long coat, scarf, and hat, and seemed to be shivering slightly. It was only early fall, and not cold enough for full winter gear just yet. Plus, it was only just past four, and normally, Jay and Magda showed up at five. And Magda did not look too happy to be there. What was up?

They had worked together for years, and Magda seemed to love the work. But sometimes Sally felt she was ready to just quit. That would have been difficult for Sally. She, Jay, and Magda made a great team. And she and Bill had always been particular about who worked there. Though, Sally admitted that she didn't have a huge choice of young or youngish people to staff the bar. Most left town as soon as they graduated college. The town had been getting older and older ever since she had come to Berry Springs, with half the workforce seemingly on the verge of retirement.

Sally parked her car on the side of the building and walked around to the front door.

"Hi, Magda. What are you doing here so early?"

Magda didn't look at her, but just said, "Can we go inside?"

Uh oh.

Magda handed her the keys back, and Sally unlocked the door. As Sally entered, she was astounded by what she saw. The place was sparkling. And everything was perfectly in its place. She had never seen it like this.

She turned to Magda. "Wow, you two have done an amazing job. When did this happen?"

Magda looked at the floor. "Well, we decided to clean up last night after the police left."

Right, she had had to give Magda the keys to lock up.

Magda finally looked up.

"It was Jay's idea, and he did most of the work. I was exhausted and left about a half hour after closing."

Sally kept smiling but was thinking that that didn't sound like the helpful Magda she had come to know.

"What's up, Magda? Why were you standing outside waiting for me when you had the keys?"

"Well, I didn't want to scare you if you walked in and heard somebody moving about the bar."

"But it's not warm outside."

Magda just shrugged her shoulders.

"Let's sit down. I want you to tell me what's wrong," Sally offered.

They sat down at the bar. Sally waited for Magda to start talking.

"Well, it's difficult to say."

Sally felt a lump in her throat.

"I'm strong. Please tell me," Sally replied, sounding not too convincing to herself.

"I've decided to quit," Magda said meekly, looking at her hands.

Sally took a few seconds to compose herself before responding.

"That's an awful shame to hear. I thought you loved working here."

Magda finally looked at her. Her lower lip was trembling. "I do. I do. I'm just so scared about all the deaths."

Sally hugged her. "I know. It's awful, but you aren't in danger." Although she wasn't too sure that was entirely true with the growing body count over the past week. She hoped Magda didn't notice the wavering in her voice.

"How do you know that?" Magda shouted at her.

"Well…"

Magda pointed her finger at Sally. "There you see, you don't. Anyway, Jeff and I have been talking, and well, we decided to get back together. Once this has all cleared up, we're getting out of Berry Springs."

Sally pursed her lips. She wasn't sure the young woman had thought this through. "Magda, Jeff is probably going to jail. He has admitted to preparing the syringe that killed Bill. He could be gone a long time."

"Well, we're getting back together and getting out of this place. If Jeff is in jail, I'll go somewhere and wait for him." She was hysterical. "Wherever that is, it won't be here in Berry Springs."

"Magda, Magda, calm down. I want to help you. Do you think running away is going to help? You love it here."

Magda jumped off the bar stool. "You know, you really are a nosey parker. Why don't you just leave it to the police like you're supposed to? You're going to ruin so many lives with your snooping, you know that? I've made up my mind. I quit," she shouted and ran across the bar, pushing Jay, who'd just arrived, out of the way as she stormed out the door, leaving Sally sitting alone, shaken.

"What's happening?" Jay looked at Sally for an explanation.

"Magda quit," she replied bluntly.

"What? Why?"

"That's between her and me." Sally was still upset and didn't want to share every detail of the conversation she had just had with Magda.

"She's worried about everything going on in town, isn't she?"

Sally looked at him.

"We've been talking."

"And you didn't warn me she was upset?" Sally could feel her face turn red.

"She asked me not to say anything. She thought she might be a victim."

"That makes no sense. I'm trying to find out who killed Bill, Father O'Malley, and Gillian. It has nothing to do with her."

The same thing she had just told Magda. Though she wasn't sure that was entirely true. The part about Magda not being in any danger, that is.

Sally noticed that Jay flinched when she had said Gillian's name. Sally put off pursuing the Gillian angle right now. He might have flinched because he still had feelings for her and was upset she was dead. Anyhow, the bar would be open soon, so they wouldn't be able to talk about that then, anyway.

"How are we gonna manage tonight's shift without her? Let alone find a replacement?"

"We'll manage. Now, let's get to work. It's almost opening time," Sally replied.

* * *

At midnight, both were splayed out on the couch in Sally's office. It had been a crazy evening with only two people working. And it hadn't even been a weekend. But during the evening, Sally had made a decision. She turned to Jay, who had his eyes closed. She wasn't sure if he had fallen asleep.

"Jay, are you awake?"

He opened his eyes.

"Yeah."

"Jay, I've made a decision. I'm going to close the bar for a week until I've finished the investigation. Magda's leaving tonight told me I need to finish this thing before we can get back to normal."

Jay stared at her. "Close the bar? Why? I can handle it without you. A couple of my buddies can help out," he suggested.

"No. Let's not do that. It will only be for a few days, and I'll still pay your wages. I need to help the police figure out who killed Bill, Gillian, and Father O'Malley. For Bill. For myself. And the time here running the bar in the evenings is taking away from that."

Jay shook his head. "But what about our customers?"

"Well, everyone knows I'm investigating, and I would think most of them will want to know who did this to Bill and the others."

He didn't seem to want to give in. But again, what did it matter? It was

176

her bar.

"Listen, I know this is difficult, but it needs to happen. I know that now."

Jay sat looking at the floor for a few seconds. Sally let him think.

Finally, he looked at her with a blank expression on his face. "Okay, I don't like it, but I'll go along with it. If you want, I can make some signs for the door and prepare some posts for our social media page."

"That would be fantastic. Now get yourself home and get some sleep. We both need it."

Chapter Thirty-Eight

The decision Sally had made the night before had not been easy for her. When she got home, she downed a double bourbon and staggered to bed at two a.m. The weight of the past week and a half had finally hit her, and she didn't wake until she heard her phone ringing.

Leaning over to grab it, she saw it was her friend Nancy from the Little Rock record office.

She slowly put the phone to her ear and sleepily said, "Good morning, Nancy."

"Hi, Sally. Did I wake you? It's already two in the afternoon."

Wow, she had slept that long?

"Yeah, rough night at the bar, you could say."

"Well, I finally got the information you wanted. I'm sorry I didn't call or write yesterday as I promised. It took even longer than I thought."

Sally was now wide awake. She scanned her bedside table for a pen and paper and grabbed both.

"Don't worry about it. What did you find out?"

Sally was too excited to complain to Nancy about the day delay. And why should she? Nancy was doing her a very big favor and possibly putting her job on the line for Sally.

"I got a call from the Little Rock diocese this morning, and they managed to find Diane's original employment record, including the form she filled out years ago."

"Little Rock?"

"Yeah, she started working for the church in Little Rock, not Berry

Springs."

"What does the record say?"

"She filled it out as Diane Collins."

"Okay, so she changed her name. Why would she do that?"

Nancy continued: "I thought that too, so I did some more digging. It turns out Diane was adopted when she was just a baby."

Sally could barely contain her excitement as possibilities began falling into place.

"Adopted? So Collins is her adopted name?"

Sally heard a keyboard clicking.

"I think so," Nancy said. "The adoption record is sealed, and I have no access to that."

Sally's excitement dropped to her toes. "Oh, that's too bad. That seems like a dead end."

"Collins mean something to you?"

"Nothing. Thanks, Nancy, for checking. Bye."

Sally was about to hang up when Nancy stopped her.

"Hold on a minute, I'm not finished."

"You found something else?"

Sally heard the beam on Nancy's face in her voice. "Well, actually, yes. While the adoption record was sealed, the lawyers or clerk at the time forgot to seal the birth record."

"You found her birth record?"

The weariness caused by the aftereffects of bourbon was long gone.

"I am proud to say I did. She was born Diane Fletcher on March 5, 1963 to a Carol Fletcher. The father is not named. The birth record also indicates that the baby was immediately given up for adoption to a Clark and Beverley Collins.

"Wow, Nancy. You're a rockstar. Thank you."

Sally hung up and whistled out loud. She'd heard that last name before, and it was just the break she needed to solve this case.

Chapter Thirty-Nine

Sally was on cloud nine after digesting Nancy's discovery. Her hunch about Margaret not being the brains behind the killings seemed to have paid off. It had to be Diane, who must be the daughter Momma Arnold gave up for adoption all those years ago. Sally knew Momma Arnold's first name was Carol. And she had talked about her Daddy Fletcher making her give up her baby for adoption. It all linked.

It must have taken a lot of digging for Diane to find out who her birth mother was and then track her here in Berry Springs. And Diane had been here for years without saying or doing anything. So why now? Sally guessed she was planning her revenge. But why did it take so long?

Sitting at her kitchen table, she thought about what she should do next. The safest option would be to contact Detective Finnegan and tell him what she found out and let him determine what to do. Or she could just drive over to the Arnold place and tell Momma Arnold, née Carol Fletcher, what she had found out.

She sipped her coffee and rubbed her legs. They were still not quite back to normal after the ordeal of being kidnapped and escaping. Sally looked back at the last week and a half and still felt herself reeling from all that had happened. And yet, she was somehow pleasantly surprised and proud of everything she had done. She was close to finding the killer and avenging Bill's death. And getting on with her life.

The one big question remaining was whether Diane was the killer. Or whether she had gotten someone else to do her dirty work. You don't need strength to poison someone, so Diane could easily have done it to both Bill and Gillian. But she couldn't picture Diane bashing Bill on the head and lifting his bulk into the dumpster. And she didn't think Diane would have been able to stab Father O'Malley.

And come to think of it. Diane wasn't even at the bar that Saturday night. Did she have an accomplice? But who could it be?

As for Bill's murder, it had to be someone strong who was at the bar that night, Sally surmised. Based on the estimated time of poisoning and death, it could only be someone left at the bar from around eleven p.m. on. That didn't leave a lot of people.

She pulled out her notebook and jotted down some more notes.

Father O'Malley: but he was killed himself, and he was definitely not strong enough to lift Bill into the dumpster

Zeke Parker: got into a fight with Jeff, may have been upset at Bill breaking up fight and was definitely strong enough.

Margaret Jackson: may have been seen behind the dumpster picking up the syringe, but don't think she is strong enough, and what is her motive. Though she did kidnap me.

Mayor Milkowski: mayor killer. I don't think she is strong enough. And what would her motive be?

While she was thinking about this, she made a decision. She would call Detective Finnegan and tell him what she found out about Diane. She would also suggest that they go to Momma Arnold to tell her before they talked to Diane. Maybe she could give them some clues to go on. And she had forgotten to ask to see the notes Momma Arnold had said she received from her long-lost daughter.

Looking at the time, Sally was relieved she had closed the bar temporarily. Otherwise, she would have had to drop everything and head over there soon.

Close the bar temporarily. Wait a minute.

That made her think of the other people at the bar that night: Magda and Jay, her bartenders.

She had always focused on the customers, but Jay and Magda were there too. She couldn't imagine either of them wanting to kill Bill, their boss, but she had to keep an open mind.

Putting this new thought aside, she reached for her phone and dialed Finnegan's number.

"Hi, Detective. I have some important information for you."

* * *

It hadn't taken long for Detective Finnegan to make a decision. He told Sally to stay put at home. He would send an officer over to pick her up, and then they would head over to the Arnold's place. Finnegan and Soder would join them there with another two cars with an officer each, just in case. Sally didn't think anything would happen, but Finnegan wasn't taking any chances. And Finnegan had let drop that Randall Wentworth had gotten Margaret out on bail.

They pulled up to the Arnolds. Finnegan and Sally got out while Finnegan told the rest of the officers to stay in the cars.

They walked up to the door, and Sally knocked.

Steve Arnold opened the door.

"Do you have news?" he asked. His hands were shaking, and Sally was always wary around him. He was unpredictable, and that made him difficult to handle.

Finnegan stepped forward and put his foot in the doorway.

"No, we're here to have a chat with your mother," he replied, puffing out his chest.

"My mother? What does she have to do with this? She didn't kill anyone."

Steve tried to move forward to push them out of the doorway, but Finnegan's bulk prevented it.

"No need to get upset, Steve. We're just here for a chat."

Momma Arnold came out of the kitchen, a blue flowery apron around her hips. When she saw it was Sally and Finnegan, she stabbed her finger at her son. "Steve, let them in!"

Sally was impressed by how she handled her beefy sons. She was definitely their momma.

Steve stamped his foot and stood aside.

Momma Arnold came forward and ushered them into the kitchen. Freshly baked chocolate chip cookies were cooling on the large wooden table, with more baking in the oven. Momma Arnold took off her apron, and they all sat down.

"Would you like a cookie?" she asked.

Finnegan greedily grabbed two. Sally's stomach wasn't quite up to eating right then, so she just shook her head.

"Mrs. Arnold. We're here with some important information."

Steve had come in behind them and stood near the doorway, his arms crossed, and a tough-guy look on his face.

What a baby, Sally thought.

Finnegan turned to Sally. She nodded.

"Momma Arnold. I think it would be better if we talked alone." She glanced over at Steve.

Momma Arnold understood the signal from Sally. "Steve, go into the living room. I need to talk to them alone."

"I'm not going anywhere."

"Steve, get your ass out of here," Momma Arnold yelled.

At that, he moved toward the door and slammed it hard on his way out. They all heard the living room door slam just as loudly.

"So, what is it?"

"Remember our conversation here in this kitchen on Sunday morning?"

Momma Arnold glanced nervously at the detective.

"That was in confidence, Sally." Momma Arnold's friendly greeting seemed to have turned sour. Sally felt bad that they had sprung this visit on her, but it was now a matter of life and death.

"I know, but you want us to find Bill and Gillian's killers, don't you?"

Momma Arnold nodded, a tear in her eye. "Of course, but what does this have to do with me and our conversation Sunday?"

She seemed to have forgotten her misgivings she had admitted to Sally. But maybe it was just the nervousness of the detective knowing about her secret. *What happened in the Arnold family stayed in the Arnold family.* Sally

DEATH IN THE OZARKS

knew it had taken a lot of strength for her to admit her secret to Sally.

"You told me you had gotten some threatening letters from the daughter you gave up for adoption. Can you show us those letters?"

Momma Arnold looked down at the table and nibbled on one of her cookies. She was breathing heavily. Finally, she got up and went over to the sideboard next to the table. Opening the left-hand drawer, she brought out a packet of letters.

Sally was surprised she kept them right there in the kitchen. Wouldn't one of her children have been able to easily find them and read them?

She tossed the packet on the table, and Sally opened the bundle and read a couple of them. She handed the rest to Finnegan to peruse. All of the letters were typed on plain white paper, no signature. Sally didn't think the police would find any fingerprints on them. They were all dated, and as she went through them, she saw that they got shorter and shorter, but angrier and angrier.

The final one just read, *I will do everything possible to get back at you.*

Sitting back in her chair, Sally put the letters down and looked across at Momma Arnold, who had been nervously watching them the whole time.

"Well?" Momma Arnold said.

Detective Finnegan spoke first. "You are sure these must be from your daughter?"

"Yes, as I told Sally, there is a reference to her correct birth date, and she also knows my maiden name. How else would someone know that? The adoption record was sealed."

"Well, we have found out that your daughter is someone here in Berry Springs, like you suspected," Sally explained. She quickly thought about what she could or should say. She certainly didn't want to get Nancy in trouble. Luckily, Finnegan took over.

"Well, ma'am. We found that while the adoption records were sealed, the birth certificate wasn't."

Momma Arnold turned to look at him, her eyes wide.

"Who is it?" she demanded.

"Diane Gregory," Sally replied.

184

Momma Arnold went red. It looked like she might explode. "What? She got Father O'Malley to convince Bill to change his will, I'm sure, and now she's the one who killed my babies. That bitch."

The quiet, serene cookie-baking Momma Arnold was gone.

Sally wasn't sure how to defuse the situation. She looked over at Detective Finnegan, but he didn't seem like he had an idea either. "Momma Arnold, we're not sure it's Diane who killed them," she tried.

"But if she was involved. I'll kill her," Momma Arnold said coldly.

At that moment, the door burst open, and Steve reappeared. This time, with a shotgun aimed directly at Sally and the detective.

Chapter Forty

Finnegan jumped up. "Steve, put the gun down," he said calmly.

Sally froze in her seat. Even Momma Arnold seemed surprised by the outburst and remained silent.

"Adoption. Diane. Killers. What the hell is going on here, Momma?" He took a step forward. The gun barrel only inches from Sally's face.

Momma Arnold jumped up when she heard her name and ran over to her son. "Steve, I'll explain everything. Just put the gun down."

Out of the corner of her eye, Sally noticed Finnegan slowly reaching for the gun in his holster. Steve apparently noticed it, too, because he swung the gun around and pointed it at the detective.

"Don't even think about it. Sit the fuck down," he barked. Sally saw spit dripping down his chin.

Finnegan put his hands up and sat back down.

"Okay, Sally. Tell me what's going on," Steve yelled.

Sally was shaking and glanced over at Momma Arnold, who hadn't moved from Steve's side.

"I, I..." Sally stuttered.

"Steve, put the gun down, now," Momma Arnold repeated.

Sally saw Momma Arnold reach for the barrel, and she waited for the bang. Her stomach lurched, and she thought she might be sick. She took a deep breath but couldn't speak.

"No, not until you tell me what's going on. Who killed Bill and Gillian?" Steve bellowed.

Finnegan edged forward with his hands up. "That's what we're trying to find out, son." Steve flicked the barrel up, as if telling him not to move. "We're not here to arrest your momma."

"But what does this have to do with Diane? What is this about an adoption?" he said, waving the shotgun around.

"Put the gun down, Steve, and I'll explain everything. Please, I don't want anyone else to die. Hasn't there been enough death?" Momma Arnold pleaded.

Steve looked at her, then at Sally and the detective. The gun was still pointed at Finnegan. Momma Arnold held his arm and stroked it. Steve looked at Sally again and then back to the detective.

"I think your momma will explain everything to you. We just want to help find Bill and Gillian's killer. Not to hurt you or your momma any more than you have been," Sally pleaded.

Steve aimed the gun at Sally's face.

She was going to die.

Momma Arnold grabbed his arm, pulling the gun toward herself.

"Please, Steve. Don't do this." Tears streamed down her face.

"Momma, is it your fault my brother and sister are dead?"

Steve looked down at her with tears in his own eyes and dropped the gun on the floor.

It went off.

Chapter Forty-One

The explosion made them all hit the floor. There was a loud shattering of glass as the kitchen window was smashed, and cold air swept in. Sally quickly looked around, but it didn't seem anyone was hurt. Finnegan grabbed the shotgun off the floor, pushed himself up, and handed it to Soder, who had rushed in at the sound of gunfire and shattering glass. Finnegan handcuffed Steve, who had now collapsed in a heap under the kitchen table. The officers that had accompanied them took Steve outside and put him in the back of one of the police cars. They quickly drove him away to a jail cell.

Sally got Momma Arnold to move into the living room to get away from the frigid draft.

Momma Arnold collapsed on the sofa.

"Oh, Sally, what is happening?"

Sally sat down beside her and held her hands. "Don't worry. I'm just glad no one got hurt."

Perhaps it would have been a good idea for Momma Arnold to have told all her kids about her past a lot earlier. Finding out like that was bound to upset them. But she kept her mouth shut and let Momma Arnold sit in silence.

Soder and Finnegan came into the living room, and when the door opened, Momma Arnold looked up with wide eyes.

"What will happen to Steve?"

Finnegan walked over and sat down on the armchair near her.

"Don't worry. He threatened a police officer, but luckily no one got hurt.

We'll keep him in jail overnight to let him cool off. I'll talk to the district attorney, and we'll probably just give him a warning."

Sally knew Steve was getting special treatment because his last name was Arnold.

"Oh, thank goodness," Momma Arnold replied.

Looking at Sally, Finnegan continued. "Okay, we have to get back to Diane. We need to get her to talk about what she knew about the three deaths and what her part was in all of it."

"You really think she was involved?" Momma Arnold asked.

Sally thought this was disingenuous, considering they had just read the threatening letters Diane had sent her biological mother.

"I'd like to bring her in for questioning," Finnegan said.

Sally coughed. "Detective, I have an idea," she said.

Finnegan slowly turned toward her. "Oh?" was all he could say with a look that said he didn't like to be interrupted.

"Well, at this point, we don't have any proof Diane was involved. Yes, we've found out that Momma Arnold is her biological mother, and we can also assume that Diane sent the threatening letters. But there's no concrete proof she was involved in setting up the killings or being involved in the murders of Bill, Gillian, or Father O'Malley."

"So what do you propose?" Finnegan said, raising one eyebrow.

Sally hoped she could convince him. She had spent the last week and a half balancing trying to solve the crimes herself and staying on his good side.

She turned to Momma Arnold. "We will need your help. And it might be dangerous."

Momma Arnold stared at her with a look of determination. Sally wasn't sure if she was going to have another outburst like she did in the kitchen, but to Sally, it seemed Momma Arnold had pulled herself together.

"I want to find out who killed my babies. I'll do whatever it takes."

Sally turned back to Detective Finnegan. "Okay, I propose that Momma Arnold call Diane and ask her to come to the house. Then…"

Finnegan put his hand over his eyes. "Are you kidding me?"

Sally put up her hand. "Wait. Let me finish."

Finnegan shrugged.

"I'm not suggesting she call Diane and tell her all she knows. I'm proposing she call Diane to invite her over here to have a special memorial of the three that have died. She will tell Diane I will also be there, and we can reminisce about Bill, Gillian, and Father O'Malley."

"So, use me as bait?" Momma Arnold said, quickly understanding what Sally was getting at.

Sally turned to her and nodded.

"Well, yes, but Finnegan and Soder will be hiding in the next room. We'll have to come up with a signal to warn them if we think something is getting out of hand."

Sally looked at Finnegan, and he was obviously mulling it over.

Soder was about to say something, when Finnegan responded to her proposal. "It's dangerous. She could poison one or both of you."

"True, but don't you think she will be more likely to talk openly here than when being questioned at the police station? And maybe we will get a clue about how Margaret was involved or who actually killed our friends."

Sally was really working herself up. She knew this was a great, albeit dangerous, idea, and she wasn't too sure they would get out of it alive. But then someone had to do something, and maybe taking this big risk would pay off.

Momma Arnold nodded vigorously while Detective Finnegan sat in thought. He gave Soder a look that said he shouldn't interrupt or offer his own opinion.

After a few minutes, Finnegan looked up.

"All right. Let's do it."

Chapter Forty-Two

Momma Arnold reached for the phone, one of those old-fashioned phones with an actual cord. Sally looked at her phone and dictated Diane's home phone number.

Momma Arnold swallowed nervously, and they all waited for Diane to pick up. Momma Arnold held the receiver close to Sally so she could hear what Diane said. Sally tried to breathe as quietly as possible.

"Hello," the voice on the phone said.

She was home.

"Hi, Diane. It's Momma Arnold."

There was silence on the other line.

Gotcha, Sally thought.

"Oh, uh, hi. What are you calling for this late in the day?"

Sally looked at her phone. It was only six o'clock.

"Well, you know, I've been thinking. I'd love to invite you over tomorrow for lunch. With Bill, Gillian, and your Father O'Malley gone, I thought it would be nice to get together and reminisce and support each other during this difficult time."

"Well, I...I...I'm not sure," Diane replied.

"It would mean a lot to me if you came over. I've also invited Sally. It will just be us three, and we can have a nice time together."

"Sally? Sally? I thought Sally went away." Diane's voice cracked.

"Now, why would you think that Diane? Of course, she hasn't gone away. She's trying to help us find who killed our friends and family." Momma Arnold had turned on her soothing Momma voice. Sally hoped the honey would sweeten the offer.

"Well, I would like to get over to the church in the afternoon to see if there is something to do…but I guess I can come over for a short while."

Sally gave a thumbs-up to the officers, who nodded.

"Oh, that is just wonderful, Diane. How about one p.m.? You know where we live."

"Of course. Okay, sure, I'll be there tomorrow at one. Thanks for the invitation."

Diane hung up.

* * *

Thursday at noon, Sally and the officers were back at the Arnold place preparing for their afternoon operation. Sally and Finnegan were alone in the living room.

"Well, I talked to the district attorney," Finnegan explained. "He does want to charge Steve with threatening a police officer, so we're keeping him in jail."

Sally raised her eyebrows. "Charge him? I thought, as an Arnold, he would be scot-free."

"Yeah, well, the DA wants to run for mayor or something. You know citizens in Arkansas always like politicians tough on crime."

Sally nodded in understanding.

Momma Arnold came in, and they both went silent.

"I'm so glad Jack's away on business in Little Rock, so I'm all alone in the house for this, um, operation," Momma Arnold added slowly, her face drained.

"That's good for the lunch with Diane. Don't want any more interruptions," Finnegan said.

Momma Arnold looked like she would burst into tears. Sally gave Finnegan a dirty look. Finnegan took that as a signal to go out in the hall and confer with Soder.

"I've got everything ready, Sally. If you want to have a look," Momma

Arnold said, leading Sally into the kitchen.

Sally surveyed the large spread Momma Arnold had prepared for lunch. Pumpkin soup was bubbling on the stove. Looking in the oven, she could see roast chicken and potatoes. And then she admired the pumpkin pie cooling on the countertop.

"Wow, what a lunch you've prepared, Carol," Sally said. "And you've even opened a white wine for the occasion."

Momma Arnold beamed, Sally noticed, in spite of her apparent nervousness.

"Well, I do like to cook. And I wanted to make it as convincing as possible for Diane."

"Good thinking."

Finnegan and Soder came into the kitchen.

"Well, we've been looking for the best place for us to hide while you talk to Diane," Finnegan began. Turning to Momma Arnold, he explained, "We will wait in the large hall closet. I was thinking maybe the living room, but if you all spontaneously decided after this lovely lunch to go there, as it might be more comfortable, we would have to run and hide somewhere else. And the back of the hall closet backs onto the kitchen, so we'll hear your signal."

Sally and Momma Arnold nodded in agreement.

"So what do we use as a signal, Detective?" Sally asked.

"Why don't you say *New York*," he suggested, "Probably not a word you would be using in conversation today, and not something obvious like *help*."

Well, he did have a sense of humor.

Sally laughed. "True, Okay. *New York*, it is."

Soder looked at his phone. "Boss, it's almost one. We should hide."

Finnegan nodded, and they made their way to the hallway. Sally heard the closet door open and the shuffling of the officers trying to squeeze themselves inside; with Finnegan's bulk, it was going to be a tight fit.

Just in time, in fact, as the doorbell rang.

Momma Arnold jumped. Sally went over and hugged her. "It will be okay. Just be the friendly host you always are, and we'll have a nice time together without getting hurt. If Diane does try something, the police are already here."

Though, Sally herself didn't quite stand behind what she was telling Momma Arnold. If Diane slipped something in their food or drink, they might not notice. She would keep an eagle eye on her the whole time and hope for the best.

Momma Arnold took two deep breaths to calm herself, smoothed her graying hair, and walked out into the hallway with Sally.

Momma Arnold waved to Diane through the glass in the window and smiled. Opening the door, she gave Diane a big hug.

Sally noticed Diane seemed to pull away a bit too early, but then maybe she was just reading things that weren't there.

"Oh, Diane. Thank you so much for coming," Momma Arnold said as they walked to the kitchen.

"Well, I was a bit surprised by your call to be honest. But after I thought about it a bit, I thought maybe it was a good idea. All this death can really be depressing," Diane replied, not looking at either of them.

"Let's sit down and get settled. I've made us a hearty lunch, and we can chat and enjoy each other's company."

She served the pumpkin soup, and the three slurped in silence. Sally wanted to let Diane start the conversation. Momma Arnold kept looking over at Sally to take her cue. Diane sat between them and looked at Sally, then Momma Arnold, then back at Sally. To any outsiders looking in, the awkwardness was almost sitting at the table with them.

Finally, Diane broke the silence. "This is delicious."

"Why thank you, dear. I'm glad you like it."

Sally didn't remember the last time she had had a real full meal like this, so she was making the most of it. The last week and a half had been a blur.

"You didn't have to go to all this trouble for little old me," Diane said, smiling.

"Of course. I always like to serve my guests good food and drink. Would you like some white wine with the main course?" she asked.

Diane nodded, and Momma Arnold poured them each a small glass of the chardonnay she had been chilling in the fridge. Sitting back down, she turned to Diane. "How have you been, dear? It must be difficult now that Father O'Malley is gone."

"He was such a sweet man. Life will not be the same without him," Diane replied. She looked like she would burst into tears.

Sally couldn't figure out if she was actually sad or just playing a part. Then again, maybe she was being too analytical.

"He was. He really welcomed me to the church and Berry Springs when I moved here all those years ago," Sally added.

She felt a stabbing in her stomach. Bill's death had hurt her, but she just now realized how important Father O'Malley had been to her. Sally smiled wanly and took a sip of wine to calm her nerves. She looked across at Momma Arnold, who appeared to be as strong as steel. The nervousness before Diane arrived seemed to have disappeared.

"Will you be staying on at the church?" Momma Arnold asked.

Diane froze. "I will always stay here in Berry Springs. It's where I belong." She gripped her wine glass in both hands, the skin turning white.

"Of course you do. I was just wondering if you thought of making a change after everything that's happened. It's enough to unnerve the strongest of souls," Momma Arnold continued.

"Well, I will be coming into a lot of money soon, and I was thinking of buying a small hotel here."

At the mention of money, Momma Arnold looked like she was going to get up from the table and do something she would regret. Sally stared at her. *Do not give into your emotions now, Momma Arnold.* Fortunately, the matriarch picked up the signal and settled herself, albeit reluctantly.

Close call. This "friendly" lunch wasn't quite going as planned. On the other hand, they had wanted Diane to confess to something, and maybe she would.

"So, are you any closer to finding the killer or killers?" Diane asked Sally. *Here we go.* Or was Diane just playing her?

"Well, I have a few leads. And Detective Finnegan has questioned several people who were at my bar that night or who saw something behind it."

"Really, that's interesting. Anyone I know?"

"Um, sorry, Diane, I can't tell you that. Police confidentiality."

"But you're not police, " Diane replied, her voice almost sinister.

"I'm helping the police to find the killer or killers and the person behind it. They think there was a mastermind, pulling all the strings."

Sally dropped that nugget in to see how Diane reacted. She lapped it up.

"Well, there are certainly a few clever people in this town, like me," Diane replied. "But why do they think that?"

Had Diane just slipped?

"Oh, sorry, Diane, I can't tell you that. Again, police confidentiality."

"I want to know, Sally. Please tell me. I won't tell anyone, will I?"

Sally hoped Momma Arnold would finally serve the roast chicken and potatoes to defuse the situation. Diane was getting quite demanding.

Though wasn't that the reason that they had asked her to lunch.

Sally wondered if her plan had been such a good idea after all.

As if she read Sally's mind, Momma Arnold got up and plated out the main course. She handed Diane her plate first and then served Sally and finally herself.

When all had food, though, it seemed that Diane wasn't going to let it drop. She was staring at Sally, seemingly waiting for an answer.

"Let me ask you a question, Diane. Did you see anything when Gillian was killed? Anything that might help find the killer or the person behind it all?"

Diane cut a piece of chicken and stuffed it in her mouth. She looked at her plate the whole time. Sally didn't want to just blab out the question that was on her mind. Diane might do something drastic, if it was her behind all the killing. That is, if she had a vial of poison in her pocket.

Looking up finally, Diane said, "Now, honey. I told you everything I know about how I found Father O'Malley. There was so much confusion at the time when Gillian died. How could I have seen anything? Anyway, it was a dreadful day for me at the funeral. You know that."

Her voice was unsteady.

"But you were standing not too far from the Arnolds. Don't you remember?"

At the name *Arnold*, Diane stiffened.

CHAPTER FORTY-TWO

"Yes, I was near *them*," she replied.

"And you didn't see anything?"

Diane just shook her head.

This is going well.

Sally was thinking about her next question when she jumped in her chair. Her phone was buzzing in her backpack on the floor. She reached down to pull it out of her backpack.

"You're too late," Diane sneered.

"What have you done?" Sally and Momma Arnold yelled in unison, dropping all pretense of a friendly memorial lunch.

Chapter Forty-Three

Sally looked down at her phone. It was Jeff calling.

Was Diane manipulating Jeff? It was all too weird.

She looked at Diane, who was still in a cold sneer and said a bit too loudly, "Oh, it's my *New York* aunt calling, " as if they were still having a quiet lunch together.

She got up from the table to move into the hallway to take the call. Diane's eyes followed her out of the room, but she didn't get up from the table.

"Forget about it," she just yelled after Sally.

At the same moment, the closet door opened, and Finnegan and Soder lumbered into the kitchen. Diane sprang from the chair and tried to run out the back door. Soder got her before she reached it.

"Hands off me. I'm innocent, you bastard!" she yelled.

Finnegan sauntered over.

"Innocent of what? We've got you, Diane Fletcher."

Diane swore.

In the hallway, Sally picked up the call while trying to listen to what was going on in the kitchen. She had left the kitchen door open on purpose.

"Jeff, what's going on? Why are you calling me? Aren't you at school working?"

Jeff was breathless. "Sally, help. Please. Magda is missing." His sentences were staccato, and he seemed out of breath.

"What? Magda? How?"

"We were supposed to meet for coffee this afternoon, but she never showed up. I went to her apartment, and there was a typewritten sign on her door that read, 'I've got her.'"

Sally quickly ran through a very short list of names in her head.

Well, Diane was with them. Could it be Margaret? That was the only other person she could think of.

"Who do you think's got her?" she asked Jeff.

"Sally, Bill's killer. It has to be! But who is that?"

"Okay, Jeff, calm down. Are you still at Magda's?"

"Yeah, I'm still here. I only just found the note."

"Okay, I'm with Finnegan and Soder now, and I'll let them know what happened. I'll call you back as soon as I can."

"Oh, thank you, Sally. Please hurry."

Sally felt a lump in her throat. All her friends were being killed. It had to stop now.

She headed into the kitchen. Soder had handcuffed Diane, who looked like she had gone feral, thrashing in the chair.

"What's up, Sally?" Finnegan asked.

Looking directly at Diane, she said. "That was Jeff. Magda's missing, and he's worried she's been kidnapped, or worse."

Diane sent darts at Sally.

"Like I said, it's too late."

That was it. Sally lost it. She ran across to Diane and shook her. "What have you done with Magda?" she demanded.

Finnegan pulled Sally off Diane. "Sally!" He held onto her arms. "Calm down. This won't help Magda."

Sally took a deep breath and took a few steps back.

"You'll definitely be sorry soon," Diane sneered again.

Where was this Diane coming from? This was the real Diane, it seemed.

"Okay, Soder, get Diane to the station for questioning." Finnegan jerked his thumb toward the door, and Soder dragged Diane up from the chair. She fought the entire way, so Soder had to nearly manhandle her to get her to the door, outside, and safely locked in the back of his police car.

* * *

Sally and Finnegan jumped in Finnegan's police cruiser. Her little Datsun would be no help, and his blue lights flashing would get them to Magda's apartment quickly. They sped east from the Arnold's toward town, then south down Route 10. Sally hoped they weren't too late, even if Diane told them they were. She tried to remain optimistic.

The entire drive to Magda's, she sat rigid in the seat, her hands gripping the seat cushion. She shivered, even though the heat in the car was on full blast, Diane's words echoing in her mind.

They pulled into Magda's apartment complex and found Jeff anxiously waiting right at her door. He had a backpack with him and was wearing a brown blazer, fancy blue shirt, and khakis.

Sally scanned the note tacked to the door.

"Weird. Just one sentence. Typewritten again. Why even leave a note and not just take her?" Finnegan wondered aloud.

"That's easy," Sally said. "Whoever it is likes to show off. Wants to show how they are one step ahead, bragging about it, you could call it."

Jeff shook his head. "Bragging about killing and kidnapping. Sick."

Sally agreed.

"Do you think it's Margaret?" Finnegan asked.

"Margaret Jackson?" Jeff cried in disbelief.

"I'll explain later," Sally replied, trying to block out the talking to think who the likely suspects were and where they might have taken Magda. It seemed likely Margaret was their best bet, and maybe she had taken Magda to the same house she had held Sally. But where was that house?

She took another look at the note tacked on the door and noticed a small black smudge in the lower left-hand corner.

"Jeff, do you happen to have the note you got with you?"

This was a long shot. Why would he carry it around with him?

"Actually, yes." Jeff reached into his pocket. "I've been keeping it with me to remind me not to gamble."

Sally nodded. "Has it worked?"

Jeff looked at his feet. "Well, a little."

Sally took the paper from him and unfolded it. Yup, sure enough, the same small black smudge in the lower left-hand corner she had remembered seeing when Jeff had first shown her the paper the week before.

"Okay, so this was done on the same printer. Both papers have the same mark in the corner."

She held up Jeff's note to the one on the door for Finnegan to see.

He nodded. "So what does this tell us, Sally?"

That was a good question.

"My gut tells me we should assume Margaret took Magda on Diane's order and took her to the house where I was kept. We should start there. Otherwise, we are just grasping at straws, trying to figure out who else it is. We know, of course, that Diane was with us today, so she can't be holding Magda."

"Good thinking," Finnegan agreed.

Jeff hopped from one foot to the other. "Come on, we need to find Magda," he cried.

Sally squeezed his shoulder. "Jeff, yes, we want to find Magda, but we have to have a plan. Otherwise, we're just driving around. And you know yourself there are tons of dirt roads here that could lead to a house or shack. We don't have time to try every one."

Finnegan agreed with a nod. Apparently, she was in charge today.

"I know. I know. I'm just so worried. And scared." He looked like he was about to burst into tears.

Sally turned back to the detective. "I don't remember exactly where the house was, Detective, but I remember the general direction. Is there any way we could get help on our search?"

"Yeah, let's get back to the station, and I'll call in backup," Finnegan replied.

All three jumped in Finnegan's police car, and they flew back to police HQ.

Chapter Forty-Four

On the way, Finnegan called Soder on his radio to issue an all-points bulletin for Magda. They would have to deal with Diane later.

Meanwhile, Sally tried to call Jay. For some reason, she was worried he might be next. Unfortunately, it went right to voicemail.

Back at the station, Finnegan pulled Soder into his office. Sally stood next to the desk. Jeff waited outside for them.

"The APB is out?" Finnegan barked.

"Yes, boss. No word yet."

Of course not. It had only been three seconds.

"Detective. Shouldn't we get going?" Sally pleaded.

She knew the general area of where she was kept and thought they should start searching there now.

"Um, didn't you just tell Jeff that we should have a plan first before running around like chickens with our heads cut off?"

Sally shrugged. "Okay, yeah. I see your point."

Finnegan turned back to Soder.

"Put a trace on Magda's phone. If it's on, we should be able to triangulate her position. Then have the guys send that info to my car."

"Sure thing."

"And then get two officers to come with you and meet us at the parking lot. Oh, and pack your car with enough bulletproof vests for everyone." Finnegan motioned him to get out with one hand and pulled out a map of the area from the desk with the other. He smoothed it out on the tabletop.

A map, how quaint, Sally thought.

"Yeah, I know," Finnegan said, as if reading her mind, "but a big map is easy to read. You know, get an overview. Then I've got my tablet in the car to follow the route."

They both stared down at the map, and Sally showed him where she had turned right onto Route 10 at the intersection of Route 36 south of town.

"Okay, so the house must be somewhere east and south of Route Ten."

Sally pointed to a town within that area.

"The only town there is Jefferson on Bangor Creek," she noted.

"That's a heavily wooded area with houses few and far between. We're going to need more than my three officers."

He reached for his cell phone and punched a number.

"Hi, this is Detective Finnegan from Berry Springs. We've got a kidnap victim we need your help to find. Can you send an officer or two to help with the search?"

Sally could only hear a muffled voice on the phone.

"Yeah, meet us at the intersection of Route Ten and Route Thirty-Six in thirty minutes." He hung up. "Well, we've got the cavalry."

Sally hoped it was enough.

Soder ran back in. "Okay, trace on the phone is on, and the two officers are waiting outside for me."

"Thanks." Finnegan pushed his bulk off his chair. "Soder, have someone get a statement from Jeff and keep him here until we find Magda. If he has something to do with it, we don't want him getting out and warning anyone."

"But Jeff called it in," Sally answered.

"Sure, but that might have been a diversion," Finnegan replied.

"True," Sally agreed.

"I'll be right back," Finnegan told Sally.

She wondered what was so important, but didn't want to push him.

He came back in ten minutes in a police uniform.

Sally's eyes widened.

"Yeah, I rarely wear this, but we're on a manhunt. I want to be quickly identified as police if things get ugly."

They headed out.

In the car, Finnegan punched in the coordinates of the search area on his tablet. As he pulled out, Sally saw another Berry Springs police car behind them with Soder and the two officers to help with the search. They headed south to meet the Jefferson officers.

When they pulled into the small parking area at the intersection of Routes 10 and 36, Sally saw two Jefferson police cars parked there. Three of their officers were standing in front of their cruisers.

As Sally walked over to them with the detective, Soder, and the Berry Springs officers, she could tell the other police weren't that happy about this special duty. She always thought cops stuck together, but guess not.

"Thanks folks, for helping out," Finnegan began.

The three Jefferson officers just stared at him.

"Well. We don't have much to go on," Finnegan admitted. He pulled out the map from the station to show the search area. "There are a lot of dirt roads and remote cabins here, and she could be held in any one of them."

Sally pulled out her phone.

"Her name is Magda," Sally said, showing them all a picture of Magda she had taken last summer. Sally knew they had to hurry, or it would be too late. She didn't want another murder on her hands.

Finnegan drew a large circle on the map and broke it into four parts, numbering them. "Okay, everyone, take a photo of the map now. We're going to break into four teams of two and systematically search the area."

Each officer took a photo and noted their number as Finnegan split them up.

He and Sally would be Team One. Soder and one of the Berry Springs officers would be Team Two. Teams Three and Four would be the Jefferson officers, along with the remaining Berry Springs cop. This officer gave Finnegan a look that could kill. Finnegan frowned and jabbed a finger in the direction of the Jefferson police. She reluctantly walked over to them.

With a nod from Finnegan, the teams headed out.

Sally checked her phone. It had now been two hours since they had met

Jeff at Magda's apartment, and the sun was getting lower in the sky. She prayed Magda was still alive.

Chapter Forty-Five

Finnegan drove quickly to their part of the search grid, and they started down the main road in the middle of it. He slowed to a crawl so they wouldn't miss any side roads. The woods were thick here, and a dirt road was easy to miss. Not every house had a mailbox at the end of the driveway, so they couldn't use that as an indication.

Finnegan looked left while Sally looked right.

At the first dirt road, Finnegan turned left, and they drove to the end, which ended in a clearing.

Nothing.

Driving back to the road, Sally feared they would never find her. There was so much area to cover.

"This is going to take forever," she said.

"Maybe we'll get lucky. And we're not alone in the search."

Sally nodded as they headed farther down the road.

They checked the next few dirt roads and found nothing. On the next road, they saw a mailbox at the end of the driveway and a name on it: *Roberts*.

The name meant nothing to either of them, but they drove down the driveway anyway.

"What if Magda is here and they see the cop car?" Sally asked after they had driven one hundred feet.

"Good point."

Finnegan stopped the car when they could see a house in the distance through the woods.

"Detective, let me go. Your uniform might act like a beacon."

Finnegan shook his head.

"No way, you want to get yourself killed?"

"It will be faster. Trust me," Sally pleaded.

Finnegan looked out the window, drumming his fingers on the steering wheel. Sally hoped he would let her go. It was the only way, in her opinion.

He turned back to her. "All right. Suit yourself," he said and waved her out.

Sally slowly opened the door and crept down the driveway, trying to stay in the shadows and near the trees.

It was only about two hundred feet to the house, so it didn't take long. When she got to the end of the driveway, she found an old log cabin. No lights were on, and there were no vehicles in the driveway or a garage to hide a car. She checked around the back of the house, but didn't see a light or a car. The house was right at the edge of thick woods, so no car could have driven in there.

She walked back to the police cruiser. "Nothing," she said as she got in.

Finnegan backed down the driveway to the main road, and they continued on.

The next three roads also had mailboxes, but none with names either of them recognized. Again, Sally did the checking while Finnegan waited in the car a few hundred yards away.

At the third house, a small one-story cottage, Sally saw lights on and a black pickup in the driveway. She took a deep breath and slowed her steps. If Magda was being held there, she didn't want to notify the killer. She trod lightly the rest of the way to the house.

Snap.

She stepped on a twig. The stillness of the woods made it sound like a gunshot. She waited a few minutes, hoping the people in the house didn't hear. She also considered Finnegan might come running if he thought there had been a shooting.

Listening closely, she heard nothing and continued toward the house.

There was a light coming from the front room with curtains partially drawn. She ducked down and waddled toward the lit window.

Peering up, she saw an old couple watching TV. They had their backs to the window and seemed engrossed in the show they were watching.

She walked around the rest of the house and peered in all the windows. It was dark by now, and the moon was bright, so she could see clearly. None of the other rooms were occupied as far as she could see. She debated breaking into the house to check the basement, if they had one, but she didn't think the old couple was holding Magda, so she headed back to the car.

Climbing in, she shook her head.

Finnegan started up the car and headed back to the main road.

He stopped at the end to contact the other teams and find out if they had discovered anything. Obviously, he didn't trust them, Sally thought. Otherwise, if they had found something, wouldn't they have contacted him?

"Nothing, boss, a lot of woods with no houses or roads." Soder's voice crackled over the radio.

Team Three had found a few houses, but no one home. Team Four had just driven down many dirt roads and found nothing. This was going to take all night.

"Should we just keep going down this road or try another?" Sally asked.

As Finnegan was considering this, his radio fizzed. "HQ here, Detective. We have a signal on Magda's phone."

Sally clapped her hands.

"Where is it coming from?" Finnegan asked.

The officer gave him the details. "It's within two miles of those coordinates."

Finnegan punched the numbers into the tablet and found they were within Team Four's search area.

"Great work."

Finnegan radioed Team Two and Three and told them to meet again at the parking lot where they started the search.

"Okay, boss," Soder replied.

"Okay," the Jefferson Team Three replied.

Though he had only spoken to them moments ago, Finnegan couldn't reach Team Four.

Chapter Forty-Six

Finnegan kept trying to get Team Four on his radio, but no luck. He then tried his cell phone. Team Four included one of his own officers, so he tried her number. No answer.

"Do you think the kidnapper got them?" Sally asked.

Finnegan appeared optimistic. "I don't think so. Maybe they're not in the car. And you know what cell service is around here, especially if you're traipsing around the woods."

"True." Sally hoped they were okay but, in her gut, was worried they'd met a more serious fate.

Where was that negativity coming from? She didn't want to go down that path. But three of her friends were dead, and what was stopping the killer from adding more dead bodies?

The teams regrouped at the small parking lot where they had started the search and divided up Team Four's section. Now that the search area was narrowed, finding Magda should be easier, though it was still a heavily wooded area with houses few and far between. Sally put on a brave face as they headed back to the cars to head out again. Time was running out.

They all headed east on Route 36 for five miles, then turned right on an unmarked side road that went right through Team Four's section.

Sally scanned left and right, thinking Magda was in the woods somewhere.

They reached a fork in the road. Team Two, with Soder and Team Three, headed left to cover the northern part of the area while Sally and Finnegan continued south.

Sally kept tapping the armrest. Finnegan clenched the steering wheel and kept glancing over at her. She knew this was driving him crazy, but she had to do something to try and calm her nerves.

It wasn't long before they found a side road on the left with a mailbox.

"Oh, please let her be here," Sally pleaded.

They drove down a gravel path until they came close to a house. Finnegan had switched off the headlights when they started down the path so they couldn't be seen. Using binoculars this time, as there was more of a clearing in the trees, Finnegan searched, but no cars were parked outside.

"No lights on. No cars. Another dead end," he said.

He backed up the car slowly down the path to the main road and continued farther south.

Sally glanced at the tablet on the dashboard and saw they weren't too far from Jefferson. Then she saw a street sign on the right.

"Stop," she cried. "There's a street."

Finnegan slowed down and turned down a paved road. There were three houses set far apart. Sally held her breath as they slowly passed each one, looking for lights on.

The first house was dark, with a two-car garage. There was a mailbox at the end with a nameplate on it, but it was dirty with age. Since it didn't look like anyone was there, they didn't bother to check it. At the second house, they saw lights on and an SUV in the driveway.

"Let me go and check," she said.

Finnegan shook his head. "No, I'm going this time. We have to be close to where Magda is. I don't want you getting hurt."

Sally had wished he had been more adamant at the last house where she crept through the woods.

Finnegan parked across the street away from the house and got out. Sally watched him as he walked toward the house and up to the lights. He glanced in before ducking down quickly.

The curtain opened wide, and an older woman peered out. The moonlight was hitting her face directly, so Finnegan would have been backlit, blocking her view.

She quickly closed the curtain again.

Finnegan stood up and walked back to the car, shaking his head. Before continuing, he picked up the radio.

"Any news, Team Two and Three?"

Both reported finding nothing.

"Team Four, come in, Team Four." They waited a few minutes, but still no response.

"Come on, let's go to the last house and then keep going. We have to find her," Sally said.

Though Sally wasn't really sure, Magda was in one of the houses on the street. It didn't seem like anything sinister was going on here.

Finnegan started up the car. As they drove the last few hundred yards to the end of the street, they saw the house was dark.

Finnegan turned the car around when there was a pounding on Sally's window.

Finnegan slammed on the brakes.

Sally shrieked and looked out to see Magda, her face bloody with a black eye. Finnegan unlocked the doors, and Magda jumped in the back.

"Sally, oh Sally, you found me!" Magda yelled.

"Where did you come from?" Sally asked her, reaching back to give Magda an awkward hug.

Magda pointed to the first house.

"We didn't see any lights, so we assumed no one was there," Finnegan explained.

"He kept the lights off the whole time. I was tied up in the basement. I managed to get out while I heard him in the bathroom right above the corner it was kept. He killed two cops."

Sally felt like her gut was punched.

Finnegan turned red. "Killed what?" he yelled.

"I heard a door slam, then two voices yelled, 'Police, put down your gun.' Then gunshots." Magda was sobbing.

"How did you hear that if you were in the basement?" Sally wondered aloud.

"I was near the front of the house, under a small window. I kept yelling while I was there, thinking someone might hear. Of course, there's no one around this area. The houses are set too far apart for anyone for noise to carry, even on this street." Magda took a deep breath before continuing. "That's how I got these bruise marks. He heard me. We have to get out of here before he finds out I'm missing. Please." Each sentence came out in a staccato.

"But we didn't see a cop car?" Finnegan noted.

"After I heard the gunshots, I heard him pull a car into the garage."

Finnegan drove to the end of the street, past the house, and parked just at the edge of the main road. Trees next to the house blocked the view to where they were sitting.

"What are you doing? Drive! Go!" Sally pleaded.

"We need to get this guy. I'm calling backup. We can't just leave and let the guy escape."

Finnegan radioed Teams Two and Three and gave them their location. "Don't turn onto the street. Park just before and get your guns out. The suspect is at the first house on the street. Armed and dangerous."

Sally noticed he didn't mention the dead colleagues. She considered that might make them do something they would later regret.

Sally then turned to Magda. "Who was it who took you?"

Magda shook her head, crying. "It was…it was…Jay."

Chapter Forty-Seven

"Jay! Our Jay?" Sally pounded her fist on the dashboard. "How did I miss this?"

"Everyone did, Sally. He called me and said he needed help closing the bar for the week and putting the signs up."

"But you quit. Why did you agree to help?"

Magda didn't look at her. "Well, I felt bad about the way I was to you. I didn't mean to yell like that. I was so scared about Jeff and all that was going on here, I just lost my head. I thought if I helped Jay, maybe I could try and make it up to you."

Sally took her arm. "Magda, I know. I understand. We've all been through a lot."

The radio on the dashboard crackled. "We're here, parked on the side of the road about a hundred yards before the road."

Finnegan picked up the radio.

"Okay, wait there. I'll come and meet you."

Opening the door, Finnegan looked at Sally and Magda.

"Lock the doors. Stay put. Let us deal with this," he ordered.

Sally shook her head. "No way am I staying here. I'm coming with you. Magda can stay locked in here," Sally declared.

"Are you crazy? You're staying here," Finnegan replied, his face flushing.

Sally opened the door, got out, and walked toward the house.

"Shit!" she heard him mutter behind her. He slammed the door, caught up to her, and grabbed her arm. "Get back in the car," he told her through clenched teeth.

They both glanced toward the house.

"No, and let go of me."

Sally shook him off and continued to where the other cops were waiting.

As they walked by the house as quickly as they could, Sally glanced at the mailbox.

This time, the moonlight hit the mailbox, and even through the dirt on it, Sally managed to make out the name on it.

It said: *Fletcher*.

"Well, there might be many Fletchers in these parts, but this seems a bit too much of a coincidence," Finnegan whispered to her.

Sally nodded.

They reached the other cops. "Okay, the suspect is inside the first house," Finnegan explained. "We have Magda in the car. She managed to escape, but the suspect is armed and dangerous. We'll split up. Soder and I will go to the front door. I want you two to go to the back," Finnegan said, pointing to the two Jefferson cops from Team Three.

"What about me?" Soder's partner in Team Two asked.

"Cover the garage," Finnegan replied.

The officer nodded.

"Any word from Team Four, boss?" Soder asked.

Sally could see Finnegan hesitating. If he told them what probably happened to the other cops, they may get too emotional just before surrounding the house.

On the other hand, they deserved to know what happened.

"It looks like the suspect may have shot them. That's what Magda thinks she heard," Finnegan admitted.

"Fuck," the Jefferson cop growled.

"We don't know that for sure, but I wanted you to be warned. We're going to have to check the garage after we get him."

Sally noticed that Finnegan waited a few moments instead of just going to the house immediately. She wasn't sure the Jefferson cop was going to cool down enough, but Finnegan did the best he could.

"Soder, get the bulletproof vests."

Soder passed around the vests, including one for Sally. They all slipped them on and got ready to head to the house.

Sally could feel the tension in the air. Or maybe it was just herself. This was it.

As they walked back toward the house, Finnegan said, "Sally, stay behind me. I don't want you getting hurt."

This time, she obeyed.

When they reached the house, Finnegan motioned for the Jefferson officers to head toward the back. His Berry Springs officer walked toward the garage.

"Okay, you stay here on the side of the house," Finnegan told Sally in a whisper.

She grunted and reluctantly hid behind the bush at the edge of the porch.

Finnegan and Soder quietly walked up the steps to the front door, guns drawn. Both men looked at each other, but stayed silent. Finnegan looked around to see if a window was unlatched or open for a way to get in without alarming Jay. Though they had no idea which room he was in as the house was still dark.

"Damn," Finnegan muttered under his breath.

The house was old, but the windows were fairly new and sealed. There would be no way to get in without smashing the window or breaking down the door.

He headed toward the window.

Sally watched, frozen in terror, through an opening in the bush.

He motioned Soder to stand back but kept his gun poised at the door. Finnegan took off his coat and wrapped his right hand with it.

He took three deep breaths and smashed his hand hard into the window. It gave way instantly.

There was a loud sound from the back of the house. It sounded like a door flying open.

Shots were fired, and they continued as Jay came rushing around the side of the house toward Sally.

"Jay, stop!" she shrieked.

He looked over at her, his eyes wide, but he kept running.

The police at the back of the house were in hot pursuit.

"Stop. Police."

They fired warning shots into the air. Jay hit the street and ran toward the woods near the side of the house.

Finnegan fired.

Jay went down.

"No!" Sally yelled, running toward Jay.

"Stop right there, Sally," Finnegan shouted, but she ignored him.

Sally reached Jay, who was on the ground clutching his leg.

Finnegan had shot him in the knee, but Jay's gun was pointed right at her.

Chapter Forty-Eight

Sally froze when she saw the gun. She was now about five paces from him.

Jay groaned. "Stay where you are. All of you!"

"Jay, what is going on?" Sally cried.

"I'm getting revenge. That's what's going on."

Sally took a step forward.

Jay waved the gun, and she stopped.

"I will shoot you. I don't care."

Sally looked down at the ground and saw a pool of blood spreading. She needed to get him to a hospital as soon as possible.

"Jay, you need a doctor. You're bleeding."

"It's too late for a doctor, Sally."

Sally could feel the police behind her and hoped they weren't going to do anything stupid. She didn't want to see Jay die, no matter what he may have done. Jay was like a son to her.

"Jay, drop the gun," Finnegan yelled from behind her.

"Jay, no!" Magda protested.

Why did she leave the car? Sally thought, glaring at Magda.

"Jay, stop. Why are you doing this? Why did you kidnap me?" Magda pleaded.

Sally was going to yell at her for leaving the car, but she realized if she took her eyes off Jay, even for a second, he may shoot her, so she stayed put and kept her eyes pointed at Jay's gun. She no longer knew what he was capable of.

"Magda, get back in the car, please," Sally cried.

"Shut up, Sally. Shut up, everyone. I'll shoot all of you." Jay waved his gun.

Sally was praying Magda would listen to her.

She heard a car door open and slam, and she relaxed only slightly.

"Jay, look how many cops are surrounding you with their guns drawn. Do you think you will get out of this alive if you don't drop the gun?" Finnegan yelled.

Sally couldn't move. Her eyes were locked on Jay's gun.

"I'm not going to jail. You won't get me. All those people deserved to die."

Sally felt her stomach lurch. "You, you killed everyone?"

She could barely say the words.

"Yes." He looked her directly in the eyes as he spat out the words. "They deserved it. But you won't get me for it."

Sally watched as he raised his gun and put his finger on the trigger. It was now pointed away from her to the right, toward Soder.

Her heart was beating hard in her chest, she could barely breathe.

Jay yelled, "For Momma!"

Bang!

The gun fell, and Jay's head hit the asphalt.

"No!" she cried, sprinting the last few paces.

She looked down at him. His eyes were cold.

She spun around. "What have you done?"

It was one of the Jefferson officers who had shot Jay.

"What the hell were you doing?" Finnegan demanded, stabbing his finger in the cop's face, apparently not worrying whether the cop would shoot him, too.

The Berry Springs officer moved over to stand next to her boss.

The Jefferson officer put his gun in his holster, crossed his arms, and stared at Finnegan with a look of steel. The other Jefferson officer stood next to him, his hand on his holster.

"He was obviously going to shoot one of us, so I got him first."

"Shit, we wanted him alive."

The Jefferson officers started to move away from the house toward the road.

"Where do you think you're going?" Finnegan asked.

"Back to Jefferson headquarters. The suspect has been neutralized."

"No way in hell. You're staying here until we get backup, paramedics, and Forensics on the scene. And Soder here will get your statement."

With that, Finnegan walked over to Sally to move her away from Jay's body.

"No, I'm not leaving him."

"Sally, come on. Sit in the car with Magda and take a break."

She didn't want to leave Jay. She was numb, not knowing what had happened or why. What a tragic end to a young life.

Finnegan led her to his car, and she sat in the front seat, eyes straight ahead while Finnegan radioed into HQ. She wondered why he had wanted backup. Would the Jefferson cop shoot a fellow officer? She didn't think so. But emotions were running high.

From her viewpoint in the cruiser, she then watched Finnegan walk over to the garage and open it. Inside was a police car. Oh, all this death, including two police officers. The bodies piled up like a stack of cards. She hoped this would be the last of the killing for a while. Or better yet, forever.

She watched as Finnegan gathered the other officers around to bow their heads for the lost officers from Team Four. They had each lost a colleague tonight.

Sally heard Finnegan saying some words. She wanted to get closer, but felt it was best to leave the cops with their own. This had been a terrible conclusion of a terrible two weeks.

The police officers seemed to all be in tears. She had to look away.

She turned to Magda. "Oh, Magda, I'm so glad you're safe."

Magda touched her arm.

"I am so relieved you found me. I thought I was going to die. Oh, Jay. Did he kill all those people?"

"It looks like it," Sally said, shaking her head.

It only took the Berry Springs teams twenty minutes to reach the scene. Sally and Magda waited in the car while Finnegan talked to his teams. She saw the paramedics hovering over Jay's body, though Sally didn't think there was anything they could do for him.

After a few minutes, they stood up and walked back to their ambulance.

It was time for Forensics to take over.

Sally watched in the rearview mirror while Magda had turned around to see what was going on. Sally saw her staring in the direction of Jay's body the whole time.

Finnegan walked over to his police car and opened the back door.

"Magda, I want the paramedics to check you out. Come with me, please."

Magda reluctantly got out of the car and followed him over to the ambulance.

This gave Sally a few moments to think. Running through everything she had seen during her investigation in her mind, a lot of it was starting to make sense, even if it was all so tragic.

One death had turned into six.

Finnegan returned a few minutes later.

"Okay, the paramedics are taking Magda to the hospital for observation. I'm heading to Berry Springs HQ to question Diane. Do you want to come? Or should I take you home?" Finnegan asked, "By the way, we also picked up Margaret again."

Sally was exhausted, but they were so close to finding out the truth, there was only one response she could give.

"Of course, I'm coming with you. I want to know the truth."

Chapter Forty-Nine

Back at the station, Sally sat in Finnegan's office while he arranged the interrogation rooms with his team. Sally was glad he was questioning Diane, the church assistant, and Margaret, the head of sanitation, separately. That way, the police could play one off each other rather than have them in one room.

Soder came in with a coffee. "Here you go."

"Thanks, Mark. Did you spike it?"

They both laughed. It felt good to relieve some of the tension after the fraught past few hours.

"You okay?" he asked.

"I guess I'm glad it's over, well, almost over. But Jay. How did he get involved?"

"The craziest two weeks we've had here in a while," Soder said.

Sally nodded. She hoped she would have plenty of time after this to rest. She'd give anything for "normal" life to resume. Not that it could ever be "normal" again without all the friends she'd lost these past two weeks.

"I just don't get it," she said. "He was always so helpful at the bar, though sometimes in a weird mood, but that was just Jay. Now he's gone too."

"Who knows," said Soder. He gave her shoulder a gentle squeeze and wandered back to his desk.

Her nerves were frayed, and she felt like she would cry. God, she wanted to cry. To let it all out, the emotions she'd been suppressing for the sake of the investigation. She just had to hold it together a little longer. It was almost over.

She put her feet up on the coffee table and sipped her coffee. There was a dull pain in the back of her head. Even so, she was certainly not going to miss watching Margaret and Diane getting questioned. The anger she had felt just after Bill was killed was still simmering inside, and she wasn't going to take any crap from either lady. This was war, and she was determined not to let up until she found out the truth. She knew there was enough evidence and her testimony to keep both in jail for a long while. Drugging and kidnapping someone were serious offenses in themselves, and this might be considered attempted murder. Who knows what Margaret would have done with her if she hadn't escaped. And she was sure Diane had planned it all.

But how and why was Jay involved?

Finnegan came in and broke her thoughts. "Sally, we're ready. Follow me."

She had an idea.

"Detective, can I talk to you for a moment?"

"Now?"

"Yeah, um, well, I would like to be in the room with you while you question each of the suspects."

"No way, you're a civilian."

She got up and stood right next to the detective to reiterate her point. "I've been helping you with this investigation, in spite of my anger and sadness at Bill's death. And didn't I help with the crucial information on Diane's background? Where would you be without it?"

Finnegan took a step back and thought for a moment.

"You're right, of course, but I'm not sure I like it. Let me talk to Randall Wentworth. He's representing both. We're starting with Diane."

"Okay."

Sally grabbed her backpack and followed him down the hall.

Finnegan opened a door and showed Sally in. One wall was covered in a one-way mirror. She looked through it and saw Diane, along with her attorney, Randall Wentworth. An officer was standing in the corner watching Diane the entire time.

In the small anteroom she was in, there was a high table and chair next to the one-way mirror. She arranged her notebook and pen and sat in the room alone, looking into the interrogation room.

Finnegan and Soder entered the interview room. Soder sat down across from Diane while Finnegan motioned Wentworth to follow him outside.

They joined Sally a few seconds later, standing by the one-way mirror opposite Diane.

"Randall, Sally has asked to be in the room for the questioning."

Randall furrowed his brow. "Not going to happen," he said, turning to Sally.

"Randall, please let me help. I know both Diane and Margaret and maybe I can get them to talk better than the cops."

Finnegan gave Sally a look of death when he heard that.

She was really pushing it a bit far with her boldness, but her bartender voice and ear might get them somewhere with the facts faster. She couldn't just sit and watch. She just hoped she wouldn't try to punch either of the women.

Randall considered her request. "I don't know. If you are in there, I want you to say nothing until we tell you to. Let the police start the questioning. Can you do that?"

Sally nodded vigorously, glad she had won. It would be hard to say nothing, but if it got her in the room, she'd agree to anything.

The three walked next door to the interrogation room.

When Sally walked in, Diane stared at her.

"What's she doing here?" Diane asked.

Randall Wentworth sat down next to Diane. "As you know, she has been working with the police on this investigation. I agreed she can listen in on the questioning," Wentworth explained. "Don't worry."

Diane shrugged her shoulders and looked across at Finnegan, who had taken a seat next to Soder.

"Whatever. I'm not saying anything anyway," Diane said. "I mean, I have nothing to say." She turned to Wentworth. "Randall, get me out of here," she demanded.

Wentworth shook his head. "Diane, the police have a right to question you. They have some important evidence, and you need to answer their questions."

Turning back to Finnegan, she said, "Okay, let's get this over with."

Soder started the recording device.

Sally inhaled slowly and let out a controlled breath. She was ready for this, wasn't she?

Finnegan smiled at both of the ladies before opening the blue folder he had brought with him and looking at it for a few minutes, holding it up so Diane couldn't see the contents. Sally watched him as he flipped over page after page, most of them blank. He scribbled a few notes, also nonsense—from Sally's position, it looked like a shopping list. Sally glanced at Diane, who began drumming the table. Randall Wentworth put his hand on her shoulder, and she stopped. The stalling tactic was working.

Finnegan finally closed the folder, put it down, and looked up.

Diane leaned forward, teeth bared.

"Diane, you've been in this town for years. Even if people don't go to the church, they know Diane Gregory, or should I say, Diane Fletcher. And people trust you."

Wow, Finnegan started right with a direct shot. Sally didn't think this was the best idea, but she had agreed to stay quiet and just observe. That wasn't going to be easy.

Diane stood up, but Wentworth pulled her back.

"Uh, Fletcher? My name is Diane Gregory," she replied not too convincingly.

Finnegan pulled out the last piece of paper in his folder and slid it across the table. Sally noticed the official seal. Finnegan had been quick in getting the official documentation that Nancy had dug up, even if Sally still hadn't revealed to him how she had gotten it, which she hoped she would never have to.

Diane stared at the paper.

"Okay, so. I don't know any Fletchers. I'm Diane Gregory. You know that, Detective," she replied.

"You were put up for adoption by someone in Little Rock, weren't you? You became Diane Collins. And now you're Diane Gregory."

Diane squirmed in her chair.

"People trust you. Or should I say, *trusted* you? Look what you've done to the town you claim to love."

Finnegan was really pushing it.

"I think people deserve whatever they can get in life, Detective, don't you?"

Her sickly, sweet voice made Sally shudder.

Who was this Diane?

"What do you think you deserve, Diane?" Finnegan retorted.

"Everything. The world owes me everything," she sniggered.

She jumped up and went for Finnegan when the officer pulled her back.

"One more outburst like that, and I'll handcuff your arms and legs. You understand?" Finnegan barked.

"You think this is helping, Diane?" Sally interjected.

Finnegan glanced back at her, and his look said it all. She mouthed a silent "Sorry" and stepped back.

Diane sneered, crossed her arms, and stayed silent.

"Good, then I can continue," Finnegan said. "I have to admit, you are very smart, Diane."

At this, Diane grinned. "Of course I am, Detective."

"Well, yes, you managed to organize all these killings and make other people do your dirty work."

Diane's grin turned into a frown. "Oh, please, Detective. You don't think I'm going to fall for that trick. I had nothing to do with anything that had happened. Father O'Malley was a friend."

Sally saw a tear in her eye, which she actually thought might be genuine. *Unstable genius*, Sally thought.

"Well, let's start with Bill. Bill Arnold."

Sally wondered when Soder was going to join in the questioning. He had not said a word and spent the entire time looking at the blank notepad in front of him.

"What about him?" Diane asked, glancing over at Sally.

"Why start with Bill? What did he ever do to you?"

Sally was impressed at Finnegan's cool. This seemed to be his favorite thing to do. Try to trip up suspects to get them to confess. He really seemed to be enjoying himself.

"You know, I really don't like idiots. There are a lot of idiots in this town," Diane replied.

"Bill was an idiot?" Soder asked.

Ah, the man speaks.

"Of course. It was so easy to…" She caught herself before continuing.

Finally, we're getting somewhere. Sally had barely moved the entire time, and her left foot was falling asleep. She hoped she would be able to sit down soon and question Diane herself.

Finnegan leaned back in his chair, and it creaked. He now had a smirk on his face.

"Ah, um, Diane, easy to what?" he asked.

Diane shook her head and said nothing.

"Easy to kill Bill?"

"What? I didn't kill Bill or anyone else. I'm not that stupid," she said, stabbing her finger at Finnegan.

"Okay, but you planned it all, didn't you? What a great plan. Kill everyone off to get the Arnold money. Get Bill to change his will in favor of Father O'Malley, then kill him off, too."

Diane said nothing.

"But one thing confuses me, and maybe you can help me understand it. How did you think you would get the money? Seems a bit of a stupid plan. Get revenge for Momma Arnold putting you up for adoption, but that plan doesn't end up with you getting any money though. You're named in Father O'Malley's will; this is true, but the Arnolds are fighting that. And you know as well as I do that what the Arnolds want, they get, in this county. Stupid, Diane. Just stupid."

As Finnegan spoke, Diane got redder and redder in the face. "Don't call me stupid," she said. "I had it all worked out. But that bitch over there interfered."

Diane pointed at Sally.

"Why would you hurt me, Diane? I was your friend." Sally couldn't help herself. She looked at Finnegan. "Sorry, Detective. I just had to say something."

Finnegan didn't raise his voice and just let Diane stew.

"Good point. Sally was getting too close to the truth, so you had her kidnapped. Wanted to kill her too, I bet," he continued.

"She got away. Margaret is an idiot, like the rest of them. Should have..." Diane shut her mouth, realizing she had begun to reveal it all.

So much for the smarts she claimed to have, Sally thought.

"Should have what?" Finnegan pushed.

"I'm not saying anything else. I didn't do anything."

* * *

Finnegan, Soder, and Sally regrouped in the hallway.

"Let her simmer a bit. She's already starting to unravel. I want to work on Margaret now and see what she has to say. We can then take that back and use it on Diane," Finnegan said.

"Great work in there, Detective," Sally replied.

She was really milking it. Finnegan had given up too quickly, but she wanted to stay on his good side, and Finnegan was beaming.

"She seems to waver between protecting herself and wanting to reveal her 'genius,'" Sally said.

Finnegan nodded.

"It's a bit scary though. I thought she was going to implode," Soder commented.

"You never really know people. Even in a small town like this," Finnegan replied.

Heading down the hall, Sally was cooking up an idea of how to get them both to confess, if Finnegan was as successful with Margaret as he had been with Diane.

When they arrived in the interrogation room where Margaret was being held, they looked through the small glass window in the door and saw Randall Wentworth already there, conferring with his client. Sally was more and more aware of how much he must know about almost everyone in town. It was an unnerving thought.

Wentworth stopped talking when the three of them walked in.

"Oh, joining us again, Sally?" Wentworth said, looking down at her through his polished metal glass frames.

Margaret just stared at her blankly. Wentworth must have filled her in.

Sally smiled at them and took her place behind the table where Finnegan and Soder had just sat down. Soder reached over and started the recording device.

"So, Margaret. Do you know why you are back here?" Finnegan began. She shook her head.

"No, I got out on bail on Tuesday, so why am I here now?"

"Well, we still have the witness statement that says you were seen picking up an envelope containing the syringe behind the dumpster at Sally's bar the night Bill was killed."

Finnegan held up an envelope.

"There are traces of strychnine in this envelope and your fingerprints all over it. We found this while searching your house."

Finnegan grinned like he was a cat that had just gotten the canary.

Margaret just stared at him, but said nothing.

Finnegan continued, "And we know that you kidnapped Sally. Even if your buddy, the mayor, got you out."

At the mention of the mayor, Margaret leaned over the table and pointed her finger at Finnegan.

"You leave Jennifer out of this. One phone call, and you're fired."

Finnegan just laughed. "Yeah, I bet an obstruction of justice charge would really help her lofty career goals. Get in your seat!"

Sally could tell he was getting impatient. Probably more with the course of the investigation than with Margaret's teasing. If she had been able to, she would have told him to take a deep breath and calm down.

Margaret dropped in her seat reluctantly. Wentworth leaned over and whispered something in her ear. She looked at him and scowled.

"Okay, so you told Sally and me that you had gotten up to go to the restroom at the bar." Finnegan resumed his line of questioning. "Couldn't you have also gone outside, gotten the envelope with the syringe, and then brought it in to kill Bill?"

Margaret laughed. "Do you know how long that would take? Someone would have seen me leave."

"Well, we do have the witness who saw you behind the dumpster, remember. Would that work? Or maybe the fact that the restrooms at Sally's bar are near the back door meant you could slip out easily."

Margaret stayed quiet.

Finnegan continued. He seemed to be warming up, Sally felt. "You went outside. Got the syringe and handed it to the killer."

"How do you know I didn't do the killing?" Margaret blurted out, then slapped her hand over her mouth.

"Ah-ha," Finnegan said. "Bill, Father O'Malley, Gillian. Three people dead, Margaret. You and Diane are going to jail for a long time."

"Too many idiots in one town," she replied.

That seemed to be a theme with Diane and Margaret. Getting rid of the idiots. Though Sally admitted that was the most inane reason she had ever heard of wanting to kill someone. It definitely wasn't as grand as love or money or revenge. Sally couldn't help but air her confusion. "Margaret, isn't that a pretty dumb reason to kill people?"

"Sally." Finnegan raised his voice.

"No, let her talk, Detective," Margaret replied. She turned to Sally. "Well, dear. If we get rid of the idiots, there's more money for the rest of us."

"But there's no guarantee of that. What did you expect to get out of it? You're not an Arnold or a member of the church," Finnegan said. He leaned over the table as far as his bulk would allow and stage-whispered to Margaret. "You know, we have Diane in a room down the hall. She's telling us everything. So why don't you cooperate too, Margaret."

"Bullshit." Margaret spat in his face.

He threw up his hands. "I'm just telling it like I see it. She planned it all, and you did her dirty work. You're like her little slave, aren't you? That's what you got out of it. The thrill of being someone's worker bee, isn't it?"

He wiped away the spital with a handkerchief, then tucked it back into his pocket.

Sally thought he was really pushing it. Just throwing accusations at Margaret.

"And you weren't even the killer. You're just the puppet, a nobody in this little small-town drama."

Margaret clenched her fists.

"I'm an important person in town," she cried. "Jennifer and I..." She slammed her mouth shut.

"You and Jennifer what?" Sally asked. She could figure out what Margaret was about to say, and that would explain a lot, including the mysterious call she had overheard.

"You and Jennifer are a couple?" Sally guessed.

Finnegan just stared at Margaret, who looked like a deer caught in the headlights, but she said nothing.

"Wow, Sally, what are you saying?" Finnegan asked, turning around to look at her.

"Oh, come on, Detective, you aren't five years old," Sally replied.

He shook his head and refocused on Margaret.

"So that's how you got caught up in all this murder? Blackmail? Diane found out you and the mayor were more than employee and boss? And forced you to help her?" Finnegan demanded.

Margaret looked like she was about to speak, but just pressed her lips together tightly. Sally couldn't tell whether she was going to yell or cry.

Finnegan ignored her and continued, "Like I said. Diane is down the hall telling us all about it."

Sally wondered when he was going to mention Jay. Finnegan hadn't said anything about Jay confessing and getting killed to Diane. Was he going to mention it to Margaret? It seemed like a big piece of evidence that should be thrown in their face. Sally wanted to bring Jay up, but Finnegan was in charge here, and she was at least glad she could be in the room.

"Without me, none of it would have worked," Margaret replied, apparently forgetting she didn't want to talk about her involvement or why she did it.

CHAPTER FORTY-NINE

"Ah, so you were involved." Finnegan sat back like a cool cat.

Wentworth leaned over to Margaret to whisper something to her again. She pushed him away. She turned back to Finnegan but had her eyes on Sally. "If she hadn't interfered, we would have gotten away with it all." Margaret realized she'd said too much and shut her mouth.

"Tell us all about it, Margaret," Finnegan said, staring her down.

She crossed her arms.

"Forget it."

"What about Jay?" Finnegan asked.

Finally.

"Jay, the bartender? Another idiot."

Sally's patience was wearing thin.

She began moving forward at one point, and Finnegan coughed, signaling her to keep quiet.

Geez, this is going to go on all night.

Will she ever confess?

Chapter Fifty

Sally was surprised Finnegan had finally gotten Margaret and Diane to tell all the day before. To be honest, he seemed to be surprised himself.

Now that the drama of the last two weeks was over, perhaps she and the rest of the town could get back to their regular lives. Though Sally knew that nothing would be the same with Bill, Father O'Malley and Gillian Arnold murdered.

As she felt a main part of her job as bartender was to bring people together and make them feel comfortable, she had invited everyone involved and affected by the events to a get-together at her Sally's Smasher. It was Friday, four PM and everyone planned to get there at five, a couple hours before the regular opening that day at seven. Maybe they could all help each other to process what had happened. And maybe they would all become closer because of it.

Soder and Finnegan were already there, seated at the bar. Altogether there would be ten people in total when the others arrived.

Sally had invited Annette and Zeke, Momma Arnold, and Magda. She had left the invitations for the mayor and Randall Wentworth to Finnegan. He had gotten both to agree to show up as well. The mayor didn't like basically being told what to do, but Finnegan had explained it was an evening to bring closure.

Sally stood behind the bar where she had set up quite a spread of food. And she had made sure the liquor stock was full both upstairs and down. She wanted to offer a place to relax, unwind, have a drink, and eat some yummy food.

Right on the dot at five, the door jingled, and one by one, guests arrived.

Momma Arnold arrived first. Sally was glad to see she had come alone. While Sally had specifically invited just Momma Arnold, she was worried she might bring one or both of her sons. That might have turned unpleasant if something someone said set them off after they had had one too many. It was supposed to be a relaxing get-together, but talking about the murders and events could be a trigger for the Arnold boys.

Sally strode over to the door and gave Momma Arnold a big hug. She led her to one of the round tables near where Finnegan and Soder were seated. Momma Arnold nodded as she took her seat. Sally quickly placed a glass of wine in front of her.

Zeke, Annette, and Magda arrived next. There were hugs all around as they got seated. When Magda started to head to her station, Sally stopped her with a shake of her head.

"I'm the only one working right now," she told Magda with a smile.

At 5:15 PM, the mayor swept in with Randall Wentworth. She smiled at Sally as they walked to a table, but Sally quickly noticed that the smile didn't reach her eyes.

Finnegan turned his chair to survey the room while grabbing a bunch of chips from one of the bowls in front of him.

The room was quiet as they seemed to expect Sally to say something before they began the feast.

Momma Arnold was fidgeting with her purse, while Annette and Zeke held hands and looked down at the table they were at.

Sally coughed, and everyone looked at her. "Thank you everyone for coming," she began. She rubbed her hands together and then smoothed her ponytail. She was ultra casual with jeans and a worn blue sweatshirt with the Sally's Smasher logo on it. It had been a one-year bar anniversary gift from Bill. "It's been a very difficult two weeks for all of us. I'm glad to say the confessions are out, and we can all breathe a sigh of relief. I'm sorry for all of us, but I wanted you all here so we can close this murderous chapter in Berry Springs and move on together," she continued.

She waved her hand across the bar.

"There is plenty to eat. And, of course, a ton to drink."

The last remark got a chuckle out of everyone.

"Come on, dig in, and let's have some fun."

Sally finished talking but continued to smile, and her eyes looked at everyone one by one.

The only sound in the room was Finnegan chomping on the chips.

Finally, Zeke got up, leading Annette over to the food. This got everyone else up except Momma Arnold. While the group grabbed plates and began spooning on chili, roasted vegetables, and all the other delectable choices, Sally plated a selection of everything for the town matriarch. She spooned some chili into a bowl for herself and brought both over to Momma Arnold's table.

"Why thank you, Sally."

"It's time to eat and try to move on," Sally said, starting to scoop some chili, blowing on it before putting it in her mouth.

"I'm just glad it's over," Momma Arnold said between bites. She ate like a bird, but seemed to be enjoying the food nonetheless.

Sally decided to leave the biggest question for another time: What would happen to Bill Arnold's money? But she didn't want to spoil the ambiance. Glancing around the room, she was glad to see everyone chatting away and enjoying the food.

Zeke, Annette, and Magda were at one table. And she was pleased when she saw the mayor and Randall Wentworth get up to sit with them.

Soder and Finnegan were chatting at the bar, chugging their beers. Sally wasn't surprised to see the bowl of chips empty.

Turning back to Momma Arnold and her chili, she said, "Yes, aren't we all. I just wish I had been able to solve everything sooner. Maybe Jay, Father O'Malley, and Gillian wouldn't be dead."

Momma Arnold sniffled at the mention of Gillian, but seemed to be putting on a good matriarchal show of power and resilience.

"You did what you could. And for that, I'm thankful."

Noticing Momma Arnold's empty glass, she reached over to pick it up to fill it.

"Oh yes, so attentive you are."

It gave Sally an excuse to move around the room without being rude.

At the bar, she filled up Momma Arnold's glass and filled Soder and Finnegan's mugs with beer.

"Hey Sally, thanks again for the invite," Soder said.

"And the chips," Finnegan added.

The three of them laughed.

She headed over to drop off the glass of wine for Momma Arnold before grabbing a chair and sitting with the rest.

The conversation stopped as she joined them, but they were all smiling.

"What a nice idea you had," Annette said, smiling.

Sally really hoped they would be friends, but the shock of Bill's will leaving part of the bar to Annette was something Sally was still going to have to get used to. She hoped her smile in reply seemed genuine.

"A bar is a place to relax and be with friends. And we definitely all need to relax," Sally said.

Everyone nodded.

"Is everyone enjoying themselves?" she asked.

"It's so nice to be able to sit down and be waited on," Magda said.

Another bout of laughter.

"I just can't believe Jay, Diane, and Margaret did all this," Magda continued.

Sally had needed someone to talk to the day before after everything had come out and had called Magda.

Everyone in the room knew Jay was dead, but only Magda, Sally, and the police knew what he had confessed to just before he was killed. He claimed to have killed them all, but Sally now knew he hadn't organized it all himself. Margaret had definitely kidnapped Sally, and the questioning of Diane and Margaret the day before had offered some important clues about what they had done beyond that.

"Diane and Margaret, we all heard about. But Jay?" Annette asked, looking at Sally.

My how news travels fast.

She still couldn't believe Margaret had kidnapped her and Diane had planned it all to get revenge on the person who abandoned her at birth.

As for Jay, Sally decided to avoid the question.

"As I was just saying to Momma Arnold, I wish I had solved it sooner."

"How could you know what they were planning?" Zeke remarked.

"True, but there must have been clues along the way," Sally said.

"Yeah, the sweet church assistant, a murderous planner, and adopted daughter revenger," Magda said coldly.

Sally glanced over at Momma Arnold to see if she had heard what Annette just said. It didn't seem like it.

Randall coughed. He was obviously uncomfortable having his client talked about.

Sally wasn't planning on grilling him about what he knew, knowing he wouldn't be able to say anything anyway. But she would have loved to.

"Adopted daughter?" Annette asked.

Most details of what Diane and Margaret had done had made it around town. Apparently, this information had not.

"Well, um. This seems to be at the center of it all," Sally began slowly.

The others leaned forward.

"Momma Arnold is Diane's biological mother," she said in a whisper, not wanting to get Momma Arnold's attention.

"What?" Annette cried.

Sally nodded, wondering if Momma Arnold would try and build some kind of relationship with Diane, even if she were in jail or even on death row.

While the confessions the day before had revealed all, there was one important piece of information Sally still needed to share with Momma Arnold.

She had planned the evening to be relaxing for everyone. And if someone wanted to ask a detail about the confessions the day before, she would be willing to provide that information, that is, if Randall Wentworth didn't stop her.

But it was that information that Jay had revealed just before he died, that was making Sally nervous. She knew she had to tell Momma Arnold she had a grandson, by the daughter she had given up for adoption who tried to destroy her life. But she wasn't sure how to break the news to her, and she wasn't sure if this get-together was the right place.

Annette seemed to be reading her mind.

"So Diane was behind all this?" she began.

Sally nodded again.

"But, what about Jay?" Annette asked again.

"Someone injected Bill with strychnine, using a cleverly small, thin needle. He probably wouldn't have felt anything, and it would have been done in a split second."

"I asked about Jay," Annette replied.

Sally looked over at Finnegan as she spoke. "Well, someone who was at the bar after eleven p.m. poisoned Bill."

"The question is how the syringe was brought into the bar. It was small, true, but we know that someone prepared it and planted it behind the dumpster in the back, and someone else picked it up. Too much danger of someone seeing the syringe change hands in the bar."

Magda rocked in her chair.

"Who planted it?" everyone at the table asked at once, ignoring the fact that Sally still hadn't answered Annette's Jay question.

Magda's eyes pleaded with Sally, but there was no time to keep secrets.

"It was Jeff," she said matter-of-factly. "He had the poison in his garden as fertilizer, and he had special needles for his insulin injections."

There were a couple of intakes of breath.

Everyone sat in silence before Annette spoke up again.

"But why Jeff?" she asked, seemingly forgetting her question about Jay.

Sally kept looking over at Finnegan and Soder at the bar, but they seemed in no mood to explain anything at the moment. Both were laughing and slapping their thighs.

Glancing at the next table, she saw the mayor and Momma Arnold sitting together in silence, sipping their drinks.

"Margaret was blackmailing him to do it. He had a major gambling problem, which Margaret had found out when she saw him at the casino."

"Jesus," Zeke grunted.

Magda was stabbing Sally with her eyes, but Sally just looked at her and shrugged.

Randall got up and walked over to sit with the mayor and Momma Arnold.

"So, who poisoned Bill?" Annette pleaded. Her love for him clearly still strong.

As she spoke, Zeke turned red and looked away.

"Well, someone had to pick up the syringe behind the bar after Jeff planted it," Sally continued.

"So it was the murderer?" Annette asked, clearly anxious to get all the details out of Sally as quickly as possible.

"Actually, it was Margaret. But she wasn't the murderer."

"But, who did Margaret give the syringe to?" Annette asked.

"Well, she could have slipped it to someone inside, but that might have been seen. It turns out there was one person walking around the bar that night but who left his post at some point," Sally explained.

Sally looked over at Magda. "When I talked to Father O'Malley, he told me that you, Magda, had served him drinks at one point."

"Well, um, yeah, I guess."

"Now, why was that? Jay had table duty that night."

It was easy to put two and two together.

"You mean, Jay, what?" Annette said, "No, no, it's not true."

"I'm sorry to say that you are right, Annette. A part of me didn't want it to be true, but everything points to Jay. As you know, he died yesterday. And he confessed to the murders."

Sally choked up as the realization of Jay's death hit her again. Her mind had been occupied with getting all the facts out, but this was too much for her.

"Jay jabbed Bill with the syringe and then went on with his bartending tasks. Bill had mentioned a headache to Jay, according to what he told me," Sally continued.

"Which is just sick," Annette commented.

"Jay must have enjoyed watching Bill suffer. When the place cleared out, he followed Bill outside. Watched him start his motorcycle so he was distracted, bashed him over the head with a tire iron just to be sure he really died, and dumped him in the dumpster for me to find a short while later." Sally was glad Momma Arnold and Randall Wentworth were sitting at the other table. The group here wanted every gory detail, and neither of them would have wanted to be witness to that. In particular, Momma Arnold needed to move on without knowing all that had transpired.

"But what about Father O'Malley? Jay did that, too?" Annette asked.

Sally continued the narrative.

"So, that Tuesday afternoon, Diane claims she got a call to come to the church again, which, as she told us, was unusual as she usually worked mornings."

"Now, the strange thing about this is, Detective Finnegan and his team found that no calls had been made from the church office, the parish, or Father O'Malley's cell phone at the time Diane claimed to have gotten the call. Now, what does that mean?" Sally asked.

Hearing his name, Finnegan came over, followed by Soder.

"Telling the tale, I see, Sally," Finnegan said as he pulled a chair over and sat his bulk down. Soder stood in the corner watching.

Zeke piped up. "Um, either she is lying, or someone was impersonating Father O'Malley and called her to lure her to the church?"

Sally nodded. "It's strange, though," she continued. "If Diane is lying, why did she run out of the church and not just get away? Or if it was someone else luring her there, why wasn't she killed?"

Several heads nodded.

"It just doesn't add up. For me, there is only one obvious conclusion: she was lying about the phone call and ran out to get sympathy after she or someone else had killed Father O'Malley, to deflect attention away. She had a key and could let the killer in."

Zeke interjected. "I don't get why Father O'Malley was killed. What did he have to do with all this?"

Annette grunted. "Oh please, Zeke, it's obviously to do with the will."

Several heads nodded again.

Turning to Sally, Annette said loudly, "I'll sell you my share of the bar. You deserve it."

Now, there were a few gasps at the outburst revealing a secret Sally hadn't wanted to be known around town.

But she was relieved there would be closure. She went over and gave Annette a big hug.

"Now you get back to finishing your story, Sally," Annette said, patting Sally's arm.

Sally got up and took a center spot in the room again.

"Diane let Jay in that day. Father O'Malley would have heard a noise and come out into the hall, and that's when Jay stabbed him."

As she said the last part, Sally thrust an imaginary knife into the air.

She was really getting into her narrative, but her last sentence was loud, and Sally saw Momma Arnold, the mayor, and Randall Wentworth turn to them. Momma Arnold started to cry.

Sally got up and walked over.

"Oh Sally, I just can't take this."

"I'm sorry. We were just going through the events of the evening. I didn't mean to upset you."

"I know everyone wants to know what happened, but oh, oh," Momma Arnold said, taking a sip of wine in between sniffles.

The chatter at the other table stopped as everyone heard Momma Arnold's plea.

Zeke put his foot in it by calling out: "But what about Gillian?"

Annette slapped his hand.

Sally looked down at Momma Arnold, who nodded.

Okay, she was going to finish the story.

"That's the most confusing and the most interesting. We were all there for the funeral, except Jeff, along with a ton of other people. The poison that killed Gillian was fast-acting, so anyone could have slipped it into her drink. On the other hand, it was probably administered by a person standing near where Gillian was standing. Now who could that have been?"

240

Everyone stared at everyone else.

"Gillian was standing with the bishop and me," Momma Arnold said, looking around the room.

"I don't think it was the bishop. And it wasn't me, for that matter!" Momma Arnold declared.

Sally loved how she pivoted between the grieving mother and the powerful town matriarch.

"No, I don't think so either. The closest table was where Diane was chatting with Father O'Malley's sister. And I don't think it was his sister, who barely came to Berry Springs."

Sally stopped talking for that all to seep in.

"So that means, um, Diane did it!" Magda exclaimed, looking quite pleased with herself but surprised at the same time.

Sally nodded. "She certainly had a good motive to get rid of Gillian and Bill."

"But Jay said he did it all," Annette reminded everyone.

"That was just to shield Diane," Sally explained.

"But why?" the mayor said, suddenly adding herself to the conversation.

Sally took a deep breath and patted Momma Arnold's shoulder.

"Well, I don't think I should tell everyone that right now," she said, not too convincingly.

"Honey, I'm ashamed of what I did to Diane, but you don't have to protect me," Momma Arnold told her quite firmly.

Sally wasn't so sure, though. She would be happy when she heard the final piece of the puzzle. She thought back to the last words Jay had said before he was shot dead and decided to just get it all out there.

"Well, he was under the spell of the planner for the same reason the planner did all this."

The room was silent as everyone finally worked out what it all meant.

"What? What? I had a grandson?" Momma Arnold howled.

Chapter Fifty-One

L ater that evening, after everyone had left, Sally sat with Finnegan and Soder around the coffee table in her office at Sally's Smasher biker bar. All three had their feet up with mugs of beer in their hands. It was the first time in two weeks that she felt she could really relax.

Now that the murders were solved and Diane, Jeff, and Margaret were in jail awaiting trial, the entire town could breathe a sigh of relief. Everyone seemed to want to kick up their heels that night because the bar had been packed.

"Cheers. To a job well done," Finnegan said, raising his glass.

Sally and Soder did the same.

Sally smiled. "I'm just glad it's over. It wasn't the most fun experience I've ever had. But I'm glad we now know what happened. I would hate to think any of the deaths would have gone unsolved."

Finnegan patted her shoulder. "Your instinct is really good. Maybe you should think about joining the police force."

Sally laughed. "Uh, yeah, I don't think so. It was more my determination to find the killer or killers of my friends that kept me going. Even if there were many points over the last two weeks where I thought the search would be impossible or I couldn't go on."

"Yeah, and getting kidnapped probably didn't help," Soder added.

"That is true," Sally agreed. "I wonder if we will ever find where I was kept?"

Finnegan pulled out his trusty map. "Actually, we got that out of Margaret after we brought her and Diane back to the station yesterday."

Sally leaned forward to see where he was pointing to. "Wow, it's just a few miles north of where Magda was held. Who owns it?" she asked, the pain in her legs returning and reminding her of her harrowing experience.

"Margaret. It was where she grew up."

Shivers ran down Sally's spine. So, where she was tied up was Margaret's childhood bedroom. Sick.

Shaking off that feeling, she turned to Finnegan and asked, "So what happens next?"

"Well, the district attorney is certain she can get convictions for Diane and Margaret. Margaret, as we heard yesterday, is ready to tell all. She's been charged as an accessory to murder. Diane, however, may get the death penalty, especially because it was definitely premeditated."

"Yeah, premeditated for at least twenty years," Sally replied. "What about Jeff?" she asked.

"He'll also be charged as an accessory. He did prepare and plant the syringe. The district attorney is prepared to go a bit lighter on him. He did it under duress."

She sipped her beer, lost in thought. Would the town recover from all this death? She hoped so. It had been her home for so long, she couldn't imagine living anywhere else. She woke from her reverie with a thought. "One thing I've been trying to figure out—although maybe I already know—who tried to run me off the road when I was headed to Jeff's?"

"That was probably Margaret. There are so many silver pickups in town. She could easily have taken one from the sanitation department yard," Soder offered.

"True. That makes sense. She seems to be the one who did all the dirty work to set everything up," Sally replied. Looking at Finnegan, she asked, "What about the Arnolds? I mean Momma Arnold."

"You mean the money. Well, if Diane is on death row, it shouldn't be too difficult for a judge to hand the money to the Arnolds. The Arnolds are a powerful family in the county, after all. Even if Diane's will is valid, the Arnolds will certainly fight that too."

Sally loved small-town politics, sort of.

"So what's next for you, Sally?" Finnegan asked.

"What do you mean?"

"Well, you seem to be pretty good at detecting. If you're not interested in joining the force, any thoughts of closing the bar and going into private detection as a full-time job?"

Sally laughed and shook her head. "No way. This has been a lot of fun, I admit, but I love my bar and bartending. I wouldn't want to give that up."

Though that doesn't mean I won't take up another case if it comes around, she thought.

A Note from the Author

I hope you have enjoyed *Death in the Ozarks*!

If you are interested in learning more about me and my writing, please have a look at my website (https://www.erikmey.com)

Be well!

Acknowledgements

Thank you to Cindy Bullard, my literary agent, and to Shawn Reilly Simmons and everyone at Level Best Books for helping to bring Sally Witherspoon into the wider world. I am eternally grateful!

About the Author

Currently in Austria, Erik S. Meyers has been an American abroad for years and years who has lived or worked in six countries on three continents, the longest in Germany. He is an award-winning author and communications professional with over 25 years of expertise in a variety of corporate roles. Reading and writing are his passions, when he is not hiking one of the amazing trails in Austria or elsewhere.

SOCIAL MEDIA HANDLES:
  Facebook: https://www.facebook.com/ErikSMeyersAuthor/
  Instagram: https://www.instagram.com/erikmeyauthor/

AUTHOR WEBSITE:
  https://www.erikmey.com

Also by Erik S. Meyers

The Accidental Change Agent
  (https://www.amazon.com/-/en/dp/B08BSR9CDS/)

Caged Time
  (https://www.amazon.com/Caged-Time-Tarniss-desire-faith-ebook/dp
/B08VRCR5FS/)

Printed in the USA
CPSIA information can be obtained
at www.ICGtesting.com
LVHW090823120224
771341LV00020B/77